NCIS:™
NEW ORLEANS
CROSSROADS

Also available from Titan Books

NCIS: Los Angeles™: Extremis
by Jerome Preisler

NCIS: Los Angeles™: Bolthole
by Jeff Mariotte

NCIS:
NEW ORLEANS
Crossroads

Jeff Mariotte

Based on the CBS television series
created by Gary Glasberg

TITAN BOOKS

Once again, this one's for Marcy,
with love.

NCIS New Orleans: Crossroads
Print edition ISBN: 9781783296347
E-book edition ISBN: 9781783296354

Published by Titan Books
A division of Titan Publishing Group Ltd
144 Southwark Street, London SE1 0UP

First edition: March 2017
1 3 5 7 9 10 8 6 4 2

This is a work of fiction. Names, characters, places, and incidents either are
the product of the author's imagination or are used fictitiously, and any
resemblance to actual persons, living or dead, business establishments,
events, or locales is entirely coincidental. The publisher does not have any
control over and does not assume any responsibility for author or third-
party websites or their content.

A CIP catalogue record for this title is available from the British Library.

Printed and bound in the United States.

PROLOGUE

When Caydee Spurgeon glanced over at Roger Mitchell, sitting with his back against a brick wall, pale as death, face buried in his hands as if afraid it might fall off, her older sister's parting pearl of wisdom rang in her head like an ancient prophecy of doom. "When a couple takes their first trip together," Bree had said, "it's make or break. Either you come out of it crazy in love, or you want to murder each other. There's no middle ground."

That was how it had worked for Bree and Spence. A weeklong climbing and hiking trip to Lake Placid had culminated in a proposal at the top of Mount Marcy, New York's highest peak. Seven years and two babies later, they were still, in Bree's words, "deliriously happy." Bree might have been exaggerating the "delirious" part—they had their ups and downs, as any married couple did. But they were still together, and happy more often than not. Caydee loved her nieces, and was glad the hiking trip had turned into so much more.

But this Mardi Gras trip with Roger was turning out very much the other way—which, in retrospect, she figured her sister had been trying to warn her about. Murder was looking better all the time.

They'd only been here for three days so far. The first day had been nice, walking around, exploring the sights and the shops. But it had gone downhill since, and yesterday had been the worst. Roger hadn't wanted to leave the French Quarter all day. More specifically, he hadn't wanted to leave the French Quarter's bars, and even when he could be persuaded to, he carried a go-cup with him. Increasingly inebriated as afternoon turned into night, he'd become just one more loud, obnoxious drunk among many others. He had pressured Caydee to bare her breasts for some cheap plastic beads offered by a trio of different loud, obnoxious drunks, and when she had refused, he'd sulked and called her a prude. She had pointed out a couple of strip clubs where he could see all the breasts he wanted, and she went back to their hotel alone. He had stumbled in a few hours later, smelling of cheap perfume and vomit—which still flecked his shoes, she noticed—and fell onto the bed, fully dressed.

Now she was wondering if she could exchange her ticket for an earlier flight, so she wouldn't have to sit next to him all the way back to Ohio. She had already decided to break up with him; the only question remaining was whether it would happen in New Orleans or back home in Dayton.

She turned her attention back to the parade. She was standing under one of the gorgeous shade trees lining St. Charles Avenue, and it was the real, actual Fat Tuesday, and a Mardi Gras parade was passing by right in front of her eyes in all its color and spectacle. Seeing this had been a dream for years, and she wouldn't let a bad boyfriend decision ruin it for her.

She was astonished by the beauty and complexity of some of the costumes, both in the parade and among the spectators. Music and laughter and cheers filled the air, and her eyes almost ached at the riot of colors—especially the variations on purple, green, and gold, the "official" colors of Mardi Gras, according to the pre-trip research she'd done. This was so different from the seedy scenes in the French Quarter the night before that she could hardly believe she was in the same city.

Across the street, people thronged the balconies of the Buccaneer Hotel, which was where she had wanted to stay when the idea of the trip was initially broached. Roger had dithered, as he so often did—that should have been a sign, she realized now—and the Buccaneer had sold out long before they'd made their reservation. Instead, they were at a dump called the Crescent Palms Motel, in a marginal neighborhood, miles from the parade route. She wasn't sure whether the cockroaches or the bedbugs would win the war for dominance of the room—the roaches had size and weight, but the bedbugs had strength in numbers. Either way, she knew who the loser was.

She noticed a man sitting by himself on one of the third-floor balconies. He looked like a serviceman, wearing a khaki uniform of some kind. He was African American, slender, maybe in his late thirties, she guessed, and the reason he stood out to her was because it looked like from his chair, he could barely see the parade passing below him. Something else seemed to be on his mind. He looked worried, even afraid. Caydee found herself checking up on him often, hoping that whatever was weighing on him would leave him alone so he could enjoy the hotel room he'd obviously paid a small fortune for.

A gasp coursed through the crowd like an electrical charge as the next float lumbered into view. This parade was put on by the Krewe of Poseidon, and the sea king himself loomed over the float. Poseidon was fifteen or twenty feet tall, she guessed, a papier-mâché giant with shaggy hair and a long, flowing beard made of silvery feathers. That beard looked soft, not like the one Roger had been growing out for the past few months, which sometimes made her feel like she was making out with a Brillo pad. Clutched in Poseidon's raised fist was a trident that looked like real metal and towered another seven or eight feet above the figure's head.

People on the float were tossing "throws" to the audience lining both sides of St. Charles: more plastic beads, doubloons, rubber tentacles and sharks, even a few shoes. Caydee had caught a strand of beads earlier, and had got her foot down on a tentacle before anyone else could, but for the sake of her fingers, she hadn't tried to pick it up until after the people around her had stopped stomping at it themselves. Now it was safe in the pocket of her jeans and the gold beads hung around her neck. No nudity necessary, thank you very much, Roger.

She was watching one of the Krewe dressed as a masked pirate tossing out gold-colored plastic chalices when a sudden motion on the balcony across the street caught her eye. It was the serviceman again, she realized, but he was no longer sitting in that chair, well back from the edge. Instead, he was standing at the railing—no, not standing. Lunging, climbing… she couldn't even tell. He was a flurry of movement, all khaki and dark skin, and was that someone behind him? Was he trying to escape the balcony, or—

Then Caydee stopped trying to figure out what was happening, because none of it made any logical sense. The man was perched for an instant on the railing, and then he was *flying*, soaring through the air. But he was airborne for just moments before his course altered again, and then he was plummeting toward the street.

No, not that far. Because the float was passing just beneath him, and the tines of Poseidon's trident broke his fall. She blew out the breath she'd been holding, but it caught in her throat when the tines erupted out the other side of him. As blood began to drip down onto the float's passengers, Caydee started to scream.

So did everyone else.

Almost everyone else.

Sitting against the wall, head in his hands and oblivious to the scene in the street, Roger just moaned.

1

Dwayne Cassius Pride—"King" to special friends, and, more often than not, less respectful names to people he had arrested—had enjoyed a lot of Mardi Gras celebrations. A lifetime of them, in fact. He had been to the balls, listened to what seemed like thousands of musicians and bands of every style, size, and degree of talent, and watched parades from every angle: looking down from rooftops or balconies, riding on the floats, sitting at a restaurant table with a good meal in front of him, a beer, a Sazerac, or a glass of fine wine close at hand.

The floats could be fun, and most of the millions of people who'd watched the parades and participated in the long stretch of celebrations held between Epiphany and Ash Wednesday would never have a chance to experience riding them. He would always be happy that he had been able to. But the experience was limiting, too—the crowd passed by in a blur, his view partially blocked by the requisite mask; the sound was a ferocious roar in which individual voices, much less the notes played by the float's musicians, were utterly lost; and the constant motion of dipping into the containers of throws and tossing them overboard made the whole experience into a kind of grueling ordeal. It was nonetheless a blast, of course, and not an experience he would ever regret. Nobody who rode on a float forgot it; in the days immediately following, they remembered every time they tried to lift their hands above chest height, and the ringing in their ears reminded them at every otherwise quiet moment.

This year, Pride was more than content to watch from the sidewalk, like the hundreds of thousands of visitors and locals lining the parade route. He had arrived early and staked out a spot near the corner of Napoleon and St. Charles. The parade made a turn there, enabling the spectators to get a good look at each float from multiple angles. The marching bands slowed for the turn, too, so the crowd got to hear a little more of each performance than they would elsewhere on the route.

The morning was cool; spotty showers the night before had dampened the streets, but fortunately hadn't lingered past sunrise. Still, Pride had worn a brown leather jacket until the press of bodies and the sun pushing through cloud cover warmed the day. Now he held it slung over his shoulder. He stood with family, by blood and by choice: daughter Laurel and fellow NCIS special agents Chris Lasalle and Sonja Percy, Jefferson Parish medical examiner Doctor Loretta Wade, and forensic agent Sebastian Lund. Investigative computer specialist Patton Plame sat among them in his wheelchair, with purple, green, and gold streamers threaded between the spokes of his wheels. Pride had hoped Tammy Gregorio, his team's newest addition, could be there, but Washington, in its infinite wisdom and mercy, had chosen Mardi Gras week to summon her to lead some specialized training workshops.

The Krewe of Zulu parade had passed by earlier. The Krewe of Poseidon parade had just finished; next would come the Krewe of Rex. Shrove Tuesday was a legal holiday in Louisiana and, with any luck, the day's NCIS workload would be light to nonexistent. Over at CFA, the bar Pride owned, manager and bartender Michael Buckley was no doubt already being run ragged. It would only get busier toward evening, so Pride expected he would be helping out there later on.

Then he heard the screams echoing from farther down St. Charles Avenue, and he winced. They didn't necessarily portend trouble for NCIS, but they assuredly meant that somebody's day had just gotten a lot worse.

"Come on, folks," he said. "I don't know what's going on down there, but whatever it is, I expect NOPD could use a hand."

"I hope it's just *your* hands that are needed, and not mine," Loretta Wade replied. "Mardi Gras parades should be memorable, not fatal."

"I think we're all hoping that," Pride said. "Only one way to know for sure, though. Let's go learn things."

"He was *gigged*!" Lasalle said.

"Excuse me?" Sonja said. "What do you mean by that, Country Mouse?"

"I wouldn't expect you to know, City Mouse," Lasalle countered. "But gigging is when you go fishing with a multi-pronged spear."

"Like a trident?"

"Exactly like a trident."

Sonja shook her head. "The things you learn…"

"Hang with me, Percy. I'll teach you *lots* of things."

"I just bet you will. Only most of them, I probably don't want to know."

The police department had cleared St. Charles Avenue and rerouted the later parades, much to the consternation of people who had been lining the street since before sunrise to claim prime spots. Considering the size of the crowd, Pride thought the NOPD had handled the situation as well as they could. There had been complaints and a few scuffles, but most people had complied, especially once the reason for the shift spread through the crowd. Then the problem became the morbidly curious, those more interested in seeing the victim than watching the rest of the parades. The NOPD had pushed them back to the ends of the block, sealing the area with CRIME SCENE tape and as many uniformed officers as could be spared.

EMTs and firefighters had worked together to free the victim from the trident and bring him down to the street, and Loretta was performing a preliminary investigation on the body. Pride stood with Sebastian, who shook his head sadly. "I've seen some compromised crime scenes before," he said, "but never one that probably had five thousand people walk all over it between the crime and the investigation."

Pride nodded toward the still-bloody trident atop the float. "That's the crime scene, not this street," he said. "That float, and that balcony over there."

"Yeah, on top of that trident? You remember that I'm not great with heights?"

"I won't make you climb it," Pride assured him. "You can focus on trying to figure out if this was a homicide, a suicide, or an accident."

"Yeah, that sounds better," Sebastian said. "I'll stay

here and work on—well, what you said. Thanks."

Sebastian wandered off to get a wider view of the overall scene. When he had gone, Pride surveyed the street. The detritus of the spectators remained very obvious: cigarette butts, food wrappers, empty go-cups and broken bottles and dented aluminum cans, dirty disposable diapers, abandoned parade throws everywhere. It was a good thing the victim had never hit the ground, he thought, or Sebastian would have been stuck in the lab for the next ten years, examining every item recovered from the scene for trace evidence.

"Dwayne?"

Pride's attention snapped back to the medical examiner. "Yes, Miss Loretta?"

She had opened a wallet on a clean spot on the victim's clothing, and she held a couple of plastic cards out toward Pride. "We knew from the service khaki uniform that the victim was Navy. Here's his ID. He's Lieutenant Edouard Alpuente. The address on the driver's license is in Nicholson, Mississippi."

"Nicholson?" Pride echoed.

"He must work out at Stennis," Lasalle suggested.

"That'd be my guess," Pride said, taking the cards and glancing at them. Stennis Space Center was a NASA field center—primarily a rocket testing facility—but it also served as the home base for various U.S. Navy organizations, including the Naval Meteorology and Oceanography Command, the Naval Oceanographic Office, and a small craft training center.

According to his driver's license, Alpuente was thirty-four years old. He looked younger. He was an African American man, trim, with a short, military-style haircut. His eyes were set far apart, but his most prominent facial feature was a strong chin with a cleft in it. He had been a handsome man, cut down in his prime.

"Interestingly, I also found *this*," Loretta said, interrupting Pride's review of the victim's appearance. She raised a small cloth bag, dirty red and tied at the top with string. The fabric was worn almost through in some places, and ragged at the edges.

"What is that?" Lasalle asked.

Pride took it from Loretta's hand, handing back the lieutenant's ID cards at the same time. He didn't have to open the little bag to know the answer to Lasalle's query. "*Gris-gris* bag," he said.

"*Gris-gris*? As in voodoo?"

"That's right, Chris." Pride untied the bag and poured the contents into his palm. He counted eleven items altogether: some tiny plastic bags containing herbs, a piece of root he didn't recognize, what looked like a desiccated mushroom, a couple of small metal charms, a crystal, what he guessed was a chunk of white bone, and a fragment of heavy, cream-colored paper on which was a hand-drawn sigil. "They're meant to ward off evil spirits and bad luck."

"I guess it didn't work for him," Sonja said.

"Or somebody else had some stronger juju," Loretta replied.

"Wait a minute," Lasalle said. "So this guy is working at one of the most advanced scientific facilities in the world, and he believes in voodoo?"

"It's impossible to say yet if he truly believed," Loretta said. "But if he did, it wouldn't be unheard of. Science and the spiritual are sometimes separated only by a thin veil, if any. Is it easier to believe in a Big Bang than in the power of *Li Grand Zombi*?"

"It is for me," Lasalle said. "Do you believe in voodoo?"

Loretta chuckled and shook her head. "Science is what I do," she said. "All I'm saying is that it doesn't hurt to keep an open mind. About voodoo, and just about anything else."

Pride didn't want the conversation to devolve into a philosophical discussion of belief systems, given how much work lay ahead. "What else do you have, Loretta?" he asked.

"I can say for sure that Lieutenant Alpuente was alive when he hit the trident," she said. "And that his death was quick and relatively painless, after that. The tines are barbed at the top, so the entry and exit wounds were larger than the diameter of the shafts. The barbs opened good-sized holes, and he bled out rapidly." She touched the man's blood-soaked uniform shirt. "I won't know for certain until I have him on my table, but I believe one penetrated his heart."

"Bad way to go," Sonja said. "But I guess it could have been worse."

"It could have been much worse," Loretta agreed. "The trident was part of the support structure holding up the deck, so it was solidly built. Landing on it was going to injure him, but if things had been different, he could have died much more slowly and with a great deal more pain. If it were me… well, I would choose to go fast."

In the distance, Pride could hear the roar of another parade: the music, the cheers and applause, the familiar sounds of Mardi Gras in New Orleans. America's biggest party. Those watching were having the time of their lives, and those participating were taking part in an old and rich tradition—one that helped define the city that he loved.

But he and his team were here, on a now largely

deserted street, examining the victim of a violent death. *Which is as it should be*, he thought. *Alpuente will never experience another Mardi Gras. Our duty is to figure out why, and find whoever is responsible.*

Sebastian rejoined the team, looking at the screen of his smartphone as he crossed toward them.

"I ran a quick check on the ID Loretta found," he began. "The victim is from Shell Beach, in St. Bernard Parish. Unmarried. He lives in MS, but is also renting a house over in Tremé, on a month-to-month basis."

He tapped on his screen, then looked up with a half-smile on his face. Pride felt his phone buzz in his pocket. "I just texted you all the addresses of his rental, and a home he owns in Nicholson."

"Thanks, Sebastian," Pride said. "Chris, Sonja, why don't you two go check out that house in Tremé? Sebastian and I will drop into the Buccaneer Hotel and try to find out what a guy who had a house across the state line and one here in town was doing on that hotel balcony, besides watching a parade. You okay here, Loretta?"

"I'm nearly finished. I'll get Lt. Alpuente moved to the morgue and I'll have more for you later today."

"All right, then," Pride said. "Let's get to it. Oh, and by the way—happy Mardi Gras."

2

"Pride."

Pride stopped and looked at the man who had spoken his name. New Orleans Police Department Detective Byron Menefee stood in the street, crooking a finger in a "come hither" motion. His massive shoulders were hunched as usual, his neck almost nonexistent behind them. He wore a dark blue suit jacket that might have fit him forty pounds earlier, but was splitting at the seams now, a white shirt that didn't quite close over his substantial gut, and a red tie. The flaglike colors didn't look like a patriotic display on him, but instead like the sartorial decisions of a man who chose his clothes in the dark and hoped for the best.

But he was a good detective, and through periods when the NOPD's reputation had suffered from allegations of corruption—allegations that were true, as often as not—Menefee had always maintained a clean reputation. He was wrinkled and he hadn't shaved in a couple of days and he had a hangdog expression and bleary eyes rimmed in red. Despite appearances, he was a solid cop, a longtime veteran of the homicide unit, and one of the most effective investigators on that constantly overworked, understaffed team. So Pride, who had been headed into the hotel, veered away when Menefee beckoned.

"Byron," he said. "It's good to see you. Your guys did a great job clearing the street."

"It'll be years before they forgive you for that."

"I'm not the one who decided to stage a homicide in the middle of a Mardi Gras parade."

"Homicide? Are you sure about that?" He looked at Sebastian, and Pride could read a second question in his eyes.

"This is Sebastian Lund, our newest agent. Sebastian, Detective Byron Menefee is as good a cop as cops get."

Sebastian and Byron shook hands. Sebastian was about to say something, but Pride broke in before he could get it out. "In answer to your question, Byron, not officially, but between you and me, it looks like a homicide to me. I'm open to being persuaded otherwise, but suicides tend to be private matters, and this was... well, pretty public. The victim is ours, so it won't be any trouble for you. I mean, beyond the obvious."

"Thanks, Pride," Menefee said. "I just wanted to make sure you know that we'll provide whatever help we can. Just ask."

"Thanks, Byron."

Menefee's grin twitched the ends of his mustache. "I mean, you know, if you don't count all the unis who are going to hold a grudge against you for making them shift an entire parade route."

Pride knew he was right. There were cops on the force who would take a long time to forgive the man who had insisted that it be done, regardless of whose fault the original incident had been. "So who does that leave?" Pride asked, wary of the answer.

The detective shrugged. "Well… me, I guess."

"You sure you're not mad at me, too?"

"Now that you mention it, I'm still kind of peeved at you for winning that Super Bowl bet."

"My team appreciated the beignets," Pride said. His favorite kind of bet. "So did the random people on the street who got the leftovers. We'll have to do it again next year."

Menefee chuckled and turned as if to walk away. "Oh, one more thing," he said. "I found a witness for you."

"To the trident incident?"

"To the homicide, in your words. Yeah, that."

"Who is it?"

Menefee pointed toward a young woman standing outside the yellow tape, flanked by two uniformed officers. "Her. Tourist from Ohio. She says she was looking up at the guy on the balcony. Saw the whole thing."

"Why did you take so long to mention that?"

"Hey," Menefee said. "Two dozen beignets don't come cheap."

The witness's name was Caydee Spurgeon, and as it turned out, she didn't see much at all. Menefee had the cops bring her inside the tape, and Pride met her in the shade of a tree. He'd asked Sebastian to wait some distance away; she was still shaken by what she'd seen, and two agents would feel like an interrogation, not a conversation. He let her sit on the curb, and he sat down beside her, speaking in low, measured tones, trying his hardest to be a calming presence instead of coming across like just another cop.

"How are you enjoying New Orleans?" he asked.

"The city's beautiful."

"It really is, isn't it?"

"I love the history, the architecture, the culture. The music everywhere you turn. Oh, and the *food*."

Pride smiled and nodded. "We're kind of known for that."

"Deservedly so. I wish I was here with someone else, though."

"Why? Who are you with?"

"My boyfriend." She shot a glance at the tape line. A young man sat on the sidewalk, looking her way. When he saw her turn, he gave her a feeble wave. He looked a little pale. "Ex-boyfriend, really, or he will be soon. He doesn't know that yet, though."

"I'm sorry," Pride said.

"Don't be. I'm glad I found out now, before it's too late."

"There's something to be said for that, I guess. Forewarned is forearmed, or something like that."

"I won't bore you with the whole sordid tale," she said. "But if I could change my flight, I'd let him go home alone. I'd rather not have to travel with him."

"I can make some calls," he offered.

"Really? You would do that?"

"Nothing to it," Pride said. "We like people to go home from New Orleans happy, and we'll usually do whatever we can to make that happen. It's the best way to make people want to come back."

"Oh, thank you," she said, fairly gushing. Pride was embarrassed for her, so he changed the subject.

"Can you tell me what you saw?"

She considered the question for a few moments before she answered. He was glad; it meant she was replaying the memory in her head, trying to describe it correctly. Or she was making up a lie, but he didn't get that impression from her, and he considered himself a pretty fair judge of character.

"I looked up. He was right across from me, only, you know, up there, sitting on the balcony. He was facing the parade, but I had the impression he had something else on his mind, like he was so lost in his thoughts that he wasn't really seeing anything in front of him. His chair was so far back he could hardly see it, anyway. I thought it was sad that he was so preoccupied that he wasn't enjoying this amazing spectacle, especially considering how much he must have spent on that hotel room."

"You have a good eye," Pride said.

"I was an art history major," she explained. "Which means I work in a bank now, because careers in art history are kind of thin on the ground in Ohio. But I guess I notice things. Visually, anyway; I'm not so good with sounds."

"Maybe you should look into a law enforcement career."

"You think?"

"Couldn't hurt. Police officers need to be able to scan a street and process what they see. And to remember it afterwards."

She smiled. "I'll think about that. Thank you."

"What did you see next?" he pressed.

"When I looked up there again, he was on his feet, at the rail. I thought he was clutching it pretty tightly, but then I realized that he wasn't really standing there. He was in motion. Over it."

"By himself, or…?"

"I couldn't tell, honestly. There might have been somebody else… someone behind him on the balcony.

Or it might have just been his shadow. I don't know, honestly. I mean, I've tried and tried to remember. But really, it was all so fast and so shocking and it only took a second. I saw him flying out over the rail and headed for the float, and then he landed and I... I guess I kind of closed my eyes, because..."

"Nobody could blame you for that, Caydee. I'm sorry you had to see it."

"I know I'll have nightmares about it forever."

"I wouldn't be a bit surprised. I can tell you, they'll fade, with time. But it's not something you're ever likely to forget, unfortunately."

"Anyway, after I opened my eyes again, I looked back up there. Really, I wanted to see anything except that float. But the balcony was empty. And he was... he was..."

"I know, Caydee. It's okay. Thank you for everything you've told me." He slipped a business card from his pocket and handed it to her. "There's my information. If you think of anything else, please call me anytime. If it's okay with you, I'll turn you back over to the NOPD. They'll take your contact information, so if I can do anything about changing your ticket, I'll be able to reach you."

"That's so nice, Special Agent Pride," she said. She turned the card over and over, as if looking for something on it that wasn't there, then put it in her pocket. "I don't know how to thank you."

"You just enjoy the rest of your New Orleans vacation," he said. "And when you get home, tell your friends. I mean, tell them about the good parts, not just the awful ones."

He gestured to one of the uniformed officers, who came and fetched the young woman and walked her back to the other side of the tape. The young man waiting for her didn't get the enthusiastic reception he seemed to be expecting.

The course of young love, Pride thought. He caught Sebastian's eye and headed for the Buccaneer.

"Dwayne Pride! It's been an age and a half."

"At least that," he replied with a grin. "How're you holding up, Rose? Last I saw you, you were singing at d.b.a."

Rose Vergados smiled and came out from behind the hotel's check-in counter, moving in close for a hug. She was the kind of woman for whom the adjective "willowy" had been coined, slender and as flexible as a dancer. She smelled like a tropical rain forest, floral and fragrant. "Those were good times, weren't they?" she said. "But with Paul's health issues, you know, I needed benefits. Insurance."

Her husband, Pride remembered now, had suffered a run of bad luck. Parkinson's, he thought, then colon cancer, and various complications that stemmed from those. As he so often did, he offered silent thanks that such things had not afflicted him or his immediate family. "So you work here now?"

"It's worse than that," she said with a laugh. "I manage the joint."

"I guess you've had better days than today, then," Pride said. "I'm sorry about what happened this morning."

Her smile faded and she ran her fingers through her thick, blond hair. "You could say that. Is that why you're here? That poor man? And here I was hoping it was a social call."

"I wish it was, too. Official business, I'm afraid."

He introduced her to Sebastian.

"A little while after it happened, a couple of police officers came in," Rose said. "They looked inside, but the room was empty. They sealed it off and said detectives would be over later. I'm just surprised that it's you."

"The victim was Navy, so now it's an NCIS case. NOPD's busy with crowd control, anyway."

"No doubt." Rose slid behind the hotel's front desk. The pirate theme implied by the name carried over to the décor. Gold paint was abundant, as were displays of fake treasure chests overflowing with gold pieces. Huge, framed prints of pirate paintings by N.C. Wyeth, Howard Pyle, and other artists Pride didn't recognize hung on the walls. Tall potted plants inhabited by brightly painted wooden parrots flanked the check-in counter, which had been built from aged wooden planks that might be found on a ship, in a kind of wedge shape suggesting a prow.

Rose tapped some keys on a keyboard down behind the counter, where Pride couldn't see. "The balcony the man fell from belongs to room 327," she said. "It was occupied by someone named J.B. Goodtown. That's a strange name, isn't it?"

"You must see plenty of strange names in this business," Sebastian said. "And strange people, for that matter."

"That's for sure. But that's not all that's strange here."

"What do you mean?" Pride asked.

"There's no credit card on file, or any indication that the room was prepaid. It looks like a complimentary booking. But that doesn't make any sense. We might— under truly extenuating circumstances—comp a room during Mardi Gras, even one with a parade-view balcony. But only to a major celebrity or a very highly valued regular guest. Nobody named J.B. Goodtown fits either of those criteria. And I would have to have approved the comp, but I didn't."

"When did he check in?"

"Two days ago," Rose said. "He would have checked out tomorrow."

"That's a short stay."

"Not that unusual for this time of year—a lot of people just want to be here for the parade. But yes, it's on the short side."

"Has anyone else been inside the room? Since the incident, I mean?"

"Just the two uniformed officers. One of them is still upstairs, watching it. I told the staff that under no circumstances were any of them to set foot in there without my say-so."

"That's good, Rose, thanks." Pride took a step toward the elevator, then stopped and turned back to her. "We'll need a copy of the security video, too."

"For the third floor, this morning? Of course."

"For the entire hotel. Since the morning of the day he checked in."

"That will take a little longer, Dwayne."

"Understood. Let me know when it's ready and I'll have it picked up."

"Will do. Are you two going to go up there?"

"Yes. We have to."

"I understand. Do me a favor?"

"Name it."

"Find out what happened. As soon as you can. Something like this—on a day like this, when all eyes are on New Orleans? That can kill a hotel's reputation. Just absolutely kill it. And I really can't afford to have to go hunting for another job."

"We will, Rose. That's what we do. Although, to be honest, it's not the killing of the hotel's reputation I'm most concerned about."

She blushed. "Of course. That's not what I—"

"Don't worry, Rose. We're good at what we do."

"I don't doubt that for an instant."

"Oh, also?"

"Yes, Dwayne?"

"I hope you haven't stopped singing altogether. Your 'Crescent City Blues' is the best I've ever heard, including Beverly Maher's original."

3

As Rose had said, a uniformed NOPD officer was sitting in a straight-backed chair in front of room 327. The chair was tipped back against the wall, so the officer's weight rested entirely on the two back legs, and he was flipping through something on his smartphone. The door to 327 was slightly ajar, but only by an inch or so, not open wide enough for anyone to see inside. Underneath the chair was a clipboard with a pen tied to it on a length of dirty string. The officer was a huge guy with a broad, flat face, his skin as pink as a baby's behind. Pride felt sorry for the chair.

"NCIS," he said, showing his ID and badge.

The officer started at the voice and dropped the chair back onto all four legs. "I've been expecting you guys," the officer said. "Or somebody, I guess. Not you specifically." His name tag said MASON.

"Has anyone been inside?"

Mason reached under the chair, pulled out the clipboard, and handed it to Pride. "Just me and my partner, Dev Billings."

"Do either of you know the victim?"

Mason tipped his chair back again. "I didn't really get a good look at him. He was kind of high up when I came inside. I've been here ever since."

"His name's Edouard Alpuente. He's a Navy lieutenant from SSC."

"That name don't sound familiar."

Pride wrote down his name and badge number on the visitor checklist on the man's clipboard. The pen was almost out of ink, and skipped spaces as he wrote. "You might want to get a new pen," he said, passing the clipboard to Sebastian.

"You offering?"

"I'm sure the department can afford one."

"Do you want me to stay out here?" He sounded like he was hoping to be released. Pride wasn't sure why—it wasn't the most exciting assignment of the day, but it probably beat standing with his back to a parade, telling over-excited kids to keep their feet out of the street. And there was essentially no chance that he would be rained on or otherwise drenched, which was more than the cops working the parade could say.

"Yes," Pride said. "Until we can finish processing the scene, please keep the room secured."

"OT?"

"You can take overtime up with your captain." Pride ushered Sebastian in, then closed the door before Mason could ask any more questions.

Inside the room, the pirate theme was more subdued than down in the lobby. Instead, there was a semi-tropical air to the room, with floral wallpaper and fresh flowers in a cut-glass vase, a batik bedspread, and furnishings that wouldn't have been out of place in a Tiki lounge or backstage at a Jimmy Buffett concert. French doors to the balcony stood open, and a gentle breeze blew in, carrying the blended aromas of the Mississippi River with it. Pride smelled algae and fish, diesel and jasmine, along with less identifiable odors.

It smelled like New Orleans. Smelled like home.

"Yuck," Sebastian said. "A hotel room. Grand Central for DNA transference. Ever since I started studying forensic science, it's been almost impossible for me to stay in a hotel. And when I do—well, let's just say it's really hard to fall asleep when you're wearing a hazmat suit."

"I'm sure it is," Pride replied. He knew Sebastian was a professional. He would complain—he wouldn't be Sebastian if he didn't—but soon enough, he'd focus on the task at hand.

The room didn't look much like a crime scene. The bed wasn't made to Navy standards, but the covers had been pulled neatly up. A glass-topped coffee table held magazines left there by the hotel, along with a copy of yesterday's *Nola Dispatch*.

It also didn't look like the room's occupant had planned for a long stay. On a table beside the bed was a small, framed photograph of Alpuente with a young woman. They were sitting at a restaurant, heads together, arms around one another's shoulders. They looked close; he guessed romantically involved, though it was hard to be certain from one picture. The woman was pretty, but Pride didn't recognize her and it was impossible to get much of a sense of her from the picture.

He pulled open the drawer below the picture. Inside was a laptop computer, closed and powered off, a bottle of pills—Marplan; the prescription label had Alpuente's name on it—and what could only be a voodoo doll.

The doll was made of various fabrics, stitched together with seemingly random bits of thread: white and red silks and satins for the clothing, with beads serving as tiny buttons, bunched brown twine for limbs, and a cloth head with crude facial features painted on. Pride picked it up, squeezed it. There might have been a wooden cross providing its structure, with a longer piece stretching from head to feet (the legs were sewn together), and a crossbar for the arms. It was elaborate, but not sophisticated—folk art, like most professionally sold voodoo dolls Pride had seen. This one had a name typed on a slip of paper and pinned to it: Dan Petro. The name meant nothing to him.

Sebastian was across the room, checking out the closet and a small suitcase on a folding luggage stand. "Sebastian," Pride said. "I have something for you."

Sebastian turned, his face brightening, then fading just as quickly. "Oh," he said. "Evidence. I thought for a second you meant a gift. Or, you know, something to eat." He had on a brown cardigan sweater over a Crescent City Comics T-shirt, with brown pants and sneakers, and something about the outfit emphasized his thinness. He had always been lean, but the thought passed through Pride's mind that it wouldn't hurt to buy him a po' boy or a muffuletta once in a while.

"I wouldn't recommend eating this," Pride said. "But it is a little different from your run-of-the-mill hair or bodily fluid samples." He held up the doll.

"A voodoo doll! Cool!"

"We'll need to know everything you can get out of it. Origin, any significance in voodoo beliefs. There's a name pinned to it, Dan Petro, but it doesn't mean anything to me."

"I'll do some digging when we get back to the

squad room," Sebastian promised. "Or I'll run it over to the lab."

Pride set the doll back down. "Anything in that suitcase?" he asked.

"As empty as a banker's soul," Sebastian replied. He tugged open the dresser drawers, but only one had anything in it: a tumble of dirty clothes. The closet was as empty as the suitcase.

In the bathroom, Pride found a toothbrush, toothpaste, comb, electric shaver. Alpuente had used the shampoo and soap supplied by the hotel, but the conditioner and body lotion bottles were undisturbed.

Pride had the impression that if Alpuente had spent much time in the room, he had been largely inactive. He might have read the magazines and the *Dispatch* from front to back, or watched TV, but he hadn't done anything that left a mark on the room. The other alternative was that he had taken it for some specific purpose, and had otherwise hardly used it. But what would that purpose have been? What had he been doing up here? Meditating? Sleeping? Hiding?

And what would have caused him to rent the room under an assumed name, without even putting down a credit card to verify his actual identity? At Mardi Gras, the room would have cost hundreds of dollars. Something was going on here, and Pride needed to know what it was.

While Sebastian swabbed for DNA, and checked for fingerprints, Pride stood in the middle of the room, trying to put himself in Alpuente's head. Secrecy probably meant the man was afraid of being found out. Why? He looked at the photograph of Alpuente with the young woman again. Was he having an affair? With her? They were together in a restaurant, having their picture taken by somebody. So maybe she was his girlfriend, and he was cheating on her with someone else. In that case, though, would one of the only bits of his personal life he had brought into the room have been that particular photo? And would he have left it standing on the night table?

That seemed unlikely. Pride couldn't rule it out— people had all kinds of strange ideas, after all, and when it came to sex, it was never safe to assume anything. Maybe his playmate found it a turn-on to make love in front of a picture of him with his girlfriend.

Then again, maybe it had nothing to do with sex at all. Hotel rooms could have other purposes. A secret meeting, perhaps. For what? Espionage? Drugs?

There were too many possibilities. He had to know more about Alpuente before he could narrow them down. With luck, Lasalle and Sonja would learn more at the house in Tremé.

Before he processed the room, Pride pushed aside heavy drapes and went out onto the balcony. A breeze ruffled his hair, brushed like ghostly fingertips across his face. It was laced with warmth and moisture, a harbinger of spring. He looked out at the broad expanse of St. Charles below, with the streetcar tracks running up the neutral ground in the middle of the street. Two hours ago it had been wall-to-wall bodies. Now, the street was almost empty. Loretta was there with a couple of her people, preparing Alpuente for his trip to the morgue. A handful of cops wandered around, trying to look busy. A pair of detectives interviewed potential witnesses, though Caydee Spurgeon had been in as good a spot as anyone, and seen nothing that would help. Beyond the yellow tape, stray onlookers angled for a glimpse of the victim. Beyond St. Charles, looking toward the river, Pride could see the rooftops of New Orleans.

His city.

He put his hands on the railing of the balcony. It would have taken quite a leap to reach the trident from here. The float had been on the other side of the street, so Alpuente would have had to go above the streetcar's overhead cables. Maybe an Olympic track-and-field star could have done it; Pride doubted that he could.

"Sebastian!" he called.

A moment later, the curtains fluttered, and Sebastian untangled himself from them. "You rang?"

"Look at the distance Alpuente had to cover to reach that trident," Pride said. "Do you think he could have done that?"

"It's a stretch," Sebastian said. He eyed the width of the balcony. "He couldn't really get a running start. Maybe if he started inside the room and didn't, you know, bump into the curtains…"

"But they were closed."

"Officer Mason out there probably didn't close them. He doesn't strike me as exactly the self-starter type."

"Not unless somebody pays him to be," Pride said.

"Anyway, I'd say no. Somebody distressed enough to kill himself isn't likely to make such a Herculean leap. And if he missed the trident, he might have lived, but probably with some broken bones. Lots of pain. I don't think we're looking at a suicide."

"I don't either," Pride said. He turned back to the view.

Looking out over the city, he was struck by a realization with a suddenness that made him laugh out loud. He should have known it right from the start, but he'd had other things on his mind.

J.B. Goodtown? Clearly an alias. Invented by Alpuente or someone else, he didn't yet know, but definitely a phony name.

The explorer generally credited with founding New Orleans—at the very least, when it had been officially founded in 1718, the man serving as director of the French Mississippi Company—was Jean-Baptiste Le Moyne de Bienville. He had later served four terms as the governor of Louisiana.

In French, *bien ville* meant "good town." Nobody would say it in conversation, but somebody with limited French—or with a sense of humor—might translate it that way.

So not only an alias, but an alias disguised by translation into another language. And at the same time, a historical reference to the city itself.

Curiouser and curiouser, as Alice had said after finding herself in Wonderland. Pride had hoped that by coming up here, he would discover a simple solution to Alpuente's miraculous flight, and they would be able to wrap up this case quickly. Alpuente's loved ones, whoever they were, deserved answers.

Instead, all he had found were more questions.

He filled his eyes with the city he loved, inhaled its essence, listened to its music on the air, then went back inside and closed the door.

4

The house in Tremé was painted a vibrant magenta, but the bottle tree in front caught the sun and threw it into Lasalle's eyes like daggers made of light, almost blinding him to the color of the walls. "I need sunglasses just to look at the place," he said.

"It's that tree," Sonja said. "All that glass is reflecting like crazy."

Lasalle steered around a pothole almost big enough to lose a school bus in—the streets here seemed to have been last paved around the time the internal combustion engine was invented—and pulled his truck up in front of the house. In the house's front yard was a scrawny tree, with glass bottles of every color and shape stuck on the end of almost every branch. There must have been a hundred of them, maybe more. "It's a bottle tree," he said. "Back in 'Bama, some people had 'em, too. For most it's just decoration, but a neighbor told me once that some people believed the glass bottles on the branches caught evil spirits that swarmed around the house at night, and held them until the rising sun could destroy them."

"Handy," Sonja replied, "if you're worried about evil spirits coming around. Do they make one for bill collectors?"

"I think you're gonna need bigger bottles."

"Remember Alpuente's *gris-gris* bag? I wouldn't be surprised if he believed in those spirits, too."

"You could be right," Lasalle agreed.

The house was a simple, wooden-sided affair, set off from the sidewalk by a low wrought-iron fence. Three steps led up to an open porch with a faded wicker settee and a small wooden table on it. Lasalle opened the gate and went inside, scanning the windows for motion as he did. He didn't know if Alpuente had any roommates, but caution was always a good idea.

"What the hell is *that*?" Sonja asked.

"What?" Lasalle replied. Even as he spoke, he saw what she meant.

Hanging from the doorknob on a leather thong was a withered, furry *something*.

"Oh, that," he said. "I don't know. Some kind of… hand?"

Sonja moved past him, eyeballing the object without touching it. "It's a paw," she said. "I think it's a monkey's paw."

Lasalle leaned in for a closer look. "I think you're right, Percy. So the next question is, did Alpuente put it there himself, or did someone else leave it here?"

"If it was someone else, that could explain what he was doing in a hotel," Sonja suggested. "If he was a believer and he came home to find that thing hanging on his door, he might not even have wanted to go inside. He might have just climbed back in his car and driven away. I don't think I'd blame him."

"Well, we need to go in, monkey's paw or not." Lasalle knocked on the door. "NCIS!" he called. "Anyone home?"

Only silence answered. "Break it down?" he asked.

"Sebastian said he was renting it," Sonja reminded him. "Maybe there's a landlord in the area."

"Good call. I'll check." He brought up Sebastian on his phone, and a few moments later, asked his question.

"Landlord," Sebastian said. "I had that here a minute ago. Did you know that forcing a person to 'clean up' a cluttered workspace can actually result in a significant loss of productivity? The workspace might look chaotic to the outside observer, but to the worker, it's organized chaos. People who clutter up their workspace know just where they put things, and—"

"Is that your way of telling me you lost it? Or that Loretta made you clean up?"

"No," Sebastian said. "Well, really, no and no, since you asked two separate questions. I had Lt. Alpuente's rental information on my monitor, but then covered it up with other windows. I've got it now, though."

"Give it to me."

"It's actually a land*lady*. If we still use that differentiation in today's world. Her name is Meghan Webster, and she lives… one second, here, let me map it… oh! She lives in the house directly behind him. Same property. Just go around back."

"That's handy," Lasalle said. "Thanks, Sebastian."

"Don't mention it. Although you already did, so I guess that's kind of a moot—"

"Bye, Sebastian."

"Right. Bye, Chr—"

Lasalle pocketed his phone and nodded toward the rear of the house. "She lives in back. Meghan Webster."

"Well, let's go see Ms. Webster, then," Sonja said. "She's got to have a key. And maybe there's a back door, so we don't have to mess with that nasty paw."

"You mean until we collect it in an evidence bag."

"Yeah," she said. "Until *you* collect it in an evidence bag. That's what I meant."

Lasalle laughed as he descended the three steps. "We'll see, Percy, we'll see. It's not like it's a spider."

"That's true."

"Of course," he said, glancing back over his shoulder, "there could be spiders inside it."

She couldn't suppress a shudder. Sonja was the bravest woman he knew. He had seen her knock down doors and face gunfire, watched her go undercover with murderous drug kingpins and known killers. Spiders were another thing altogether. She was no fan of nature in general, and spiders were, in her view, nature's biggest mistake. "All those eyes and legs," she had said once, "couldn't be on purpose. Somebody messed with the blueprints."

"Done deal, Lasalle," she said. "That paw is all yours."

They went around the house, following the path of a narrow driveway that ran past the low fence. Another house sat at the rear of the property, smaller than the magenta one. The siding Lasalle could see was weathered and pale, but a painter was working around the corner, his color-spattered, once-white pickup truck parked beside the house. His bare torso was speckled with sky blue, and he waved a paintbrush when Lasalle nodded his way.

Before they even reached the front door, a woman stepped outside. She was lean and leathery, with short platinum hair. She reminded Lasalle of Gulf Coast beachcombers, people whose love of the sun overruled concern about what it might be doing to them. She held a cigarette in one hand, smoke wafting up toward her eyes, causing him to think that the smoke, as much as sunshine, was responsible for the wrinkles around them and the rasp in her voice. "Help y'all?"

"Ms. Webster?"

"Who wants to know?"

Lasalle and Sonja showed their badges. "NCIS, ma'am," he said. "You rent that house to Lt. Alpuente?"

"That's right," she replied. "He done something?"

"He died this morning, ma'am," Sonja said.

The woman's skin was too sun-crisped to actually blanch, but she took a startled step back and her eyes opened wide. "No, that's not—oh my God."

"When was the last time you saw him, ma'am?" Lasalle asked.

"Well, I guess… couple, three days, maybe. Give or take. Are you sure?"

"We're very sorry, ma'am," Sonja said. "But yes, we're sure. How well did you know him?"

"Not well, I guess. He's been renting the front house for, what, four months now. Almost five. He keeps to himself, mostly, and I do the same. He's polite. Pays his rent on time. Don't throw wild parties or have drug dealers over. I can't abide drug dealers or prostitutes; I tell all my tenants, you have those people at your house, I'll evict your ass faster than you can blink your eyes."

"It's good to have citizens keeping an eye on things," Sonja said. "Do you think you can let us in the house?"

"Well, if you're… oh my God. If you're cops, was he *murdered*?"

"We're waiting for a definitive answer on that," Lasalle answered. "But it might help us if we could take a look inside."

"Ordinarily, I'm very protective of my tenants' privacy, but in this case—"

"Privacy's the least of his concerns now," Lasalle said. "We won't take long, and we won't do any damage."

"What about his things? What'll I do with those? I've never had a tenant up and die on me before. I don't even know."

"We're working on identifying his next of kin so they can be notified," Sonja replied. "They'll be in touch, I'm sure."

"Let me get the key," Webster said.

"We'll wait right here."

When she had gone inside, Sonja said, "Looks like this place could have used a paint job about ten years ago."

"The rental house is the one that brings in the money," Lasalle said. "Guess it's not too surprising that it's the one with the curb appeal."

Ms. Webster returned a couple of minutes later with a key ring clutched in her bony fist. "It's one of these," she said. "Might take me a minute to figure out which one."

"The back door would be fine," Lasalle said.

"But speaking of that, there's something... unusual... hanging on the front knob," Sonja added. "Do you know how long that's been there?"

"Well, I have no earthly idea what you mean," the woman said. "What is it?"

"Never mind, then. We'll take care of it."

At the rear of the house, two concrete steps led to a door with a big glass pane that had iron bars bolted over it. The door had been painted orange sometime in the not-too-distant past, and Lasalle could see ghostly graffiti underneath the paint. He guessed the orange had been on sale, or leftover from some other task, because it looked as natural with the magenta as butterfly wings on a brick.

Webster found the right key on her first try. She

turned it in the lock, then twisted the knob and pulled open the door. "There you go," she said. "Let me know when you're done so I can lock it up again."

"Will do, ma'am," Lasalle said. "Thanks for your help."

Inside, the house barely looked lived in. The door opened into a kitchen, with a stove, a refrigerator, and a dishwasher, but no table to eat at. Instead, there was a set of wooden TV trays in a stand, and one of them was unfolded in front of a ladder-back chair. Behind a door was a pantry that contained a lot of prepared foods, along with some bulk provisions—rice, beans, oatmeal, and the like, in plastic bins on the floor—that seemed to be Alpuente's main source of nutrition. A coffeemaker on the tile counter appeared to get plenty of use, but otherwise, Sonja figured he was one step up from the proverbial bachelor who ate his meals standing over the sink.

They moved on to a combination living/dining room, which the lieutenant had turned into a home office. There was no sofa or other comfortable seating, just a long wooden table with a computer monitor on it, and stacks of manila file folders. Maps and nautical charts had been taped to the wall in front of it, along with photographs of the coastline. The photos weren't professional—some had a thumb or finger blocking part of the scene—and Lasalle guessed Alpuente had taken them himself.

"If this is what he's here working on, it seems to involve coastal research of some kind," Sonja said.

"Way it looks," Lasalle agreed.

Sonja pointed at the computer monitor. "You notice there's no desktop unit?"

"King said he found a laptop in the hotel room," Lasalle reminded her. "Maybe that's all he uses."

"Or there was another computer here, and someone stole it."

"That's also a possibility," Lasalle admitted.

They walked through the rest of the house. One bedroom was closed off and empty, and the other had a mattress on the floor with a couple of sheets and a pillow thrown haphazardly on top. The closet contained a few uniforms and some civilian clothes, a couple of boxes held underwear, socks, T-shirts, and other odds and ends.

"I've heard of traveling light, but this is ridiculous," Sonja said as they shifted back to the living room. "'Spartan' doesn't begin to cover it."

"He does own a house that's only fifty miles away. He's only been renting here for a few months."

"I know that, but I also know if I had two houses, I'd want to feel like I belonged at the one where I spent most of my time."

"Who knows how much time he really spent here?" Lasalle asked. "From the looks of those photos and charts, he was probably in the field a lot. Maybe he went back home on weekends. This might just be where he slept during the week."

Sonja pointed toward the desk area. "And worked."

"And that." Lasalle examined the tabletop, where coffee had made what appeared to be permanent rings. "Maybe he didn't sleep that much, after all. Looks like he drank plenty of coffee."

"So do you," Sonja said. "But I'm guessing his caffeine habit didn't get him killed."

"I have a feeling you're right," Lasalle said. "I'm not sure I see anything here worth killing over."

"Unless there's something on that missing computer."

"If there really is a missing computer."

"Right. *If*. Maybe Patton can figure it out from the laptop."

"If anybody can, it's Triple P."

"Is there anything else you want to look at?" Sonja asked.

"It doesn't look like a crime scene, so I guess we should head back to the squad room."

"Don't forget your little souvenir," Sonja reminded him.

The monkey's paw. Lasalle barked a laugh. "After we close this case, maybe you can hang it from your rear-view."

"I wouldn't think of it," Sonja said. "Wouldn't want to deprive you of the pleasure. It'll go so well with that big-ass truck of yours."

5

Patton had been Sebastian's ride to the parade, and he had left the scene long before Pride and Sebastian left the hotel room. Pride gave the young agent a ride to the Jefferson Parish Coroner's Office, where he had worked until recently.

"It always feels a little weird, coming back here," Sebastian said. "I mean, not that it's been a long time or anything. But I worked here for so long, and Loretta—"

"Has ears everywhere," Pride warned. "Don't say anything you'll regret."

"Never!" Sebastian countered. "She's the best. I mean, she can be kind of a mother hen sometimes, but—"

The door swung open behind Sebastian, and Pride made a chopping motion at his own throat. "I thought I heard my name being taken in vain," Loretta said.

"Sebastian's going to process some of the evidence we found in Lt. Alpuente's hotel room," Pride said. "And I was wondering if—"

"You'll be the first to know, Dwayne, when there's anything to know. I've got Lt. Alpuente on my table now, but we've just started to get acquainted."

"I'm not trying to rush you, Loretta."

"Because you know better."

"I definitely do."

"I do have one thing for you," Loretta said. "One of the interns has been looking into Alpuente's *gris-gris* bag. She's still working on it, but she's identified the piece of root as High John the Conqueror. In voodoo, that has multiple uses. If you carry it in a red bag with a lock of hair from the person you desire, it'll make that person fall in love with you. It brings courage, luck, and power, and it wards away depression. Taken internally, it's a powerful laxative, but I don't think you'd carry it around in a *gris-gris* bag for that."

"Plus," Sebastian cut in, "there are plenty of commercially available laxatives at any drugstore or supermarket. For myself, I use—"

"That's the very definition of TMI, Sebastian," Pride interrupted.

"But speaking of voodoo, Loretta, Pride gave me a voodoo doll!" Sebastian enthused. "I mean, not to keep. Anyway, it's not as cool as my Laser Light Skeletor, but it's still pretty awesome."

"Let me know what you find out, He-Man," Pride said.

"Will do." As Pride started to leave, he heard Sebastian saying, "Hey, he made a *Masters of the Universe* joke…"

"Sorry, Loretta," Pride said under his breath. Sebastian was good at his job, and a terrific asset to the team. But Pride had a feeling Loretta was in for a twenty-minute soliloquy on the never-ending power struggle between He-Man and Skeletor.

Better her than me, he thought. *Much, much better.*

* * *

Back at the squad room, Pride found Patton Plame parked before a computer monitor, too. It was becoming an occupational hazard, he thought. Any time now, people would start evolving rectangular eyeballs, the better to see screens with.

When he heard Pride come in, Patton paused the action on the monitor and spun his chair around. "Just in time," he said. "I have to watch one more badly shot piece of parade video from social media, I'll go out of my mind. And that's without reading the comments. They're a fast track to insanity."

"Have you found anything helpful?" Pride asked.

"Lots of footage of our boy landing on the trident. If anybody captured him before he was airborne, I haven't seen it yet."

"You can keep hunting in a little while. I have a couple of things I want you to check out."

"Whatcha got?"

Pride set the objects down on Patton's table as he described them. "A laptop computer from Alpuente's hotel room. Also, this photograph shows him with a woman. I need to know who she is."

"Come on, give me something challenging," Patton said. "Take me away from these video clips. Why don't people understand that when they're shooting a parade, they should hold their smartphones horizontally? I mean, come on. You don't need a semester in film school to figure that out. Five minutes in any movie theater should do it. Widescreen, people."

"Well, we can't all be Triple P," Pride said.

"Can't anybody be that," Patton replied. "'Cept the one and only original!"

"That's why we keep you around, Patton. That and your modesty."

"I have to be modest. If I wasn't, everybody around me would develop crippling inferiority complexes."

"Just get me whatever you can from those," Pride said. "Then you can go back to film critique. I've got to drive out to SSC and talk to Alpuente's CO."

"Have a nice trip, King," Patton said. "Pretty country out there."

"Yeah, it is," Pride said.

He had made it almost three steps toward the door when it blew open. "Special Agent Pride! You're just the man I'm lookin' for!"

Pride stepped forward and the woman pulled him into a warm embrace. "Mama T!" he replied. "How are you?"

"Big as life and twice as beautiful," she said.

"You got that right. What brings you down here?"

"I need to ask you a favor."

"Name it," Pride said.

"I'm openin' up a little community center in the neighborhood. Nothin' fancy, just a place for kids to come in off the street when it's hot or rainy, somewhere safe for folks to meet their neighbors over a cup of coffee on a cold morning, you know."

"Sounds good."

"But one thing I want to do is have job-training classes. Try to get some of my people workin' again."

"That makes sense."

"So, what I wanted to ask... do you think you could come down once in a while and talk about careers in law enforcement? We need more cops who know what life on the streets is really like."

"That we do," Pride said. He didn't want to give her a facile answer; he respected her too much for that. The truth was, law enforcement folks weren't always popular where she lived.

Mama T—Teresa Combs was her real name, but everybody knew her by the other—hailed from the Lower Ninth Ward. The Lower Ninth—"Backatown" to many New Orleanians, and the "Lower Nine" to those who lived there—was an impoverished neighborhood, largely neglected at the best of times, except when NOPD wanted to run up its stats by arresting low-level drug dealers or some media outlet wanted to do yet another "exposé" on New Orleans' poorest citizens.

Before Katrina, it had been ninety-eight percent African American, a blend of poor and middle class. Although it stood on higher ground than much of the city, after the storm it seemed to take on special significance, at least among city and state politicians, as the area that took the worst of the damage. The perception wasn't remotely true, but the mayor at the time declared that the area wasn't worth rebuilding. The state reopened schools in many neighborhoods— particularly the well-to-do and mostly white ones—but not in the Lower Ninth. Written off, the area didn't get much in the way of redevelopment funds, and without schools and jobs and houses to return to, many of its residents had never come back.

Most of the city had eventually recovered from Katrina, but the Lower Ninth still had large tracts of land with no houses on them. Weeds grew rampant; gradually, the Lower Ninth seemed to be reverting to a natural state. Those who did still live there had little in the way of municipal services. They had to take a bridge to reach the rest of New Orleans. The community had to organize to get a single school opened, and centers like the one Mama T proposed were few and far between.

So plenty of the Lower Ninth's residents were justifiably wary of people wearing badges or with any other connection to the government. But Mama T's point was spot-on; the best way to get around that situation was for people from the neighborhood to join the ranks of law enforcement, to bring their own life experience to those ranks and open up some hearts and minds.

Mama T had her own reasons to distrust law enforcement. Her son Terence had been murdered, but NOPD hadn't seemed to take much interest in the case. It wasn't until Pride got involved that his real killer was caught.

"Sure," Pride said at last. "I'd be honored."

"I'll be honest, I don't know much about runnin' a school. Like, anything, really. I could use somebody with some school administration experience, who could pitch in part-time. I got some grants, so there could even be a little money in it, if you know anyone."

"Not offhand, but I'll keep it in mind," Pride said.

"You do that."

"Just let me know when you want me to come over there. I'll do whatever I can to fit into your schedule."

"How about next Wednesday night? Say, seven o'clock?"

"I could probably do that."

"You're a good man, Agent Pride."

"I don't know as I'd go that far. I make an attempt. I guess in the end, that's all any of us can do."

"I got a feeling you try harder than most," she said. She gave him another quick hug, and was gone.

"That's *the* Mama T?" Patton asked.

"That's right. Sorry I didn't get a chance to introduce you. She's kind of like a whirlwind sometimes."

"Sister knows what she wants and don't waste time," Patton said. "Triple P can relate."

"I expect you two have more in common than that. She is one determined lady. I figured I might as well say yes, because she's not the type who takes no for an answer."

"That's what I like about you, King," Patton said. "You know it's best to bend before a wind like that, else you're gonna break in two."

6

Pride was on Canal Street, almost to Interstate 10, when his phone buzzed.

"This is Pride," he answered.

"Pride, it's Rose Vergados. Where y'at?"

She wasn't asking his location, he knew. Rose spoke a blue-collar brand of New Orleans English often called "y'at," because "Where y'at?" was the most common greeting. It translated roughly as "How are you?" or "What's happening?" to people from other parts of the country.

"Hello, Rose. Do you have something for me?"

"I might," she said. "I found out who made the reservation for Mr. Goodtown."

"That's great."

"His name's Gilbert Melancon," she said. "He's been working here for about four years."

Pride made a right on Robertson, just shy of the freeway. "Is he there now?"

"He should be. He's on the schedule, and he was here early this morning. But he's not here now, and I can't find anyone who's seen him since that young man fell off the balcony."

"Is that unusual for him?"

"He's not the ideal employee, if that's what you mean. I've had to discipline him before, for arranging pot and hookers for hotel guests. It's New Orleans; some folks think those things should be on the room service menu. Gilbert said he wanted the guests to have whatever they wanted to make their stays memorable. I could have fired his ass, but I believe in second chances, you know? And maybe third ones, too."

"Nothing wrong with giving someone another chance. What's he look like? Is he a big guy?"

"Definitely," she said. "He works out in the hotel weight room sometimes. Huge arms, big shoulders. Strong."

Pride pulled over next to a weed-choked empty lot and retrieved a small spiral-bound notebook and a pen from the center console. "Make my day, Rose. Tell me you have an address for him."

"If I'd known you were that easy to please, I'd have called as soon as I heard you were divorced, Dwayne. He's in the Fourth. You ready?"

"Give it to me."

She read him an address near Conti and North White. He read it back to be sure he had it right, then thanked her for her help. Next, he called Sonja. She and Lasalle were still in Tremé—just leaving Alpuente's rental, she said.

"I'm on my way," Pride said. "You and Chris are closer than I am. Head over and pick up Melancon, if he's home, and I'll meet you there."

"Got it," Sonja said. "See you soon." She was already relaying the message to Lasalle when Pride ended the call. He put his Explorer in gear and swung left on Bienville, shooting between two sections of the wide sarcophagus sea that formed the St. Louis Cemetery, and toward the lake as fast as conditions allowed.

Maybe they could wrap this up in a hurry. Open and shut—he liked cases like that. He slowed briefly for a child in the street, then, when the way ahead was clear, he stepped on the gas.

"It's one of those shotgun houses," Sonja said. She was looking at the satellite view on her phone while Lasalle drove. They'd already put on their wireless radios—the coils from the earpiece always bugged her, but when the action was hot she was able to set that dislike aside in favor of clear communication. Both wore navy blue caps with NCIS printed in white above the peak. "I'll take the front and you take the back."

"Or I'll take the front," Lasalle said. "City mice are used to back alleys, right?"

Sonja laughed. "I don't mind the alley," she said. "I wouldn't want you to accidentally get some dust on your shoes."

"Deal. Alley's all yours."

"Deal," Sonja echoed.

"There it is," Lasalle said. "There's not much to it."

He was right. The house looked like it might have been red once, but wind and weather had stripped the paint down to a wan, sickly pale pink. High-water marks could still be seen on the walls, remnants of Katrina. It was, as she had suggested, a shotgun house, long and narrow, with only a single window on the long side. In the front, four concrete steps led to a plain wooden door. Off to its left, the shutters were folded open and a window was cracked a few inches wide.

"Smell that?" Lasalle asked as they approached the house.

Sonja nodded. The singular, sweet aroma of pot had been plenty familiar even before her law enforcement career had begun, and she'd been exposed to it many times since. "Probable cause?"

"Smells like it to me," Lasalle said.

She and Lasalle had worked together so long that no more words were needed. She drew her Glock and raced around to the back of the house. There was only one window here, so she hurried to the far side. Here she found a second door and a couple of windows. "Go," she said softly into her microphone.

An instant later, she heard Lasalle's voice. "NCIS!" he called, pounding on the door. "Open up!"

At the same time, she twisted the knob on the side door. It turned easily and she yanked it open. "Federal agents!" she cried as she bulled her way inside.

"Gilbert Melancon, you're under arrest!" Lasalle shouted.

Sonja had entered a kitchen that might have last been cleaned sometime around the close of the Civil War, from the looks of it. She waded through newspapers and food wrappers and pizza cartons, glad they weren't trying to sneak up on anyone.

Over her own noise, she heard the distinctive scraping and squealing sounds of someone scrambling out a window. "Side window!" she shouted.

"We got a rabbit!" Lasalle called at the same moment.

Sonja reversed course, went out the door, and darted toward the back and around the house. She was there in seconds, but Melancon was already in the wind. The house was in the middle of the block, so he might have gone around the house next door in either direction— down the alley or toward the street.

Then Lasalle raced up from the street side. "You see him?" he asked.

"No." She pointed up the alley. "Had to go that way."

Before he could answer, a dog started barking furiously, a few houses away. Lasalle flashed her a grin. "Oh, it's on," he said. "It's on like Donkey Kong."

"You cut him off," Sonja said. "I'll run him down."

Lasalle gave her a nod and dashed off toward his truck. Sonja tore down the alley and across the street. More dogs started to bark, though Sonja couldn't tell if that meant they'd seen or sensed Melancon, or were simply reacting to the first dog. Lasalle's truck roared down the street, and his voice came in her ear. "See him yet?"

"No," she replied. Then she spotted a garbage can spinning away from a tall, wooden fence. The can teetered and tipped over, spilling trash into the alley. "Yes," she amended. "Well, not him, but he just used a garbage can to jump a fence. Yellow house, a third of the way up this block."

"I see it."

Sonja reached the house. The fence was too tall to jump—Melancon had momentum going for him when he hit the garbage can, but if she stopped to right it, she would lose that advantage. Instead, she vaulted a waist-high chain-link fence around the yard next door.

Which was, it turned out, where the first dog lived.

It was a brindle mastiff, an enormous creature with a head that looked as big as a lion's. It had paused its barking, maybe trying to determine whether the interloper it had heard was still a threat, and appeared momentarily confused at the appearance of a second one—this time on its own turf. It didn't spend long making up its mind, though—it charged at Sonja, all slavering jaws and gnashing teeth.

Her Glock was already in her hand. She didn't want to shoot somebody's dog, but its charge was too fast; she wouldn't be able to get back over the fence in time to save herself. As it was, even a bullet wouldn't save her from the dog's initial impact. She raised the gun, but the dog's powerful legs were already launching it into the air. It hurtled toward her—

—and reached the end of its chain.

The animal's eyes bulged in seeming surprise as its forward motion came to a sudden halt in mid-air. It dropped to the grass—freshly cut, Sonja noted; the whole yard was immaculately groomed—and immediately started pawing the earth, trying to advance toward her.

"Good doggie," Sonja said. Animals weren't her favorite things to begin with, and ones that clearly wanted to devour her ranked even lower on her list. Especially if they were truly capable of it, as this one might have been. "Nice doggie. Stay."

The dog had no intention of staying. She'd already wasted valuable time, though, during which Melancon was putting more distance between himself and her. She gauged the length of its chain, measured against the width of the yard, and determined that there was a narrow strip on the far right that the dog couldn't reach.

She hoped.

It was a chance she had to take.

She raced over to that side. Her movement riled the dog all over again, and it charged, snapping and growling. For a terrible moment Sonja thought she'd miscalculated, but again, the beast drew up short. It pulled and pulled, and she saw the stake to which it was affixed give a little. The stake was steel, screwed into the ground, with a ring that the chain connected to. It didn't look like it would take much to tug it out.

"Stay!" she said again, her tone commanding. "Sit!"

The dog stayed, but not by choice. It did not sit.

Sonja sprinted for the front gate. The yard Melancon had entered was on the far side of this one—the dog's side—so even if there had been a way to scale the fence on that side, she wouldn't be able to.

She let herself out through the gate and closed it behind her. The realization occurred to her that the dog would surely be able to vault this low fence. Maybe the chain wasn't the only thing keeping it in. If she had a dog of that size and apparent ferocity, she'd make sure it was well trained. Given the appearance of the house and yard, the occupants were conscientious citizens.

Anyway, she told herself that was probably the case, because she didn't want to have to worry about the thing breaking free and chasing her down now that she'd left its property.

When she reached the street, Melancon was nowhere to be seen. Lasalle was a block further down, still in his truck. Sonja realized her earpiece had come out of her ear during the confrontation with Cujo.

"Chris," she said. "Where's Melancon?"

"There you are!" he replied. "I've been calling and calling."

"Sorry, lost my earpiece for a minute."

"You were gone a long time."

"Long story," she said. "Do you have his twenty?"

"Ducked into another yard, toward St. Louis and the Greenway. I'm heading over there."

"On my way," Sonja said. "See you there."

"You betcha," Lasalle said. "Woof!"

7

Knowing Lasalle and Sonja were going to pick up Melancon, Pride had turned on his radio, so he had heard the whole thing, including Sonja's encounter with what sounded like a big, angry dog. He was almost to the scene, but now he changed course, making a hard, screeching right on Dorgenois, jetting over two blocks, then cranking the wheel to the left. His tires left rubber on the road as he skidded into the turn on St. Louis, and then he was racing northwest parallel to the Lafitte Greenway.

Beyond Dupre, he saw someone emerge from between houses in the middle of the block. It was a big man, African American, wearing a Saints jersey and black dress pants, barefoot and moving fast. Had to be Melancon. Pride accelerated, then stomped on the brakes. The SUV fishtailed to a halt, and Pride threw it in park and jumped out.

"Melancon!" he shouted. "NCIS! Freeze!"

The man kept going, heading for the greenway. Pride was a little ahead of him, though, and he ran forward, angling to intercept him. Melancon shot him a worried glance and altered his course. The Orleans

Relief Canal, the low fence across from it, and the broad swath of grass that made up the greenway itself were between Melancon and the industrial neighborhood on the far side.

The canal was too wide to jump, but concrete beams spanned the distance. Melancon jumped onto one, and his momentum nearly carried him over the side and down. He corrected his balance and kept going.

Pride stepped onto the beam. It seemed very narrow indeed, and he was reminded of gymnasts on balance beams, doing flips and spins with what seemed like suicidal nonchalance.

Behind him, brakes screeched and a car door opened. Lasalle's voice rang out. "Melancon, there's nowhere to go! Give it up."

Sonja's voice came next. "Keep going, Gilbert. I'll gladly shoot your ass off that little beam."

Melancon paused and looked down at the water below him. "Think hard about it, Gilbert," Pride said. "How well can you swim? People drown in there. You might get away from us, but you also might never come out."

Melancon turned toward him, wearing a sheepish grin. He was a good-looking young man, not much more than a kid, really. His expression was that of someone who had just figured out he was in way over his head. "Who'd y'all say you were again?"

"NCIS," Pride said. He held out a hand toward Melancon. "Come on."

"NCIS? What's that?"

"Naval Criminal Investigative Service. Come on, Gilbert. Give me your hand. It's not safe here."

Melancon broke out into a broad, sunny smile. "Oh, okay, see, you got the wrong guy. I ain't in the Navy."

Pride took two cautious steps closer. "I know you're not, Gilbert. But Edouard Alpuente was."

At the mention of Alpuente's name, Melancon's smile vanished and he took a step to the side.

And off the beam.

Pride lunged and caught him. Melancon was heavy, though, and his weight and momentum threatened to pull them both into the canal. Pride shifted his weight back, knowing that if he lost his grip or Melancon broke free, he'd go over backward and be in for a swim.

Then Lasalle's hands were on him, steadying them both. "Easy, everybody," Lasalle said. "Let's just move carefully back over to dry ground. All together, now. All at once. Okay?"

"You good, Gilbert?" Pride asked.

"Yeah, yeah, I'm cool."

"Here we go."

Step by slow, careful step, they made their way to the end of the concrete beam and onto the grass. At the last moment, Melancon lost his balance again. He waved his arms to try to recapture it, and as Lasalle reached for him, Melancon's flailing hand knocked his NCIS cap off his head. Lasalle tried to catch it, but too late; it fluttered into the canal and was quickly whisked away by the current.

"Is that what they mean by 'Roll Tide'?" Sonja needled.

"You're funny," Lasalle said, watching it drift out of sight. He'd heard just about every joke possible about his alma mater, and most of them left him cold. He was proud of his school and its vaunted football team. Some people gave him a hard time when they found out he'd worn the costume of Big Al, the team's elephant mascot, but he had actually enjoyed those days. Also, it turned out the mascot got to spend more time with the cheerleaders than the players did, and that was a bonus. "I think it's what they mean by 'easy come, easy go.'"

"See, thing is, I didn't know y'all were police," Melancon said. They were back at headquarters, in the interrogation room. Pride and Sonja sat on one side of the big table. Melancon sat opposite them, facing the two-way mirror. "I had, like, a stressful morning, you feel me? So I was enjoyin' a bowl and then somebody crashes into my crib hollerin' about NICS or whatever. 'Course I booked."

"NCIS," Sonja reminded him. "And I distinctly announced us as 'federal agents.'"

"Yeah, well, that don't sound the same as police to me."

"Maybe you need to get out more," she said. "Broaden your horizons. You're in a lot of trouble here, and adding a resisting arrest charge isn't going to help you out of it."

"Let's talk about Lt. Alpuente," Pride said. "You got him a room at the hotel under a phony name. Why?"

Melancon blinked a few times and let his gaze wander from Pride to Sonja and back. "We old friends," he replied. "Grew up together, down in Shell Beach. Moms and me moved to New Orleans when I was ten, but Eddie and me still stayed in touch. He asked if there was anything I could do, so I moved him to the top of the wait list and comped him the room. That against the law?"

"Your employer might frown on it, but that's between the two of you. My question is, why the alias?"

"That's what he asked for. I asked him why, and he just said he needed to disappear for a few days. Said the best way to disappear was in a crowd."

"That's true sometimes," Sonja said. "But maybe not so much in a crowd where everybody's taking pictures on a smartphone."

"He almost never left the room while he was there," Melancon said. "I tried to see him one day, knocked on his door, and he just told me to stay away from him. So I did."

"Did you see him this morning?" Pride asked.

"Only after—you know. When they brought him down, I recognized him right off. I freaked. Figured I was fired for sure, and maybe worse. So I took off, boogied on home. I was just smokin' a little, trying to mellow out after seein'…" He swallowed hard, and his eyes brimmed with tears. "…seein' him like that."

"So you're saying you have no idea how or why he took a dive off his balcony?" Sonja pressed. "You didn't see him at all today until after he was dead?"

"Eddie was my *boy*!" Melancon slammed his palm down on the tabletop. Then he seemed to ratchet his emotions down a few notches. He sniffled and knuckled his eyes. "No way I would have hurt him, if that's what you're thinkin'. Or let anyone else do it."

"Let's take a break," Pride said. He was afraid that pushing Melancon more would just shut him down, when what he needed was for the young man to open up further. "Do you want something to drink, Gilbert?"

Melancon cracked a smile. "Like a Huge Ass Beer?"

"Like some water, a cup of coffee—"

"Chicory?"

A man after Pride's own heart. "What other kind is there?"

"Never mind, I'll take a col' drink."

"What kind?"

"Coke, RC, whatever you got."

"Be right back," Pride said. "Come on, Sonja."

Pride loved the squad room. The thought struck him as he headed for the kitchen, Sonja following behind. On warm days, its brick walls seemed to release the sweet, dry aroma of the horses and hay that had been kept here in years gone by. It had, for a while, been a bittersweet place for him; moving into his apartment upstairs had been a painful acknowledgement that his marriage to Linda had failed, after twenty-three years. In those early days, every brick in the place, every stick of furniture, every picture or poster or electronic device had seemed to be taunting him, telling him that the most important commitment he had ever made had turned out to be worthless.

Gradually, though, he had reoriented his thinking. His marriage had not, he told himself, been a failure. They'd had plenty of good years, more than many people got. They'd brought Laurel into the world, and no union that accomplished such a feat could be considered unworthy. He hadn't been ready to give up, but after trying unsuccessfully to get him into couples therapy, Linda had decided that the cord needed to be cut. Linda had moved on, and so had he, eventually reaching a place of peace with the decision. Sometimes the things that hurt the most were for the best.

His marriage hadn't lasted, but he was no commitment-phobe. He was committed to Laurel. He was committed to his job, to the pursuit of something like justice, to doing what he could to make sure that people who had been damaged by the world had somebody on their side.

More often than not, the victims weren't the only ones damaged; if you dug deep enough, you discovered that the perpetrators weren't unscarred, either. There were days that Pride thought his biggest challenge was breaking the cycles that led to more poverty, more violence, more heartbreak. A cop could catch a criminal and throw him in jail, but how many more crimes would be prevented if that criminal had come from a stable home, got a decent education, and learned a trade?

Lasalle and Patton were busy at their desks, so he didn't disturb them as he passed through the bullpen.

In the kitchen, he glanced at his Hogs for the Cause poster. The annual event raised money to help families battling pediatric brain cancer, which was about as good as a cause could be. It reminded him that whatever troubles he had, they were small indeed. What mattered was not dwelling on them, but taking action to fix those things that were within his power. He couldn't cure cancer, but he could catch bad guys, and make sure they were no longer able to harm the innocent.

He took a couple of Cokes from the refrigerator and turned around to see Sonja standing behind him, regarding him with a puzzled look. "I never understood that thing about 'a penny for your thoughts,'" she said. "Any thoughts you can buy for a penny aren't worth much. I figure it'd take ten or twenty bucks easy to buy yours right now."

"Sorry," Pride said. "I guess I was kind of lost there for a minute." He glanced around the kitchen. It, like the rest of the field office, was home, now—home in a way the house he and Linda had shared in the Lower Garden had never really been. That had been Linda's house, and he'd often felt like he didn't quite fit in it.

Here was sanctuary, peace, a place to truly belong. Sure, it was lonely sometimes, but never for long. "I was thinking about this place."

"The kitchen?"

"The whole thing. Kitchen, courtyard, squad room. Upstairs."

"What about it?"

"I don't think you'd understand, Sonja."

"Try me."

"Just... how special it is. To me. How at home I feel here."

"I get that," she said.

"You do?"

"I think so. I mean, you had a home before, when you were married, right?"

"Sure."

"And that was your place. Like they say, home is the place that, when you come to the door, they have to let you in."

"That's what they say, more or less."

"But you always had to leave home to go to work. Had to leave work to go home. Always leaving someplace to be someplace else. Half the time it probably felt like you didn't want to leave whichever you were at, and the other half you probably couldn't wait to get away."

"That pretty much sums it up."

"But here, you got it all. I mean, some people would chafe, feel like they could never escape. But our work takes you out of here a lot. Whatever time of day or night you get back, you're always coming home."

"I hadn't really looked at it that way."

"See? Not as dumb as I look."

"I never said you—"

"And you never would, because you ain't dumb, either." Sonja broke into a laugh. "I'm just giving you a hard time, Pride. What do you want to do about our boy Gilbert in there? Ready to take another whack at him?"

"I get the feeling there's more that he's not telling us. A lot more, maybe. I'm going to go back in—alone—and try a different approach."

"Let me know if you need me."

"I will. You can watch through the glass if you want."

"I'll do that, I'll need a cold drink, too. Can't watch you two enjoying yours without having something to sip on."

"There are plenty in the fridge," Pride said. "Help yourself." He started for the door, then stopped. "Oh, and, Sonja? Thanks."

"For what?"

"For explaining me to myself."

"Hey, you know what they say. It's a dirty job, but someone's got to do it."

8

Pride went back into the room and put the two bottles of Coke on the table, condensation running down their sides. He sat across from Melancon, scooted his chair in closer, and pushed one of the bottles toward the young man. "You doing okay?"

"When do I get to go home?"

"That's hard to say."

"Am I under arrest or somethin'?"

"Not yet."

"So I can leave, if I want to?"

"That's what the law says."

Melancon studied him for a long moment. "Don't seem like you think that's a good idea."

"Do you think you should be under arrest?"

"I didn't do nothin'."

"That remains to be seen, Gilbert. You have to be straight with me, here. I want to help keep you out of trouble if I can, but I need your cooperation, okay?"

Melancon nodded. "I guess."

Pride took a long pull off his bottle and let the young man watch him. When he'd set his bottle down, Melancon tipped his own back and drank.

"That's good. Nice and cold."

"That's the way it should be. I like things that are how they should be, Gilbert. But we have a situation here that's not how it should be, don't we?"

"Meanin' Eddie?"

"Meaning Eddie."

"Not much we can do for him now, is there?"

"We can find out the truth about what happened to him. That's the best thing we can do at this point. Let the truth speak for him."

"How we do that?"

Pride shifted his gaze away from Melancon, rolled his bottle between his hands. "It starts with you, man. There's something you're not telling me. I don't know why you're holding it back, but it's the missing link. If you want to help your friend, you've got to come clean."

"I don't know what you're—"

"Yes, Gilbert, you do. You might be the only one who knows it. Whatever it is, is it worth your friend's life?"

"I didn't know he'd get hurt," Melancon said. "You got to believe that. If I did, I—" He swallowed hard, but didn't continue.

"I get it, believe me. I don't think for a minute that you meant for him to be killed, or played any intentional part in that. But he's dead, and I need to find out what happened. So you need to tell me. What happened, Gilbert?"

Melancon sniffled and wiped his nose with the back of his hand. "He told me he needed a room, like I said. Wanted it under a fake name, so I hooked him up. Least I could do for a homeboy, right?"

"Absolutely."

"So I was at the desk when he checked in—I told him when to come, so I would be there. I gave him his key, and he went upstairs. A few minutes later, this dude comes up to me and says he'll give me five hundred bucks if I text him any time Eddie leaves the room or comes back to it."

"Who was the dude?"

"I don't know him. He never even told me his name. Just some guy. He told me he wanted to make sure Eddie was okay. Keepin' tabs on him, like. But he said don't let on to Eddie that he's watchin' out for him. I said I'd do what I could, and he gave me a number to text."

"Does that sound like something on the up-and-up?" Pride asked. "Some mystery man wants to keep an eye on your friend?"

Melancon swallowed. "Five bills is five bills."

"I'll need that number," Pride said.

"It's on my phone."

Melancon hadn't yet been arrested. He'd been patted down for weapons, but allowed to keep his phone. "Show me."

Melancon dragged his phone from a pants pocket and brought up the texts. They were simple:

Out.
In.
Out.
Back.

No responses had been made.

Pride wrote down the number. "Be right back," he said. He left Melancon alone again, and took the number to Sonja, asking her to run it down. Then he returned to the interrogation room.

"Now we're making some progress," he said. If Melancon was telling the truth, this was their first real break in the case. It was a long way from solved, but it could be a giant step in the right direction. "We'll find out whose number that is. What else can you tell me about the guy?"

"He was huge. Big, muscular, like an athlete. Football, basketball, somethin' like that."

"White, black, what?"

"Black dude. Hair in cornrows. Got a little gold in his grill, but not a whole lot."

"That's all you can tell me?"

"I wasn't datin' him, I just met him for about five minutes once. He was big, that's the main thing I remember."

"If you think of anything else—"

"I'll let you know. I didn't want nothin' to happen to Eddie, you know? I thought I was helpin' him out. Like maybe this dude would help keep him safe, or whatever, like he said. Anyway, I really needed that cash. My moms, she lost her job. She was in a wreck, and now she's in a chair. Like that cat in the other room, only his is a little fancier, you know what I mean? We got hers from the Goodwill. Without a job, she's about to lose her house. The five hundred helped her keep it a few more months."

He stared down at the tabletop, as if the answer to all his problems might have magically appeared there. "Now I'll most probably lose my job, and I won't be able to help her anymore."

"That's up to your boss. I know her; she's a good woman. But you might have pushed her a little too far this time. Anyway, you have a bigger problem than that right now."

Melancon looked up again. Tears spilled from his eyes. "You chargin' me? How'm I gonna help my moms then?"

"If we determine that your mystery man killed

Alpuente, then you might be an accessory to murder, Gilbert. That comes with a prison stay. I sympathize with your predicament, believe me. But you should've thought about taking care of your mother before you agreed to inform a complete stranger about your friend's whereabouts. I know you didn't think harm would come to him, but sometimes unintended consequences can be the worst kind. For Lt. Alpuente, in this case, and for you. I'm not charging you yet, but you hang tight for a while, okay?"

"I'm not goin' anywhere."

"If it comes to that, I'll do my best to make sure you're treated fairly."

"I appreciate it, Agent Pride."

Pride left him in the interrogation room and went back into the bullpen. As soon as he walked in, Patton greeted him. "King, I got a hit on the woman in that photo," he said. "The one with Alpuente."

"Who is she?"

Patton tapped on the tablet affixed to his Triple P-mobile, and one of the plasma screens flickered to life, showing several photographs of an attractive young African American woman. "Her name's Michelle St. Cyr," Patton said. "Twenty-seven. She works for a civilian contracting company at SSC, in the Naval Oceanographic Office."

"Same place Alpuente worked," Pride observed.

"That's right."

"Send her info to my phone."

"Already done."

"Thanks." Before Pride could say another word, there was a chirping noise.

"It's Loretta," Patton said.

"Put her on the plasma."

The screen flickered again, and Loretta Wade and Sebastian Lund appeared there.

"I've got a couple of things for you," Loretta said. "First, we went over Lt. Alpuente's body and clothing looking for any transfer from his killer. The trouble is, he spent the last few days of his life in a hotel room. There's all kinds of transfer—I'll need to keep Sebastian here a while longer, I'm afraid, to help us process everything you all collected on the street and in the room—but nothing yet that particularly points to anyone special. Some of it we've already determined came from other guests. Some we'll probably never identify. Hotel rooms are like DNA warehouses, but unfortunately with no labeling system."

"Understood," Pride said. "What else?"

"I've completed my autopsy," Loretta replied. "There's nothing terribly surprising. We already had a pretty good idea of what killed him, and we were right. But Sebastian has been doing some math, and he's learned something that might be of help."

"Okay," Pride said. "Whatcha got, Sebastian?"

"It wasn't very complicated math," Sebastian said. "Just some rudimentary physics. Nothing Einstein level, or even Hawking level. Though there's some debate as to which is actually the better physicist. Hawking might seem to have the advantage, but he's building on the framework that Einstein and others before him laid, so really—"

Pride cut him off. "That might be a discussion for another day, Sebastian."

"Or not," Sonja added.

"Right. Anyway, my point is, like we thought, there's no way Lt. Alpuente jumped onto that trident. Not even if he was a world-class distance jumper, and

I think we would know if he was. He was launched, effectively, and with a lot of force."

"So it would have taken someone strong," Pride said.

"Very very strong," Sebastian replied.

"Thanks, guys."

When they were gone, Lasalle glanced toward the interrogation room. "Strong like Mr. Melancon in there?"

"Maybe," Pride said. "Either way, I've got some bad news for him…"

9

Captain Attila Burke had been given a name that anyone, military or not, would have a hard time living up to. Although he had risen to a high-ranking position in the Navy, he didn't try to be anyone's Attila but his own. He was slender and balding, slightly stooped at the shoulders, and he wore wire-rimmed glasses with thick lenses. Behind them, his eyes were slits. Emotion thickened his voice when he spoke of Alpuente.

"Ed was—you'll forgive the cliché—an officer and a gentleman, and the best of both," he said. He was resting his rear against the corner of his desk in his office at SSC. Through the window behind Burke, Pride could see only blue sky and the green of a tree-filled landscape. "I haven't been able to accept that he's gone. I'm not sure I ever will."

"I'm very sorry," Pride said. He was sitting in one of the captain's visitor chairs, which was an antique, straight-backed and not very comfortable.

"I don't mean—he wasn't some ideal naval officer. Not an Annapolis cookie-cutter type, or anything. Some days, I thought he was in the wrong profession altogether."

"How do you mean, sir?"

"He could be emotional. Sometimes a little high-strung. I'm not sure I'd have wanted to be on a warship with him in command. For that matter, I don't think I would want me in command, either. But ours is not a combat mission. It's a scientific one, and no less important for that."

"Can you tell me what exactly he was working on?"

"I don't know your politics, Special Agent Pride, and I don't care to. Some people—many of whom are in Congress, and who hold the purse strings for the Navy and the other branches—wouldn't appreciate what I'm about to tell you."

"Try me," Pride said.

"The most significant threat the American military faces in the world today is climate change. I'm not downplaying terrorism or any foreign actors, the North Koreans, the Russians, any of that. But those are, for the most part, potential threats, not clear and present dangers. Natural disasters kill far more Americans every year than terrorists do. Climate change is here, now, and the sooner we face it the better our likelihood of surviving it."

"I'm not doubting you, Captain," Pride said. "But can you give me an example?"

"I can give you a dozen off the top of my head," Burke replied. He ticked them off on his fingers as he recited a litany Pride guessed he had spoken many times. "In Florida, the Naval Air Station Key West and Naval Station Mayport. In Georgia, Naval Submarine Base Kings Bay. In South Carolina, MCRD Parris Island and Marine Corps Air Station Beaufort. North Carolina, Camp Lejeune. Virginia, NAS Oceana and Dam Neck Annex, and Naval Station Norfolk—the biggest naval base on Earth. In D.C., the Navy Yard. In Maryland, the Naval Academy, from which I graduated in 1993. All the way up to the Portsmouth Naval Station in Maine. And that's just the east coast."

"And the risk to these locations is—" Pride began. He thought he already knew the answer.

"Significant flooding and loss of land and vital infrastructure, due to sea level rise and storm surge. It's not just the bases I named, either. Each one exists in a community, and members of the Navy family live in those communities. If we're busy taking care of our flooding homes, how effective are we going to be as a military force? Those bases I mentioned are all at risk, according to the National Climate Assessment. We're the United States Navy, we can't very well abandon our bases on the coasts. But we need to know that those bases will be *on* the water, not *under* it, in fifteen or twenty or fifty years, and right now, that's not something I can guarantee."

"I understand."

"Our mission is a scientific one, Special Agent Pride, not a political one. I'll leave it to those at the Pentagon to fight with Congress and the public about its importance, and about what the ultimate solutions might be. What I'm concerned with is determining the exact magnitude of the threat, and suggesting the mitigation efforts necessary to prevent exposure. Protecting a neighborhood from the sea can cost tens of millions of dollars. Imagine the cost to protect all those naval bases I mentioned, and many more. It's simply astronomical."

"And Lt. Alpuente?" Pride reminded him.

Burke blinked a couple of times, as if he had forgotten there was an audience for his impromptu lecture. "He was working on the Gulf Coast, performing a detailed assessment of wetlands loss and degradation there. He would have delivered his report soon, made his recommendations."

"Had you discussed what he'd learned?"

"Not yet. Ed kept his cards close to the vest. He didn't like to venture an opinion on a scientific question until he was absolutely certain, and had determined precisely how he was going to phrase his conclusions. I'm used to him working like that, so I didn't even try to get any hints of where his research had led him. I'd have found out soon enough. Hopefully his research is still on his laptop, so we don't have to start from scratch."

"I'll get it to you as quickly as I can," Pride said. "We're still working through it ourselves."

"Thank you."

"Was he doing that research near New Orleans? He was renting a house there."

"In southern Louisiana generally. New Orleans was a convenient base of operations for his task, with plenty of available short-term housing, and he was comfortable there. As comfortable as he ever was, I mean."

"Was there something in particular bothering him?" Pride asked.

"Not that I know of. Just—well, I already said he was high-strung. A nervous type. Maybe not entirely suited to a military career, but he was smart and determined, and he made a go of it anyway."

"How well did you know him?"

"We weren't... close, if that's what you mean. We worked together. We were part of the Navy family."

"But outside of work..."

"His life was his, and mine was mine. We didn't socialize, really. I can't say that I know very much about his personal life."

"Can you tell me if he had any enemies? Anyone who would wish him harm?"

"No. No, I'd have no idea. That wasn't something that ever came up. I'm certain I would remember if it had."

"Anything you can tell me about his social life?"

Burke cleared his throat. "I wouldn't presume to comment."

"It's not like he can be hurt by gossip at this point, Captain. He's past that."

"Like I said, we didn't socialize."

"All right, then, Captain. Thank you for your time." Pride rose from his seat and laid a business card on the man's desk. "If you think of anything at all, please let me know. Anytime, day or night. When one of our own is murdered, we don't get much rest until the killer's in custody."

"I'm sure you don't," Burke said. "Thank you for that."

On the way out of Captain Burke's office, Pride felt a gaze drilling into him with such intensity that the sensation was almost physical. He caught the eye of a pretty young woman, light-skinned, with her black hair pulled back into a bun. When his gaze met her insistent stare, she looked away, down at her desk as if she'd been focusing on something there the whole time.

Pride knew in an instant who it was. He detoured to her desk. As he got closer, he realized that the sparkle in her eyes was moisture from tears she was desperately blinking back, and the redness of her plump lower lip was because she'd been chewing on it. "Ms. St. Cyr?" he said. "I'm Special Agent Dwayne Pride, NCIS. May I talk to you?"

"It's about Ed, isn't it?" she asked, her voice hushed.

She was uncomfortable even speaking with him.

"Yes, I'm afraid so."

"Not here, please," she said. "There's a coffee shop in Picayune, on Memorial Boulevard. Near the Winn-Dixie. It's called Steagall's House of Brews. I'll meet you there in... say, forty minutes?"

"That would be fine, ma'am. Thank you."

He walked away, hoping she would really show up.

Christopher Lasalle knew all about fear.

He had lived with it most of his life. The fear hadn't necessarily been for his own safety—though there was some of that—but for his brother's. Cade suffered from bipolar disorder, and had for decades. As a boy, Lasalle hadn't known the disorder's name, or even that it had one. He only knew that something took Cade away from him for days, weeks, even months at a time. Sometimes Cade was enveloped in a cloud of gloom so deep it almost sucked the color from the sky, and during those times, he stayed in his room with his door closed. He played loud music on his little stereo system, head-banging, thrashing metal or softer, mournful tunes. If Lasalle ran into him in the hall, on his way to the bathroom, maybe, or to the kitchen for a snack, Cade often looked like he'd been crying.

At other times, he was overflowing with energy. Then, the house couldn't contain him. He went out and stayed out, disappearing for long stretches, while their parents walked the floors and called police departments and hospitals and every friend whose name they knew, looking for him. When he was old enough to drive, Lasalle cruised the streets and alleyways, afraid of what he might find.

Lasalle never knew, on any given day, which Cade he would see next, if he saw any at all. He feared for his brother's safety, for his sanity, and sometimes—though he knew that Cade would never hurt him when he was in his right mind—he feared for himself, his mom, and his sister.

He and Sonja had driven down to St. Bernard Parish, to the home of Edouard Alpuente's mother and his uncle—her brother—and the fear in the house was palpable. He didn't know quite what they were afraid of, but that they were afraid was certain.

He began to feel a sense of foreboding before they even reached the property, as they passed what had once—and not that long ago—been healthy forests. Now most of the trees looked dormant or dead, nothing but oversized sticks jutting up from spits of land surrounded by fetid, still water. The Alpuente property was a ragged scrap of farmland close to the shore, outside of Shell Beach.

The house itself looked like it had been battered by Katrina, Rita, and dozens of unnamed storms since, but had forgotten to fall down. Whatever paint might once have colored its slat-wood walls had long since been scrubbed off by the weather; in places, the slats were missing altogether, the holes patched with tarps or plywood. A rickety-looking wooden dock extended out into Lake Borgne, which connected to the Gulf out in the far distance.

"Guess he didn't come from money," he said.

"Most of us don't," Sonja replied.

Lasalle didn't answer. His father had been in the oil business. He was no oil billionaire, but he was comfortable, and Lasalle had always known where his next meal was coming from.

He drove up the narrow driveway, his truck straddling the weeds that filled the space between the two tracks, and stopped in a cleared area near the house. Another truck, older than his by at least twenty years, sat there, surrounded by rusted bits and pieces of yet more vehicles. When he opened his door, a breeze blowing in off the choppy water brought an odd, sulfuric smell along with the expected lake odors. A gull wheeled overhead, its flight wobbling, as unsteady as a drunk trying to walk a straight line.

"Nothing like that fresh sea air," Sonja said, wrinkling her nose.

"I know, right?"

A woman came out of the house and descended the steps in front. She wore a simple shift that had been white, before the years had yellowed it. Age had grayed her skin and hair and hunched her shoulders, but her voice was clear and strong. "Can I he'p y'all?" she asked.

"Mrs. Alpuente?" Sonja asked. "Donna Alpuente?"

"That's right."

"We're federal agents, with the Naval Criminal Investigative Service. I'm Sonja Percy, and this is Chris Lasalle. Can we go inside?"

"Well, I... federal agents, you say?"

"Yes, ma'am," Lasalle said.

"Wit' the Navy?"

"Yes."

"I guess so, then. C'mon in."

She went back up the stairs, pulled open a screen door that seemed to be barely attached at the hinges, and held it for them. Sonja entered first, then Lasalle.

The first thing he noticed was the altar. It covered the top of a sideboard, and then some, set against the wall opposite the door and the room's lone window, so that light from both fell on it.

Lasalle didn't know enough about voodoo to know what everything signified. There were familiar objects—a corncob pipe, a tin of tobacco, a bottle of rum, money and keys, and what looked like wrapped hard candies strewn about randomly. Candles flanked a statue of somebody he didn't recognize, a man draped in a black cloak with red trim. Covering the surface of the sideboard, and pinned up on the wall behind it, was a length of red satin.

The room smelled strange—some kind of incense, he guessed. A man was sitting in a chair, his attention glued to a small TV set. He was older than the woman, but there was a distinct resemblance between them.

"That's my brother, Elmer Comeau," the woman said. "Say hello, Elmer."

"Hello," the man said. He didn't look away from the screen. The show he was riveted to seemed to be an infomercial for a product that eased joint pain, although Lasalle wasn't entirely sure about that, since it seemed to feature two men involved in a deeply spiritual discussion about whole grains.

"Please, Mrs. Alpuente," Sonja said, "have a seat."

Donna gripped the arms of a wicker chair and lowered herself unsteadily into it. She eyed Sonja with a worried expression, her lined forehead almost folding in on itself. "Is this about Eddie?"

"Yes, ma'am," Sonja said. There was no chair close to Donna's, so Sonja squatted beside her, holding onto the chair arm. Lasalle stood close by, in case he was needed. He hated this part of the job. Every cop did. "I'm so very sorry, ma'am," Sonja said, "but Eddie is dead."

The woman's chin dropped and her lips quivered,

as if trying in vain to form words. A soft, keening sound came from somewhere deep inside her.

"We're very sorry," Lasalle said.

Elmer swiveled around in his chair. "Was he killed? That's why y'all are here?"

"That's what we're looking into," Sonja said.

Lasalle found a box of tissues on a side table and handed them to Sonja, who passed them over to Donna. "We'll do everything we can to determine what happened."

"And catch the bastard who done it?"

"And that," Lasalle replied. "Would you have any ideas? Did Eddie have any enemies that you know of?"

"Everybody's got enemies, don't they?" Elmer said. "But most folks don't get killed by 'em."

Donna blew her nose, then wadded the tissue and stuffed it into a pocket. She crossed herself and muttered what Lasalle assumed was a quick prayer. There was, he knew, a lot of crossover between voodoo and Catholicism, especially in the New Orleans area. The unique blending stemmed from the combined influence of French Catholics and slaves from what was now Benin, in west Africa—a large number of whom were first taken to the Dominican Republic, where there were also French colonists.

"Is Eddie's father living?" he asked.

"No, he's been gone for, what, eighteen, no, nineteen years, now," Donna replied.

"Eddie was working somewhere in the area, wasn't he?" Sonja asked.

"Yes," Donna said. "He was down this way a lot. He used to drop in once in a while. We have a room here, told him he could stay with us. We don't see him near enough. I don't know why he wouldn't, but…"

The tears started again, and she tore another tissue from the box, burying her face in it.

Lasalle looked around the place. Besides the altar, he saw a couple of crucifixes hanging on walls, and candles with pictures of saints on them standing on a shelf. On the shelf above those were animal skulls, arranged in order from smallest—some kind of bird—to largest, which he thought was a dog or coyote.

They stayed for about forty more minutes, long enough for Donna Alpuente to declare that she would be okay. Lasalle was glad her brother would be staying with her, because he had his doubts. Elmer said he'd look after her, but Lasalle had doubts about that, too. The man had eventually turned off the TV, but once he did, he spent more time complaining about the farming having gone downhill in the last few years, and the fishing, while coming back some, not doing much better. He seemed to think Lieutenant Alpuente should have done something about it. As they pulled away from the house, Sonja shook her head.

"I can understand why he didn't want to stay there," she said.

"So can I. A rented house in Tremé would look a lot better."

"No wonder he was on antidepressants. Living in that place would do it to me, too."

"You got that right. Place was downright gloomy. They look like true believers, though."

"Believers in what? Voodoo, or Christianity?"

"Both, I'd say. Nothing uncommon about that."

"This is Louisiana, Lasalle. The only thing uncommon around here is anything that would be considered normal anywhere else."

10

From out front, Steagall's House of Brews looked like a hole in the wall. But a back door opened onto an enclosed, shaded patio that allowed for more seating than was evident at first. Pride ordered a dark roast, which was served in a heavy white mug. He took it out onto the patio and sat beside the brick wall, on which were hung, interspersed amidst the clinging ivy, faces made from twisted wire, rusted by the elements. Some were recognizably happy, sad, upset, and frightened, while others wore more subtle or indefinable expressions. Studying them as he waited, Pride was surprised at how much feeling could be conveyed by the simplest of materials.

He finished his first cup of coffee, got a refill, and returned to his seat. Still no sign of Michelle St. Cyr. He checked his phone and found a voice mail from Sonja. She said, "That phone number Melancon gave you is to a burner phone, purchased with cash three months ago at a Circle K on Lafayette. Surveillance video for that date is long gone, and the phone's a dead end."

He sent her a text acknowledging the message—he didn't want to get involved in a conversation, in case

Michelle showed up—then read some emails, and waited. Then he waited some more. Finally, the front door opened and she came inside. Pride stood and she spotted him, bypassing the counter and heading straight for the patio.

"I didn't order you anything, because I didn't know what you might want," he said as he shook her hand. "I can get you something."

"No, I'm fine," she said. He pulled out the chair opposite his and held it for her as she sat. "Well, maybe an iced chai?"

"Be right back," he said. He left her alone, ordered her drink, and asked that it be delivered to the table. Five bucks in the tip jar sealed the deal.

When he returned, she was staring at the wire faces. "They look so sad," she said.

Pride was surprised, because to him they seemed to convey the whole gamut of human emotions. He supposed it was—as they said about beauty—all in the eye of the beholder. "I'm very sorry about Lt. Alpuente," he said. "My sincerest condolences."

She attempted a smile, but quickly gave up on it. "Thank you." She hesitated for a long moment, then added, "I almost didn't come."

"I'm glad you did."

"I wasn't sure I could. But then I decided it would be easier than staying at the office any longer, pretending."

"Why pretending?"

"A romantic relationship between military and contractor—it's not exactly forbidden, but it's frowned upon. If it had been obvious, one of us might have had to change jobs, and we both love what we do. We kept it on the down-low, and those who did know about it were happy to ignore it as long as it didn't affect our work or our relationships with others in the workplace. I guess it doesn't matter so much now that he's gone, but I didn't want to make a spectacle of myself today. When the news came in this morning, I spent a long time in the ladies' room by myself, bawling my guts out. I'd finally pulled it together when you came in."

"It's okay to cry," he said. "I know that's not brilliant advice, but it's pretty much the best I've got. Let yourself grieve, don't try to hold it in, and don't forget to take care of yourself."

She tried on another smile, and this time it took for a couple of seconds. "Thank you, Special Agent Pride. I'll try to remember that."

"Did you know him for very long?"

"Three years, I guess. We'd been dating for sixteen months, next week. We were going to get married after his current assignment was finished and he was back at SSC full-time."

"I'm sorry," he said again. "I know this is hard."

"Yes. Yes, it is. But you're here to find out what happened to him, aren't you?"

"Yes, ma'am," he said. "We know basically what happened, but there are still a lot of missing pieces. And we need to know the who and the why, as well."

Her iced chai came, and she took a sip, then dabbed at her nose with her napkin. "I so wanted to be with him on Mardi Gras," she said. "Maybe if I had been—"

He cut her off. "Don't think like that. If you had been, chances are you'd have been hurt, too. I'm sure he was glad you were safe."

"Probably so. He was like that, always thinking of others."

"Especially you," Pride said. "He didn't have much in his hotel room, in the way of personal possessions, but he did have a framed photograph of the two of you."

Her eyes welled up. "I know the one," she said. "Ed always kept it by his bedside, wherever he was. I like it. He looks so happy in it."

"He does," Pride agreed. "Do you know why he went to that hotel?"

"He was hoping the crowds would protect him. He was afraid to stay at the Tremé house anymore."

"Afraid of what?"

"The voodoo curse," she said.

"Excuse me?"

"He had been cursed."

She said it matter-of-factly. Pride knew that a lot of cops—most, probably, around the country—would have dismissed the idea as fantasy. But he wasn't most cops. He was a New Orleanian, through and through. Voodoo demanded as much respect as any other belief system, and that had to include curses. They were rare, but not unheard of. "Who cursed him?"

"I don't know. I don't even think he knew."

"Tell me about it."

She sipped from her glass, then put it down on the table with a trembling hand. "I didn't even know about it at first, so I'm not sure exactly when it started. It seemed like he was keeping something from me, and it was bothering me, but I couldn't pin it down. Then, a few weeks ago, he was back here for the weekend—I have an apartment, over in Nicholson, and he owns a house there. We're—we were going to move in there after we were married."

She wiped a tear away, and continued. "Anyway, when he was back that time, we went by his house, and we saw what looked like blood in the driveway. Just drops, you know. A little trail of them. We followed it around to a kind of courtyard on the side of his house, and the ground beside a tree had been disturbed. Eddie got a shovel and turned over the dirt, and underneath it was a newborn fawn. I could barely recognize it. It was dead. Its throat had been cut. It was the most horrible thing I've ever seen, and—"

"Easy," Pride said. "You're doing great, Michelle. Breathe, and take it slow. We've got time."

"It was just… I can't even tell you. Also in the hole were some bones and this… I don't know… tangle of hair, I guess. I don't know if it was human or what. I— why would anybody do that?"

"To scare someone, it sounds like."

"Well, it worked, then. It scared the hell out of me. And Ed was scared, too. That's when he admitted to me that he had been cursed. Other things had happened, but he wouldn't go into detail about them. He told me he didn't have any idea who would curse him, but he was sure that's what it was. I wasn't sure he was telling me the truth."

"Why not?" Pride asked.

"He had been so reluctant to even tell me about it in the first place. I don't know, I thought maybe he was hiding something. He said he hadn't told me because he didn't take it that seriously, and he didn't want to worry me. But I could tell he was worried. I told him he shouldn't have to handle things like that alone. That we're partners, in everything. So when he told me he didn't know who had cursed him, or why, I thought maybe he was still just trying to protect me."

"He might have been," Pride said. "We're like that sometimes, with the people we love."

"Men, you mean?"

"Men. People. Even though we know a burden is

lighter when it's shared, we think it's ours to bear alone."

"That sounds like Eddie."

"I'm not surprised. Can you tell me what he did with those things from his courtyard?"

"He stuck them into a garbage bag and put them out with the trash," she said. "I don't know if that's even legal, but he didn't know what else to do. He didn't want them around. Neither did I."

"I don't blame you."

"Look, Special Agent Pride. I want you to know, we're rational people. Ed's a scientist, and I'm educated. We don't believe in voodoo, or much of anything, spiritually speaking. He's a lapsed Catholic and I'm a lapsed Baptist, so I guess you could say we're not very big on organized religion. But he— this really got to him. He told me to stay away from his house. He went back to the house in Tremé, said he felt safer there, but that didn't last for long, either."

"How do you mean?"

"He said he was starting to feel the symptoms of a voodoo curse."

"What are those, do you know?"

"He just didn't have any energy, like he had been drained. He had mood swings, and recurring nightmares about these strange beings that were trying to steal his soul. He had constant thoughts of death. He looked it up online and found that those things were all associated with voodoo curses."

"That sounds pretty grim."

"Yes, it was. I was worried for him. I wanted him to go to a doctor, but he wouldn't. Then I wanted to come down to be with him, but he wouldn't let me. He said I had to stay far away from him."

"So you'd be safe. He was thinking of you."

"That's the way he was."

"I wish I had known him," Pride said. "He sounds like someone I'd have liked."

"I think you would have. He didn't have a whole lot of friends—he was kind of an introvert, I guess. But he was easy to like."

"So what happened then? Is that when he checked into the hotel?"

"He called me the other day, frantic. He said he came home and there was something tied to his front door. He said it looked like a monkey's paw. He just freaked. I guess that was the last straw. He said he had called a friend and arranged for a room, but he wouldn't tell me where. He said he would be safe there, that there would be big crowds around. Nobody would find him, and nothing would be able to get to him. He stopped going to work, ate at restaurants close to the hotel, and told me on the phone that he was feeling a little more comfortable. Once Mardi Gras was over and the crowds were gone, he didn't know what he was going to do, but…" She let the sentence trail off.

Pride put his hand on her arm. "I promise you, Michelle. We'll find out what happened, and who did it."

"Are you sure?"

"We're pretty good at what we do."

She tossed him a fleeting grin. "You seem like it."

"Is there anything else you can tell me?"

She considered the question, then shook her head. "I mean, I could talk about Ed all day long. But I can't think of anything else that would be helpful to you right now."

He put his card down on the table and pushed it toward her with one finger. "This is me," he said. "Any time, night or day, if you think of anything that might be pertinent, or if you just want to talk, okay?"

"Okay," she said, pocketing the card.

"Do you have someone you can stay with for a while? Family, a girlfriend?"

"Yeah, I can… I can stay with my sister Deirdre."

"That would be good. Do that. And remember to take care of yourself. Pamper yourself. A loss like this is a terrible thing, but if you let it take you over, it only gets worse. I can tell you that he'd want you to be well and be safe."

"You're right. You're a lot like him, I think."

Pride smiled. "Thank you," he said. "That means a lot to me, really."

A voodoo curse? Pride wasn't convinced that Alpuente had been killed by voodoo. But he'd had those voodoo accoutrements with him in the hotel, so despite what Michelle had said, he had been enough of a believer to take some precautions.

Whether voodoo was involved or not, Pride intended to find Alpuente's killer. Even more so, now that he'd met Michelle St. Cyr. She was smart and strong, and it sounded like Alpuente had much to look forward to. Whoever had cut his life short had to answer for it.

He was driving when he got a phone call. He recognized the number, and answered it. "Rose?" he said.

"Dwayne, where y'at?"

"Still working the case," he said. "Is everything okay there?"

"I have all that security video you asked for," she said. "My guy Germaine pulled it together and put it on a DVD for you."

"That's perfect," Pride said. "I'll pick it up." He glanced at the clock. "About an hour?"

"It'll be at the front desk," she said.

"Great. I appreciate it."

"Don't mention it. I just hope it helps."

"So do I, Rose," he said. "So do I."

Before he ended the call, he added, "Do you have any voodoo practitioners on the staff there?"

She considered briefly. "Not that I know of. But we're not supposed to ask about religion when we hire, you know? If somebody volunteers the information, that's one thing. Nobody's said anything about voodoo that I can remember, but what somebody does on their free time is their own business."

"Understood," he said. "Thanks again for the help."

"Anything for an old friend," she said. "Let me know if there's any more I can do."

"I will," Pride said. "You can count on it."

11

Abraham Lincoln delivered his second inaugural address on March 4, 1865. A little more than a month later, on April 9, Confederate general Robert E. Lee surrendered the Army of Northern Virginia, the event widely considered to be the end of the Civil War. Five days after that, John Wilkes Booth shot Lincoln during a performance at Ford's Theatre in Washington, D.C. It took until June 23 for the last Confederate holdout, a Cherokee general named Stand Watie, to surrender his forces, finally bringing the bloodiest war in American history to a definitive end.

But upon the occasion of his second inauguration, Lincoln knew that chapter of American history was coming to a close. His speech reflected that knowledge, as well as his understanding of what the war had cost Americans on both sides. He had ended slavery and liberated those in bondage, but he knew, as well, that the road to true freedom would be a long one, full of continued struggle. He hoped his words could help heal a broken nation, but was fully aware that the healing would be a slow and difficult process.

He closed the speech—which is one of those

inscribed on the walls of the Lincoln Memorial in the nation's capital—with these words: "With malice toward none, with charity for all, with firmness in the right as God gives us to see the right, let us strive on to finish the work we are in, to bind up the nation's wounds, to care for him who shall have borne the battle and for his widow and his orphan, to do all which may achieve and cherish a just and lasting peace among ourselves and with all nations."

That presidential inauguration was the first to be heavily photographed, and Pride had a print made from one of the photos hanging in the bar he'd purchased with his share of the proceeds from the sale of the house in the Lower Garden. He had named the bar CFA, for "charity for all." He wasn't generally one to idolize politicians, but he considered Lincoln a unique figure in the nation's history—the right man at the right time, who had steered the country through its most difficult hours.

Now it was late, and he and his team were gathered at CFA, going over the day's events and bringing one another up to speed on the investigation. Lasalle and Sonja had described their trip down to St. Bernard Parish, and Pride had just wrapped up the story of his visits with Captain Burke and Michelle St. Cyr.

"A voodoo curse?" Lasalle asked. "I think we need something a little more substantial to go on than superstitious nonsense. I mean, back in 'Bama, people told stories about all kinds of things that modern science can't explain—hoodoos and witchcraft and alien abductions and everything else—but I never believed in any of that. Seems a little far-fetched to me."

"You're not back in 'Bama now, Country Mouse," Sonja said. "You're in Louisiana, and people here take voodoo seriously."

"She's right," Pride said. "I couldn't say for sure that Ms. St. Cyr believed in it—she's a rational type, like you. But I can tell you for certain that she was terrified. Lt. Alpuente's a local, and just knowing he had been cursed could have been very upsetting, never mind any effects of the curse itself."

"Well, his mother's a true believer," Lasalle said. "And her brother, too, I think. So he was brought up with it."

"They had a big old altar," Sonja added. "With a statue of Legba in the middle of it that was at least a foot tall."

"Is that who that was? In the black cape?"

"That's right. Papa Legba is the father of the crossroads. Every voodoo ceremony begins and ends with Papa Legba, because he's the intermediary between humans and the rest of the *loa*. You want to talk to the spirit world, you go through him."

"He's kind of like voodoo's version of St. Peter," Pride added. "St. Peter stands at the gate. In voodoo custom, it's a crossroads, and Papa Legba is the guardian. Anyone who wants to speak to the dead goes through him."

"You might have heard this story," Loretta put in. "When musician Robert Johnson wanted to become a great blues guitarist, he sold his soul to the devil down at a crossroads. According to some blues scholars, that wasn't the Christian devil, but Papa Legba himself."

"Y'all are serious about this," Lasalle said.

"I'm not saying that we'll solve the case by asking the *loa* who did it," Pride said. "I'm just saying, if there's a voodoo element to it, we need to give that angle due consideration. And given what Michelle told me, along with the things we found in Alpuente's pockets and his hotel room, we definitely can't write off the voodoo aspect."

"Speaking of which," Sebastian said, "I've examined the *gris-gris* bag and the voodoo doll. They're both from a shop on Rampart Street called Doctor Jim's, just across from Congo Square. It's very good workmanship, too. They're both very authentic, from what I can tell. Of course, a lot of practitioners prefer to make their own items, so Doctor Jim's sells mostly to the tourist trade. But locals shop there, too, including serious practitioners, and they swear by Doctor Jim's quality."

"That's just up the street from the squad room," Pride said. "Chris, let's you and me pay a little visit first thing in the morning."

"Oh, I also learned who Dan Petro is," Sebastian added.

"Dan who?" Sonja asked.

"On the voodoo doll, there was a piece of paper with the name 'Dan Petro' written on it. Dan Petro is a voodoo saint who protects farmers."

"Mrs. Alpuente and her brother could use some help from him," Lasalle said. "The old man said the harvests have been pathetic lately. They supplement their farm income with fishing off their pier, but that's been a struggle, too."

"I guess Dan Petro fell down on the job," Sebastian said. "Or maybe Lt. Alpuente shouldn't have left him in the drawer."

"I'm not sure he had much choice," Pride said. "He had put on his uniform, but Michelle said he had been skipping work, and there's no indication that he had any plans other than watching the parade. All the other clothes he had with him were dirty, so I'm thinking he dressed in uniform because it was all he had left. Chances are he didn't expect to leave the room, or he might have taken the doll with him."

"He didn't expect to leave it the way he did," Patton said. "And that's a fact, Jack. Look at this here." He was sitting at the far end of the table from Pride, and he turned a tablet computer so everybody else could see it. "This is from the hotel security video King brought me earlier."

He pressed the "play" triangle and a hotel hallway came into view. Patton leaned over the screen so he could see it, and tapped one of the room doors with a finger. "This here's Alpuente's room."

As the video played, a young couple came out of a room across the hall and walked past the camera. They were probably headed down to the street to watch the parade, Pride guessed, since their room faced the other direction. "Pretty good video, right?" Patton asked. "Nice and clear on those folks."

"So we have a good look at Alpuente's attacker?" Lasalle asked.

"Patience, my man," Patton said. The hallway was empty again for a couple of minutes.

"Not much of a plot," Sebastian said. "And the characterization's a little weak. It reminds me of this movie I saw last week—"

Patton cut him off. "Now lookie here." Then there was motion again, a blur of black at the bottom of the screen. A figure in black—quite tall and broad, it appeared—headed toward the door Patton had indicated. It was impossible to get a decent view, though. Not only was the figure facing away from the camera, but the image flickered and scrambled, pixelated and indistinct. At the doorway, the figure paused, then disappeared inside.

"That's not very helpful," Sonja said.

"Hopefully we'll get a better look when he comes out," Lasalle added. "What's up with the camera?"

"I wish I could tell you," Patton replied. "Keep watching."

The video kept running, the hallway empty. Then, three minutes later, the door to Alpuente's room opened again. A black form, no more distinct than a shadow, emerged and headed straight for the camera. Once again, the image was pixelated and unclear.

"What the hell?" Sonja asked.

Patton blew out a frustrated sigh. "I've been working on the video for hours, but I can't enhance it or figure out what went haywire. There's no pixelation anywhere except when that guy—least, I think it's a guy, but it's hard to tell for sure—appears. Before and after, it's perfectly clear. The hotel actually has a pretty good video surveillance system. Thing is, although I could show you more video of this guy, it's the same thing all over the building. Any time he shows up, the camera fritzes out."

"That's strange," Pride said. "And not remotely helpful."

"Maybe this will be," Patton said. He ended the first video feed and punched some keys. A different image appeared on the tablet screen, this one showing the front desk, from an angle above and behind the hotel staff. "I found when our man checked in."

A few moments after the video started, Edouard Alpuente appeared, walking up to the counter. He carried the suitcase Pride had seen in the hotel room. A young female staffer started to approach him, but was blocked by someone Pride recognized as

Gilbert Melancon. The woman stepped away, and the transaction was handled quickly. Melancon was the only hotel employee who interacted with him. Other people moved into and out of the frame, but nobody seemed to pay any attention to the exchange at the desk. A couple of minutes later, Alpuente was on his way to his room alone, leaving Melancon at the counter.

"Alpuente goes up in the elevator by himself," Patton said. "Same thing in the third-floor hallway—just him. In the rest of the video I've seen, he occasionally leaves the room and returns, always alone. A maid shows up once in a while, but never for very long. Nobody else goes near his door, except for one time when Melancon knocks. The door never opens, and he goes away after a few minutes. Then nobody else except that one mysterious figure. I don't know, maybe that dude travels with his own electromagnetic field or something that screws with the video system. I can't explain it. And I freakin' hate things I can't explain."

"I don't think you're the only one who feels that way," Sebastian said. "Pretty much everybody at this table hates things we can't explain. Except magic tricks. Magic tricks you can't explain are the best ones. It's like that time David Copperfield made the Statue of Liberty 'disappear,' only what he really did was turn the stage a little so the archway the audience was looking through showed a different stretch of empty water."

"No spoilers, Sebastian!" Loretta said.

"Spoilers? The trick's more than thirty years old, and you can find dozens of videos online explaining how he did it."

"Videos I have no intention of watching," Loretta replied. "Sometimes a person has to simply believe. The world's full of mysteries, and even the assembled brain trust here can't solve them all. Nor should we."

"I'll drink to that," Pride said. "In fact, I think we all should." He turned toward the bar. "Buckley! Set us up again, if you please!"

12

Doctor Jim's was on Rampart, kitty-corner from Congo Square. It didn't look like much from the outside, and would have been easy to miss if Pride hadn't been looking for it. The store was a narrow space between two other businesses, with a brick exterior wall that had been painted red. The door was shiny and black, with a smudged, dirty window in it. A brass plaque bolted onto the wall near the door had "Doctor Jim's Voodoo Shop" etched on it, in an elaborate script that made it hard to read. Graffiti had been scrawled on the walls of the surrounding businesses, but Doctor Jim's appeared to have been left alone. From one of the upper-floor apartments, hip-hop music blasted loud enough to rattle the wrought iron enclosing the gallery.

"This is the place," Pride said.

"Who's Doctor Jim?" Lasalle asked. "Friend of yours?"

"I'm not as old as I look," Pride said with a chuckle. "Doctor Jim Alexander showed up in New Orleans in the 1870s. He was a voodoo priest, the only real competition for Marie Laveau in her prime. She hated him for it, and they were rivals for years. Supposedly, he kept a pair of alligators in a pool in front of his house, and they came when he called them by name. At least, that's the way I've heard the story."

"I didn't know alligators could be trained like that," Lasalle said. "That must have been something to see."

"I would imagine." He caught Lasalle's gaze and held it for a moment. "You ready, Chris?"

Lasalle looked surprised by the question. "Sure."

"Okay, here we go."

Pride turned the knob and opened the black door. The smell struck him first: incense and herbs, scented candles and sweat and more, all of it combined into an odoriferous stew that might have been toxic to small children and the infirm.

Stepping from the brightness of the day into the dim lighting of the shop, he blinked a couple of times. It didn't help; his brain was overwhelmed by the sheer magnitude of what filled his senses. Every inch of space seemed to be occupied, and, as if to spite the laws of physics, some spots seemed to contain more things than could possibly fit. The ceiling was thick with hanging objects: dolls, evil eyes, crucifixes, necklaces and strings of beads, and more. Masks and statues and saints and more crucifixes of every description eyed him from every wall and cabinet. The shop was a riot of color, a whirlwind that had picked up the contents of a dozen houses and then frozen in place.

"I feel like I walked into another world," Lasalle said softly.

"You did," Pride said.

A door Pride couldn't see opened and closed and a woman appeared behind the shop's sales counter. She was heavy and dark-skinned, wearing clothes that she seemed to have wrapped herself in rather than dressed in. She wore a crimson head wrap, and the rest of her garb had too many colors to pick out any dominant one. She offered the men a welcoming smile. "Good mornin'," she said, full of cheer. "Tourists, or locals?"

"Locals," Pride said. "NCIS." He showed her his badge, and Lasalle did the same.

Her expression changed, as suddenly as if a switch had been flipped. "Oh."

"We'd like some information on one of your customers," Lasalle said.

She put her hands flat on the counter and leaned toward them, defiance on her face. "I wish I could help you, but I'm very busy."

Pride looked around the store. There might have been other customers—there were so many objects that his eyes couldn't take them all in or his mind process them all, so he supposed it was possible that people were hidden among them. "I can see that," he said. "We won't take up much of your time, I promise."

"Sir, voodoo is a religion, and as such is protected under the first amendment of the Bill of Rights."

"Yes, ma'am," Pride said. Defending the Constitution was what NCIS did, after all, and he took that duty seriously. "I'm aware of that. Can I show you some pictures?"

"I got nothing to say about any of my practitioners."

"I assure you, we won't be violating any confidences." Pride pulled his phone from his pocket and found a photograph of Lt. Alpuente on Loretta's table. He put it in front of her. "Do you know this man?"

"Oh. Oh, my. Is he—?"

Pride flipped through a couple of postmortem shots of Alpuente. "He was murdered yesterday," he said. "He had some items among his things that were purchased at this store."

"He… I might be familiar with him. I'm sorry if he was…"

"It was a particularly violent death, ma'am," Lasalle said. "We're trying very hard to find out who did it. Anything you can tell us might help."

Pride showed her photos of the doll and the *gris-gris* bag. "Are these your items?"

She eyed them for only a moment. "Yes," she said, pride evident in her tone. "Handmade. I only sell top-quality merchandise."

"We could tell that," Pride said. "Do you remember if he bought them himself?"

"Yes, I… yes, he did."

"Did he buy anything else, anything you're not seeing here?"

"I don't think so. No, that was all, I'm pretty sure. Some stuff to go inside the *gris-gris* bag, but I don't recall what exactly."

"Do you remember when this was?"

"Three weeks ago maybe. Little less, little more. I don't know exactly. I see a lot of faces come through that door, me. This is a busy shop. Best voodoo shop in town."

"I'm sure you have plenty of customers. Is there anything in particular you can remember about this one?"

She took the phone from Pride's hands and flipped back to the photos of Alpuente. "He didn't want to talk when there was anybody in the store, so he waited around until everybody else left. He needed a lot of help. He was familiar with the concepts, but… it was like he knew the language, but he didn't have no accent, if you know what I mean."

"Like maybe he was raised in a household where voodoo was practiced, but had never really been a believer?" Lasalle asked.

The woman's eyes brightened. "Yes! Maybe like that."

"Did he say exactly what his concern was? Was he getting these for self-protection, or what?" Pride asked.

"He wasn't exactly clear about that," she said. "But that was what I figured, from what he did say and from what he bought."

"Did he happen to give you any idea what or who he needed protection from?" Lasalle queried.

"He said as little as possible. I got the sense he was mighty afraid of somethin'. I told him these might help. I don't make no promises, me. Everything in my shop can do somebody some good, they use it right. They use it wrong, either it do nothin' at all, or maybe it backfires on 'em. I tell 'em, follow my instructions, or get one of the good books. But once they out that door—" She brushed her palms together in a hand-washing motion. "—they on their own."

Sonja never entered the morgue without a little trepidation.

It wasn't the dead bodies, so much. She had seen plenty of those in her career, and had even been responsible for some of them. She tried to pretend that was no big deal, all in a day's work. She never killed without reason, of course—anyone she put down was an immediate danger to herself or others. Still, their faces haunted her, sometimes, and she imagined they always would. Every cop who killed—every soldier, too, she guessed—carried those lives they'd ended to their own graves. No matter how justified it was, how unquestionably necessary, there was still the knowledge that she had cut short a life. And she'd been around the block enough times to know that no matter how evil a person was, there were other qualities inside that person's heart, better ones. You couldn't just kill the evil, you killed the good at the same time.

But it wasn't just that. Her job was to get justice for those who had been victimized. Loretta Wade sometimes said she had to speak for the dead, because they could no longer speak for themselves. But Loretta's voice carried only so far; out in the streets, it was Sonja and the other agents on the team who had to carry it further. And there had been those—too many, over her career—who Sonja had let down, whose deaths had never been solved. Not a lot, but still... one was too many. And the number was greater than one.

Then there was—

"Sonja! Just the Percy I wanted to see!"

"Sebastian," she said, turning. He was coming out of his lab, excitement animating his lanky form. "I was looking for you."

"You found me."

"Did you see what I did there? Percy, person. 'Just the person I wanted to see'?"

"Yeah, I got that. You said you had some news."

"I did indeed. Indeed, I do." He ushered her back into the lab. "What's the most adorable kind of monkey?"

"Adorable?" Sonja wrinkled her nose. "I guess one that belongs to somebody else."

"Good answer. Safe, but honest."

"Also," she added, "one that has all its hands."

"I believe they're called paws," Sebastian corrected. "Although I think their feet are called feet, so it's not like dogs, which only have paws. At least, in the famous W.W. Jacobs horror story, it was a paw."

"What story was that?" Sonja asked.

"'The Monkey's Paw.'"

"I had to ask."

"Great story. If you haven't read it—"

"In high school."

"—since high school, it's worth revisiting. This old monkey's paw can grant three wishes, and—"

"I read it," she reminded him. "It's not that easy to forget."

"No, it's really not."

"But I'm here about the other monkey's paw. The *real* one."

"Right. So here's the deal." He took a breath and let it out slowly, as if stalling for time. "Capuchin."

"Capuchin?" she repeated.

"Capuchin. That's the most adorable kind of monkey. Also, it's the kind your paw came from."

"Okay," she said.

"You might recognize them from hanging around with organ grinders. I mean, in the early twentieth century. Way before you were born, obviously, but you've probably seen pictures." He chuckled. "Probably not the best thought, considering we're in a morgue and all, but what if there were real organ grinders? People who ground organs in a—"

"I get the picture," Sonja said. "Let's go back to the monkeys."

"Okay, right. Capuchin monkeys were named after the Franciscan friars, the Order of Friars Minor Capuchin. They used to wear these hooded, brown robes, belted with a cord at the waist, and they had the hair thing going—" He indicated this by gesturing at his own head, in a circular motion—"the tonsure. Anyway, early European explorers in South America came across these monkeys who reminded them of the friars, and called them capuchins. The name stuck.

Probably to the displeasure of the friars themselves, but then again, who knows? St. Francis got along with all the animals, right?"

"So they say."

"Capuchins are smart, too. They're tool-users. They'll use rocks to break up hard foods, like nuts, and to dig with. They've even been known to chip rocks into primitive blades, although it sounds like that's more of an accidental thing. Still, not a lot of animals use tools. Ravens do—"

"Is there going to be something that will help with the case at some point, Stringbean, or should I just get a chair and wait for you to finish?"

"Sorry," he said. "Here's the thing. In Louisiana, it's illegal to own non-human primates. Or human primates, for that matter, since 1865. But that's how this particular law reads—'non-human primates.' The only exceptions, when it comes to said non-human primates—which includes all classes of monkeys and apes—are for people who owned them before the law went into effect. People who did own primates at the time of passage had to register the ones they had, and any change in status—deaths or births, for instance—had to be immediately reported to the state. I pulled the records, but there hasn't been a capuchin death recorded since 2014. Your paw isn't anywhere near that old, so presumably—if the paw came from around here, anyway—there's a one-handed capuchin somewhere. Or one-pawed, whatever."

"So all I have to do is look for an organ grinder? Who else would keep a monkey for a pet?"

"More people than you'd expect. Capuchins are cute, like I said, although they do have their drawbacks. After about five years of age, they won't keep their diapers on, for one thing."

"Diapers?"

"Diapers. And if they get bored, they might start throwing their feces, so you probably don't want them inside the house. Or you want to make sure they're constantly entertained." He sat at a keyboard and typed for a few moments. "I just sent you a list of every registered capuchin in the eight parishes encompassing the New Orleans metro area. I can go farther out if you need me to, but I thought this would get you started."

She checked her phone. Sure enough, there was a message from him. She scanned the list. A few dozen owners, spread throughout the parishes. "Thank you, Sebastian," she said brightly. "How did you know I wanted to spend my day knocking on doors and asking people if any of their monkeys have lost any paws lately?"

He regarded her, as if trying to decide whether she was serious. "Lucky guess?"

13

"Got something to show you guys," Patton said when Pride and Lasalle walked into the squad room.

"Something good, I hope," Pride said.

"Better than that."

"Better than good? Put it on the plasma," Lasalle said. "At this point, I'll take any good news I can get."

Patton rolled to a keyboard and tapped a few keys. The rotating NCIS logo on the plasma screen blinked away, and was replaced a moment later by a framed painting of some random, possibly imaginary, building in the French Quarter on a rainy day. "It's okay, I guess," Pride said, "but nothing spectacular. Doesn't quite capture the spirit of New Orleans."

"It ain't the painting that's important," Patton said. "It's what's inside the painting. Well, inside the glass, more precisely."

"Inside?"

Patton tapped at the keyboard again. The image grew larger on the screen, as if the camera was zooming in, and it refocused not on the painting itself but a reflection on the glass over it. "I still don't see whatever I'm supposed to be seeing," Lasalle said.

"You will." Patton kept working the keyboard. The image gradually enhanced, so that what had seemed to be just a dark shadow on the glass coalesced into something else.

It took Pride a few moments to understand what he was looking at. "Is that him?" he asked.

"It's the man in black," Patton announced. "Whatever he did to pixelate the image on the video didn't affect his reflection in the glass. Not that it'll help all that much."

"No, it really won't," Pride said as the image came into clearer focus. It showed the face of the man in black—but that face was covered in makeup and distorted by what Pride had to assume were prosthetics. "Unless our killer is the real Baron Samedi."

"Seems unlikely," Patton said. "But, man, isn't he a good Baron Samedi? Brother's got me half-convinced."

"Hold up, now," Lasalle said. "Baron Samedi's some kind of voodoo god, right?"

"He's a *loa*," Pride said. "*Loa* of the dead, to be more exact." He moved closer to the screen. The image on there, distorted slightly by the glass, was as convincing as any Samedi he had ever seen. The man seemed to have a skeletal face, and he wore a top hat and a necklace of bones. His clothes were black and ragged, but formal looking just the same. A thick, unlit cigar was clenched in his teeth, and cotton plugs were barely visible in his nostrils, mimicking the Haitian burial custom. In one black-gloved hand, he carried a cane with a death's head topper.

"Baron Samedi hangs out at the crossroads between life and death," Patton said. "He greets the newly dead and escorts them to the underworld. He also makes sure they stay dead and don't come back as zombies."

"Unless he has some other use for them," Pride added. "Of all the *loa*, he's the only one with the power to return the dead to life."

Patton laughed. "But if he wants you to *be* dead, Jack, you dead."

"So we've got a guy dressed as Baron Samedi," Lasalle said. "Which ties in with that whole voodoo curse angle. Now that you've got a good image of him, can we use facial recognition software to ID him?"

"Not a chance," Patton said. "The image in the reflection is distorted. Then with the makeup and prosthetics, it'll never fly."

"Maybe we can find him in other video from the area?"

"Trouble is," Pride said, "it was Mardi Gras. There were probably a hundred Baron Samedis on the streets."

"At least," Patton said. "I'm working on it, though. I get a line on him, I'll let you know."

The door opened and Sonja walked in. "Looks like someone I dated once," she said.

"For real?" Patton asked.

"The costume," she said, "not the guy in it. If it'd been this guy, there probably would have been a second date."

"You probably wouldn't want to go out with this guy," Pride said. "We think he's our killer."

"Does he own a capuchin?" Sonja asked.

"A what?"

"A monkey. Sebastian sent us a list of people who own capuchin monkeys in the eight surrounding parishes."

"Is that what that was?" Patton asked. "I saw an email that said 'Monkey List' and I thought it was what he wanted for his birthday."

Sonja explained the rules for "non-human primate"

ownership, as Sebastian had described them to her. "So if that monkey's paw was acquired locally," she said at the end, "the capuchin that provided it should be on this list."

"Unless it's an undocumented ape," Lasalle pointed out. "Because criminals tend to break the law from time to time."

"Well, we can't get a list of monkeys that don't have their papers," Sonja countered. "We have to go with what we have. At least for starters."

"She's right," Pride said. "Why don't you two start with Orleans and points north, and I'll head to St. Bernard and Plaquemines and work west? We'll have to cover a lot of ground, but there aren't that many capuchins, so we should be able to knock these out today."

"Works for me," Lasalle said. "Percy?"

"You know me. I'm always up for a monkey hunt."

Pride opened his cabinet and took his lucky Colt Python .357 Magnum out of the top drawer. "Come on, Sweet Charmaine," he said quietly, tucking her into a holster at the small of his back. To the others, he said, "Go. Learn things."

"About capuchin monkeys?" Lasalle said.

"Hopefully," Pride said, "about murder."

The diversity of legally owned monkeys—and legal monkey owners—in southern Louisiana surprised Pride, who was pretty sure that in his lifetime he had seen just about everything. Plaquemines Parish was sparsely populated, in part because about seventy percent of its total area was water. Much of its economic base had roots in the oil and gas industries, with onshore refineries and support for offshore platforms. Fishing came second, and poverty brought up the rear.

The first capuchin Pride found lived in a cage attached to a general store. The building had concrete-block walls and a tin roof, and seemed to be held together mainly by posters for the various brands of tobacco and liquor and ice cream and candy that could be found within. At the side of the road, a hand-painted sign made of plywood sheets nailed to a sawhorse promised irresistible attractions: SMOKES BEER COLDDRINKS SWEETS FEED THE MONKEY! The building was nestled up against a screen of trees, but Pride could smell swamp not too far back.

Pride stopped the Explorer in a dirt lot, with cypress logs that marked the parking spaces. A cloud of dust hung in the air, enveloping him as he climbed out of the SUV. He approached the building, waving the dust away, and tugged open a wood-framed screen door that sagged on rusted, overstretched springs. Inside, a fan blew across the counter area, which was illuminated by free electric signs provided by alcohol distributors. The rest of the store was still and close, the only customers flies and a handful of wasps building a mud nest in a high corner.

"He'p you?" the shopkeeper asked. Only the top of his head was visible, behind the counter, its shine reflecting the signs behind him on the wall.

"I'd like to see your monkey," Pride said, barely able to hold back a chuckle at the words.

Confident that he had a paying customer, the man got out of his chair. Standing, he wasn't much taller than he had been sitting, but at least he could see over the counter. With a ruffle of magazine pages, the shopkeeper laid his reading material flat on the glass that covered his liquor license and other paperwork. What seemed like acres of brightly lit naked flesh gleamed up at Pride.

"It's three-fifty for a bag o' monkey feed," the man said. He had pointed ears that stuck almost straight out from his bald head, a pronounced proboscis, and about eleven teeth, most of which were gold. Pride wondered if he had found Horny, the eighth dwarf that was never spoken of in the stories.

"You might want to put that magazine behind the counter," he said. "What if a family comes in here? Kids?"

"Then they'll see where they came from. Anyhow, the human body is a thing o' beauty."

Pride showed his badge. "I'm not asking," he said. "Stow it or lose it."

The shopkeeper scowled, but he tucked his porn behind the counter, out of view.

"Where's the monkey?"

"It's still three-fifty."

"I'm not feeding it, I just want to see it."

"Nobody sees it without they buy some feed."

"Do you remember about twenty seconds ago, when I showed you my badge?"

"Feds got no jurisdiction here."

"Take it up with a judge," Pride said, already tired of this guy. "Where's the monkey?"

The man jerked a knobby thumb toward the rear of the building. "Out back."

"Thanks." Pride started through the sagging screen door again.

"Go ahead and stick your fingers in the cage," the shopkeeper cackled after him. "He don't bite."

If he had known the animal was outside, Pride soon learned, he could have simply followed his nose. Apparently plenty of people were willing to buy monkey feed, but no one was willing to clean up the end result. The capuchin was filthy, its fur matted and caked in its own grime. Scars crisscrossed its coat. Newspaper, yellowed and rain-soaked, covered the floor of a cage that was barely four feet square, with a corrugated steel roof and a single branch stuck through the bars for entertainment. Two bowls of water sat on the paper, both contaminated by leaves and feces and cigarette butts.

The capuchin saw Pride coming. It flung itself to the nearest cage wall and hung there, gripping the bars and screeching. The sound was grating, like fingernails on the world's biggest chalkboard. He could see both of the monkey's paws, and to stand around any longer was to suffer additional assault on his nasal passages and auditory canals. Instead, he turned away. He would make a call and get an animal welfare officer out here in a hurry.

When he got into his SUV, he could still hear the monkey screaming for the treat it had been denied.

14

Pride had started at the parish's southern end and worked his way north, on the theory that after hours of monkey inspections, he would want the shortest possible drive back to the squad room and to his apartment upstairs. A shower would be nice. A full-on sterilization might be better, but he'd settle.

The northernmost town in Plaquemines Parish was Belle Chasse, which was also home to the Naval Air Station Joint Reserve Base New Orleans. The more two-pawed capuchins he saw, the more the thought worried at him that, since Alpuente was a naval officer, his killer might have Navy connections, as well. Alpuente had never been stationed at NAS JRB, but that didn't mean he didn't have an enemy there. So far, Pride hadn't seen any evidence pointing that way; if he and his team couldn't turn up something in a hurry, though, they would have to look deeper into that possibility.

He was starting to feel like the wrong primates were in cages. He had met the monkey equivalent of a crazy cat lady; a couple with four capuchins named Bert and Nan and Freddie and Flossie, all of whom were dressed in gender-appropriate baby clothes; and a Cajun guy deep in the swamps who Pride suspected was illegally breeding monkeys to use as 'gator bait. That one didn't seem to have any interest in what happened in New Orleans, but Pride determined to keep him in mind. He had no intention of cutting open every alligator in the bayou to see if any had eaten a one-pawed capuchin, but that would be a good way to hide the evidence.

There were some regular folks, too. Pride could have spent hours listening to the stories of a man who'd spent several years in South America—Pride suspected as a CIA agent, though the guy wouldn't confirm that. He had adopted a capuchin as a pet while living out in the Ecuadorian jungle. Since capuchins in captivity could live for forty years or more, once they'd bonded, he had felt like he had to bring the animal home with him. Now the two geriatrics kept each other company in a house with spectacular Gulf of Mexico views.

When he was rapidly nearing the point at which nothing about capuchin owners could surprise him, Pride discovered how wrong he was when he read the next name on the list. The name was Burl Robitaille, and while there could easily be two people in the area with the same name, once he saw the address—a couple of miles outside the Belle Chasse city limits—he was sure it was the famous one.

The address was on a road in a prosperous rural neighborhood. The homes had extensive grounds, with plenty of space between them. Most were fenced or walled, the houses invisible from the street. Pride drove slowly until he finally spotted the street numbers he was looking for, high up on a stone wall overgrown with greenery. He pulled into the driveway, expecting to see a house on the other side of the wall.

Instead, he encountered a steel gate with a guard shack beside it, almost as overgrown as the wall itself. The two uniformed men inside locked eyes, then one nodded and stepped outside, blinking in the sunlight. His dark brown hair was neatly cut and he wore a white shirt with epaulets and blue trim, a duty belt with a holster and a sidearm, a Taser, a pouch for handcuffs, and blue pants tucked into shiny black tactical boots. He had a military air to him, as did the guard who had remained inside. That one had a shaved head and a long, scraggly red goatee that grew only from the bottom of his chin, as if it had been glued there. They were both fit and stood ramrod straight, and Pride assumed they were former military. The one who had come outside walked with a swagger that was familiar to Pride, one common among men impressed with the power and authority that wearing a badge and a gun conferred upon them.

"Good morning, sir," the man said, smiling without showing anything that resembled genuine friendliness.

"Morning," Pride replied. He showed the man his badge. "Special Agent Dwayne Pride, NCIS, to see Mr. Robitaille. Is he on the premises?"

"I'll check for you, Agent Pride."

"Thanks." Pride watched him go back into the guard shack, hitching up his pants as he did. Clearly, he knew whether his boss was home; if he was watching the gate and unaware of such a basic fact, he wouldn't be much of a guard.

Through the glass, Pride saw him say a few words to his partner, who grinned as he replied. Then the first one picked up a phone and held it to his ear. His back was turned to Pride, but from the motion of his head and shoulders, it appeared that he was having a brief conversation. When he came back out, he offered another insincere smile.

"Drive right up, sir," he said. "Stay on the road and you can't miss it. Park in front of the house and Walter will let you in."

"Thank you," Pride said. He thumbed the button that slid his window closed and waited for the gate to swing open. When it did, he followed the driveway. It led through some trees and out the other side, where an imposing plantation-style mansion sat across a vast stretch of manicured lawn.

The house was so white it almost sparkled in the noontime sun. Two-story tall columns surrounded it, and dormer windows broke the roofline. It probably wasn't really bigger than the White House, but it would be a near thing. The driveway looped past the grassy lawn and led to a large parking area in front, then continued around the far side of the house, where no doubt a multi-car garage sat.

Pride parked in the front and got out, thinking over what he knew about Burl Robitaille. He was a local man who had attended a high school that was a rival of Pride's own, but years after Pride had graduated. He had played baseball and football in high school, then dropped the former and concentrated on the latter. Pride had seen two or three of his games. In his junior and senior years, Robitaille had been a quarterback with a wickedly strong arm and terrific ball control. After graduation, he had played for LSU on an athletic scholarship, then had gone pro for several seasons with the NFL—two with the Saints and four at Dallas.

After being sidelined with a shattered hip—from an automobile accident, not a football game—he had found gainful employment as the head coach at Auburn for a few years. Tiring of that, he had moved back to Louisiana, where he had parlayed his regional fame into Burl's Place, a chain of casual dining restaurants. "You have my word on it," Pride remembered, was the motto that Robitaille spoke in all of his TV commercials. The chain had spread nationwide, and Robitaille had gone from well off to phenomenally wealthy while still in his thirties. Pride had heard some talk around town about the man looking to expand beyond just restaurants; in the tradition of the rich, there was no such thing as enough, and always a way to amass more.

Pride had met him, just once and years earlier, at one of the social events that dotted the New Orleans calendar. He could barely recall the occasion, and doubted that Robitaille would remember him.

He started toward the massive front door, up four wide steps and flanked by Corinthian columns, but he changed course when he heard gunfire from behind the house. Two reports. It sounded like a shotgun. Pride broke into a sprint.

There turned out to be whole wings of the house that couldn't be seen from the driveway. Pride's run turned into a half-marathon. The shotgun cracked again, then twice more. Pride slowed his pace, and by the time he rounded the entire house, he was at a walk.

Behind the house, he saw formal gardens and something—a pool area?—enclosed by high walls. Beyond all of that lay another expanse of lawn with a low, stone wall marking its distant boundary. That's where Robitaille was, on a flat stretch of grass near the wall, with a shotgun in his hands. A two-wheeled contraption that looked a little like a cross between a Gatling gun and a futuristic cannon sat near him. Pride had seen plenty of clay pigeon throwers, but this was a more expensive version than most casual shooters could afford. As he approached, Robitaille, who had not yet seen him, lifted his weapon to his shoulder. The cannon launched two more targets in quick succession. Robitaille tracked them, led them, and, just as they began the downward part of their arc, blew them to smithereens. He was a good shot, and confident with his weapon.

"Mr. Robitaille!" Pride called when he was near enough.

Robitaille heard him. He looked over his shoulder, saw the visitor, and quickly shut off the launcher. Then he pulled the electronic ear muffs off his ears, broke the shotgun and put it over his shoulder with the barrel hanging behind his back, and started toward Pride. He was still a handsome man, with a shock of thick, black hair over a broad, friendly face. His eyes were wide-set and had a bit of a squint to them, and his nose had been broken once or twice along the way. But his smile appeared genuine, and he extended a hand in greeting before he was close to Pride. He walked with a slight limp, but otherwise seemed to be healthy and fit.

"Agent Pride," he said. "I'm delighted to see you again. What brings you to this neck of the woods?"

"I'm surprised you remember me, Mr. Robitaille. It's been years."

"I've always been blessed with a facility for faces," Robitaille said. His hand seemed to swallow Pride's whole. He was a head taller, and considerably wider. He was wearing white linen pants and a white shirt with the sleeves rolled up over meaty, tanned forearms, and over that a shooting vest studded with shotgun shells. "That didn't do me much good, to be honest, on the football field, when mostly what I saw were face masks and chin guards. But it's served me well in business, I believe."

"It seems to have. You have a beautiful home."

"Huge," the man said. "Much bigger than I need, but somehow, if you have money, you're expected to spend some of it. And people seem to have this feeling that if you don't live in a palace, you're not really all you're cracked up to be. But that's my issue, and none of your concern, so I shouldn't spend the day bending your ear about it. I expect you're here on some more pressing matter. Unless this is a social visit?"

"I'm afraid it's not," Pride said. He wouldn't have minded spending another minute or two on the social niceties, but given Robitaille's question, it would be awkward to do anything except get right to the point. "This will sound like a strange question, but do you have any capuchin monkeys?"

"Hah!" Robitaille's laugh was sudden, loud, and infectious. "I do, as a matter of fact. Are you a cap man?"

"Not particularly," Pride said. "As I said, this is business, not pleasure. Do you mind if I have a look at them?"

Robitaille studied him as if he'd just grown a second head. "I suppose not."

"Thank you."

Robitaille carefully put his shotgun down on the grass, then rose and tilted his head toward the walled-off area behind the house. "I have a small collection of exotic animals," he said. "Not quite a private zoo, *per se*, but a decent assortment just the same."

"I didn't know that about you."

"There's probably a lot you don't know about me, Special Agent Pride. And vice versa, I'm sure. We should get better acquainted sometime. I've always thought you were an interesting fellow. I mean, judging by the stories I've heard around."

"I'd like that," Pride said. "But I'll warn you, most of those stories are probably exaggerated."

"The best stories usually are," Robitaille said.

He led Pride through the formal gardens and toward a big iron gate set into the ten-foot-tall, whitewashed wall, facing a veranda at the rear of the house. The closer they got, the stronger the animal odors became. Pride heard chittering and chuffing and the shuffling of unknown creatures. He couldn't tell how many there were, but it sounded—and smelled—like a lot.

The gate was unlocked, and Robitaille opened it and ushered Pride through.

"The monkey cages are right here in front," Robitaille said. "I've got capuchins, spider monkeys, and a couple of chimps, I guess. I've got some ringtail lemurs, too. Not monkeys, but a lot of folks confuse them. If you want to see those, they're farther back."

"Just the capuchins will be fine," Pride said.

Robitaille waved at the first set of cages. As he'd said, there were multiple types of monkeys in evidence, each kind confined to their own cage. The cages were professionally constructed from chain-link fencing. They were almost as tall as the walls, roomy, and each had a tree or a fake tree with plenty of branches, as well as covered shelter and readily accessible clean water. There were also toys, chains, plastic items that Pride couldn't make out the use of, at first. Pride had seen zoos that were less appealing. "They play with toys?" he asked.

"In the trade, they're called enrichment items," Robitaille explained. "They get bored easily, but they like toys suitable for toddlers, and anything they can climb or swing on, or throw. When they're—let's say, in the mood—female caps often throw rocks at males, as if to get their attention. The fact that they actually aim and use stones in that way is quite remarkable. Scientists tried to deny it for a long time, saying capuchins weren't capable of such advanced skills, but you don't have to watch them for long to know they're clever little buggers."

The capuchins were in the second cage. There were four, and each had all their limbs. Beyond the monkey cages was a cage containing what Pride recognized from other zoos as a primate called a slow loris. Past that was another wall. The rest of the enclosures were around the corner and out of sight.

"That's all your capuchins?"

"I keep them together, yes. It's an expensive hobby, I admit, but it's a little cheaper if like animals share living space. Like kids with bunk beds."

"I'm sure," Pride said.

"Is there anything else you need to look at?"

Sebastian's monkey list had said that Robitaille owned four capuchins, and Pride had seen all four. "No, sir, I think I'm done here."

"Well, then—"

Robitaille was interrupted by a strange, almost human-sounding cry from farther back in the collection. "What's that?" Pride asked. "It sounds like a big cat."

"It's a medium cat," Robitaille corrected. "That was my lynx. Perfectly legal in Louisiana, in case you're wondering."

"I'll take your word for it," Pride said. "I'm not really up on exotic animal law."

"Not a lot of call for it in your line, I expect."

"Not a lot, no."

"I admit, Agent Pride, your visit has got me curious. I don't suppose you would care to tell me why you wanted to check on my caps?"

"You'd be correct," Pride hedged.

"Well, then, I'll let you get back to your day. I need to put away my gun and thrower—I've got a meeting in town later this afternoon." As if the idea had just struck him, he added, "You shoot, I imagine?"

"I've been known to," Pride said. He didn't bother to add that he usually shot people who were trying to shoot him or someone else. Ducks and pigeons, clay or otherwise, rarely qualified.

"Well, come on back any time," Robitaille said, "so we can get to know each other better."

"I'll make a point of it, sir," Pride said. "Thank you for your hospitality."

"Any time," the other man said. He shook Pride's hand again, his grip like a steel band. Back in the Explorer a few minutes later, Pride's palm was almost too tender to hold the wheel.

15

"You think you know a place..." Lasalle said.

"You're not a native," Sonja interrupted. "Nobody really knows New Orleans but a native."

"I'm just saying. I've been here for years. I had no idea so many people owned monkeys. The football team shouldn't be the Saints, it should be the Chimps."

"Like I said. I know a dozen joints in town where talk like that will get you beat up."

"I haven't been in a good fight in a couple weeks." He braked into a turn and passed the wheel between his hands. "It might be worth it."

"You just keep on thinking that, Christopher."

"Are we about done with your monkey list?"

"Just one more place to check," she answered. "Somebody named Ridley Danko." She read him the address.

"You're kidding me."

"Why?"

"I've arrested him before. Not just once. Like, five or six times."

"You sure?"

"Unless there's more than one character in New Orleans with that name. Which I highly doubt."

"What did he do?" Sonja asked.

"What didn't he do? It was back when I was working vice. I arrested him for dealing dope a couple times. Once for indecent exposure—drunk and peeing in a cemetery."

"That happens all the time. You arrested him for that?"

"During a funeral, in full view of everyone. On the casket."

"Oh," Sonja said. "That's a little different."

"Yeah, a little. The last time I busted him, it was for pimping. Or would-be pimping, anyway."

"Would-be pimping? What does that even mean?"

Lasalle made another turn, heading for Danko's crib in Mid-City. "Danko was always a soft touch for the workin' girls. Sometimes when they got busted, they'd call him to make their bail, even though they didn't work for him. He kept trying to put together a string, but he could never really pull it off. The girls would swear up and down that they'd go to work for him, if he bailed them out. So he did, then they'd go right back to their original pimp, or no pimp at all. Finally, one had him so convinced that he was out on a corner, hustling her. But her real pimp was on that same corner. Each of them swore she was with him, and they got into a fight. I rolled up and collared them both for soliciting and battery and causing a public disturbance."

He pulled to a stop outside a red-brick, five-story apartment building that couldn't have looked much more like a prison if it was surrounded by razor wire. Blank, square windows faced the street. To the left of the front door was a jumble of brightly colored, plastic playground equipment that looked as if it had never been used. Lasalle figured the only thing that would be sadder would be if it had been used. Of all the places he wouldn't want to grow up, this dump would be near the top of the list.

"This guy sounds like a real winner," Sonja observed.

"They say everybody's got a purpose. I think Danko's is to give everybody else someone to look at and say, 'Hey, at least I'm not *that* guy.'"

Outside the SUV, Sonja looked up at the building. "Says he's in apartment 4C. I'm surprised they allow monkeys there."

"I'm surprised they allow humans," Lasalle replied. "Come on, let's pay Mr. Danko a friendly little visit."

The elevator was broken, which came as no surprise to Sonja. Air conditioning was nonexistent, except for individual window units mounted here and there. By the time they reached the fourth floor, sweat was rolling off her forehead. The stairwell walls were covered by layers of graffiti that could have dated back to the Battle of New Orleans, as far as she could tell. The stink of urine could have been around that long, too.

"He lives here on purpose?" she asked.

"I'm sure he lives here because he can't afford better," Lasalle said. "Just like everybody else who lives here."

At the fourth floor, they squeezed their way through the eight-inch space allowed by a jammed steel stairwell door. The hallway was dark, with only one bare bulb illuminated at the far end. Many of the tin apartment numbers were missing from the doors, but a faded ghost of 4C was barely visible on the paint of one. Sonja put a hand on her holstered weapon, and Lasalle pounded on the door.

After about thirty seconds, a muffled voice called something from inside. Lasalle knocked twice more, then lowered his hands, stepping to the side of the door.

Another dozen seconds passed, then the doorknob turned and the door opened a crack. Sonja looked inside, but couldn't see anyone. "Hello?"

Lasalle pushed the door a little farther and peeked in. "Hey, little guy," he said.

Sonja looked down. A capuchin monkey stood there, drawing aside the stool it had stood on to reach the knob.

"Anybody else home?" she asked.

The monkey chattered and dashed deeper into the apartment. Chris pushed open the door the rest of the way, then closed it behind Sonja. "Danko, you in here?" he asked.

A voice came from somewhere unseen. "I'm in here. I got a gun."

"I've got one, too," Lasalle said. "So does Percy."

"Who the hell is that?" the voice asked.

"NCIS," Lasalle said. "Your old pal, Chris Lasalle."

"You? Dude, what the hell did I do now?"

"Why don't you tell me?"

They went into the apartment's main room. It was neater than Sonja had first expected. There was a couch stained with food and drink and possibly other, less appealing substances; a couple of woven vinyl folding lawn chairs; and a TV. Off to one side, a kitchenette with a half-size refrigerator, a two-burner stove, a sink, and a Formica-topped table with no chairs. On the table was a hardcover book, splayed open and kept that way by a fork laid across the pages.

A man sat in front of the book, in an electric

wheelchair. His neck was frozen at an odd angle. His skinny arms hung by his sides, the muscles atrophied, his hands folded in his lap. He had olive skin and short, dark hair that couldn't hide the scars on his face and down his neck. The capuchin skittered up the chair and sat patiently on Danko's useless hands.

"Danko?" Lasalle said. "What happened to you, man?"

Danko backed away from the table, operating the chair with a joystick he controlled with his mouth, then turned the chair around so he could see his visitors. "Fuc—" He glanced at Sonja. "Excuse me, I mean, *freakin'* 113s," he said. "Think they own the city."

"You got crosswise with the 113s?" Lasalle asked. The street gang really did own the city, or at least pieces of it. They were constantly at war with the Triads for control of the New Orleans drug trade. Lasalle knew Danko had dabbled in dealing drugs, but he had always been strictly small time. He couldn't quite imagine the 113s being aware of Danko's existence, much less having a beef with him. "You know better than that, man."

"We had a slight difference of opinion," Danko said. "Next thing you know I'm inside my car at the dump, being picked up by one of those big-ass magnets and dropped into the compactor."

"I don't know if I believe that."

"What do you mean? Look at me!"

"I mean, you having a car."

"It might have been borrowed," Danko said. "Point is, here I am. Broken neck, severed spinal cord, piss bag. Life's a blast."

"And you have a monkey doorman."

"Bella's a lot more than that," Danko replied. "She can't cook, but she can dial the phone. When I have food delivered she can open the door and open the packages and feed me. She turns the pages when I read, and works the remote for the TV. Flushes the toilet. She keeps me company. I don't know what I would do without her."

"You train her to do all that?" Sonja asked.

"Naw. This service monkey agency trains 'em. Capuchins are great as service animals. Their dexterity's incredible. And they have this built-in sense of hierarchy that makes them want to help people. All I have to do for her is make sure she has food and water, and be company for her, and she's happy as a clam."

"That sounds like a good arrangement," Lasalle said. "I'm sorry about your medical issues."

"I guess it beats the alternative," Danko said. "At least I'm breathin', right?"

"Lots of people who cross the 113s can't say that," Lasalle agreed.

"Do you have people who visit you?" Sonja asked.

"I got a case worker comes once in a while. Social Security pays a caregiver who comes over once or twice a day to do the things Bella can't. I get by okay."

"That's one way to stay out of trouble," Lasalle said.

"Only way I ever found that works."

"This monkey agency," Sonja said. "Are they located in New Orleans?"

"Naw, they're in Iowa. Ohio? One of them vowelly states, anyhow. Illinois, maybe." He pronounced the "s," so it sounded like "Illinoise."

"You've only ever had the one capuchin?" Lasalle asked him.

"Yeah. She's been a lifesaver, Bella."

"Do you know anybody else who has one, in the area?"

Danko shrugged. "I guess maybe some folks do, but I don't know who."

Lasalle put a business card on the table. "If you think of anyone, give me a call," he said. "Or have Bella do it."

"You've always been a funny guy, Lasalle," Danko said. "A regular laugh riot. You remember where the door is, right? Hope you don't mind if I don't get up."

16

"And Triple P comes through in the clinch," Patton said. "Look at this here."

Pride, Lasalle, and Sonja had all made it back to the squad room, their respective—and fruitless—monkey searches completed. Patton was so excited he could barely contain himself, and before they had even had a chance to settle in, he was streaming an image to the plasma screen.

It was Baron Samedi—or *a* Baron Samedi, at any rate. He walked briskly down a sidewalk, weaving in and out of the ranks of spectators lining a street, looking very much like a man on a mission. He was wearing black gloves and carrying a cane, just like the one in the hotel's surveillance video. "I found this guy in some video from the parade," he said. "That's on St. Charles, a block from the Buccaneer Hotel. He's heading toward it, here. He's big, right?"

"That could be Melancon," Lasalle said.

"Or any of a thousand other big guys in New Orleans," Sonja pointed out. "He might be African American, but with all that makeup on it's impossible to say for sure."

"Do you have any more footage?" Pride asked.

"Would I have said anything if I didn't?" Patton replied. "While y'all were out chasin' chimpanzees, I—"

"Capuchins," Sonja corrected.

"Whatever. A monkey's a monkey to me. Anyhow, I spliced together some of the clips I found. Once I had a read on him, it wasn't so hard to cross-reference other video and follow his progression. The last good video is this one, from before he reached the hotel. Everything from inside the hotel is fritzed out, like we saw before. Now you'll see the whole trip, from the first piece I got on through the one you just saw."

The angle changed and the video was vertical, clearly shot by someone holding a smartphone upright. Pride braced himself for another lecture on the proper smartphone video aspect, but it didn't come. They all sat in silence as the clips changed again and again— different videos from multiple angles, captured by security cameras, news crews, and parade-goers, edited into a relatively smooth progression of shots. As Pride watched, he hoped some way to make a positive identification would present itself.

Then he saw Baron Samedi stop his long walk to briefly exchange words with a man standing in a doorway. "Hold up!" he said. "Who's that?"

Patton froze the image. Samedi's mass blocked the person in the door, though. "See if there's a better shot of that guy's face."

"He's in the shadows," Patton said. "And this video is pretty low-res. But I'll try."

He advanced frame-by-frame, until Samedi moved out of the way. The man in the doorway hesitated for a moment, then stepped out and into the sunlight. "Freeze it there," Pride said.

Patton did.

"Can you enhance it at all?"

"Not much I can do with this," Patton said. "Sharpen it a little, and give it some more contrast, maybe."

"Anything you can do. I know that guy."

"Who is it?" Sonja asked.

Pride held up a hand, waiting. Patton enhanced the image as best he could, and Pride walked closer to the screen, studying it. Finally, he was satisfied.

"That's Rich Brandt," he said.

"Who?" Lasalle asked.

"He's an aide to Mayor Hamilton. His official job is something to do with code enforcement, but he's really a political guy."

"Isn't everybody around Hamilton political?" Patton asked.

"Some are more so than others," Pride said. "Brandt is pure politics, from the second he wakes up in the morning to the instant he falls asleep. He knows everybody in the state who can write big campaign checks, and he can remember the names of their spouses and their kids and their grandparents. At campaign time, he's a one-man fundraising machine. That's why he was hired in the first place. Hamilton needs someone around the office that makes him look marginally less like a political animal and more like a public servant, by comparison."

"That guy could've been asking Brandt for directions, or a smoke," Sonja said. "That was a pretty short conversation."

"Is there any more video, Patton?" Pride asked. "Anything that shows where he came from, or anyone else he talked to?"

"That's pretty much it, King. Nobody was shooting

him intentionally, he just happened to be in the background while he walked down the parade route toward the hotel. I couldn't find anything of him leaving the hotel or after, so I'm guessing he went out into the alley behind it and stayed off the main streets."

"Well, then, I guess Rich Brandt is the best lead we've got. Christopher, want to take a ride with me?"

"Into the viper's nest?"

Pride chuckled. "That's one way to describe it, yes."

When Pride and Lasalle pushed through the front door of Douglas Hamilton's office at City Hall, the receptionist looked up in surprise. "He's in conference, Agent Pride," she said. "You can wait, but it'll be a while."

"This won't take long," Pride said. "Don't worry, we'll announce ourselves."

She started to rise from her chair, as if she might vault over the desk and physically block them. Lasalle shot her a smile and a playful shrug. "What can I say?" he said. "King's headstrong."

"But—" she began. Pride was already past her, and she seemed to acknowledge the futility of trying to stop him. "Be my guest," she said.

"I always appreciate your good work on behalf of our fair city," Pride called back as he hurried down the hall. At least she had—however inadvertently—told him where Hamilton was. Conference room, not his expansive office. Pride moved down the hallway, admiring as he always did the views from the Perdido Street building—out across the Quarter to the Mississippi and beyond, and on the other side, the Superdome. Those were almost enough to make one want an office up here. Almost, but not quite. He would stick with his squad room, at ground level in the heart of the Vieux Carré, rather than viewing it from away and above.

When Pride reached the conference room, and let himself in, Hamilton had a phone in his hand. "Never mind, he's here," he was saying. "Thanks." He put the phone down.

"Dwayne," Hamilton said as they entered. "*And* Agent Lasalle. It's just like Christmas. Except neither of you look like Santa Claus, and somehow I doubt that you've come to spread good cheer."

"Relax, Douglas, we're not here to see you." Pride looked around the room. Four men and two women were seated around the long wooden table, with a set of engineering plans unrolled on its gleaming surface before them. Rich Brandt was one of the men, and to Pride's surprise, so was Burl Robitaille.

"Twice in one day, Agent Pride," Robitaille said, standing and extending a beefy hand. "This is a pleasant surprise."

Pride took the offered hand. The handshake once again felt like Robitaille intended to squeeze juice out of him. "Yes it is, Mr. Robitaille. It's good to see you again." He fixed Brandt with a steady gaze. "But really, we're here to talk to Mr. Brandt."

"We're a little busy, Dwayne," Hamilton said. "Most people make appointments. If you've forgotten the number, I can—"

Pride cut him off. "This won't take long. Mr. Brandt, would you like to step outside for a moment?"

"Now hold on, Pride," Hamilton said. "Is Rich under arrest? Because if not—"

"No, Mr. Brandt is not under arrest, Mr. Mayor,"

Pride said, speaking slowly, as if explaining algebra to a third-grader. "We have a few questions for him, that's all."

"If you'd like to have a seat in the lobby, I can get the city attorney up here in about three minutes."

"I don't think that's necessary, Douglas," Pride replied. "Like I said, we're not arresting anyone. We just have to ask him about yesterday."

"About yesterday? What about it? Rich has nothing to hide. Do you, Rich? Still, I think I'd like the city attorney to be here."

Brandt's head swiveled as he eyed Pride, then Hamilton, and back. He was dressed in a sharp, tailored suit, and his neat brown hair was probably the result of a two-hundred-dollar haircut. "Ahh… no. I don't think… what is this about?"

Pride hadn't intended to ask him in front of everyone else, but it didn't look like Hamilton was giving him much choice. Ignoring the mayor's protests, he pulled his phone from his pocket and showed Brandt the video clip he'd asked Patton to send him—just the few seconds during which Baron Samedi and Brandt had a conversation, and then Brandt stepped into the sunlight. "That's you, right? Yesterday, during the parade?"

Brandt glanced at the mayor again, as if unsure how to answer the question.

"It's not a trick, sir," Pride said. "Either that's you or it isn't."

"I, uhh… I guess it is."

"Good. Now that we've established that, who's the other guy, in the Baron Samedi makeup?"

"I… just some guy. He asked me for directions, I think."

"You think. You sure you don't know him?"

"Pride," Hamilton said. "If Rich says he doesn't know the dude, he doesn't know him. You said he was in makeup, anyway, so how could you expect him to—"

Pride interrupted him again. "Looked like more of a heart-to-heart than just directions," he said. "And do I really need to remind you, Mayor Hamilton, that somebody was murdered yesterday, in front of thousands of spectators, during a Mardi Gras parade? That could be the worst thing to happen to New Orleans tourism since Katrina. I would think you'd want us to wrap the case up quickly."

"I do, I do," Hamilton said. "Why didn't you say it was about that?"

Hamilton knew as well as anyone what the value of tourist dollars was to the city. Sometimes he reminded Pride of the mayor in *Jaws*, a politician who would feed his own family to a shark if it meant keeping tourists coming to the island on a summer holiday weekend. Pride appreciated Hamilton's dedication to the city; the hotels and restaurants, gift shops and musicians, among others, depended on that tourist traffic. But he was firmly convinced that Hamilton's interest was not so much in those businesses as it was in his own political fortunes. To Hamilton, it was always a case of, "Ask not what you can do for New Orleans, ask what New Orleans can do for you."

Baton Rouge was the state's capital, but New Orleans was its heart and soul, and to most people around the country, that was what people thought of when they heard "Louisiana." The mayor had a lot of power in New Orleans, and there were plenty of ways he could enrich himself. And if he could use the city as a stepping-stone to higher office, so much the better. Pride was convinced that Hamilton's ambitions were nearly boundless, and that the man would cut corners or finesse the law in any way necessary to achieve them. That knowledge gave Pride a certain amount of leverage over Hamilton; to some extent, he could play the man by appealing to his ambition and greed.

"It is about *that*, Douglas. Mardi Gras. I would appreciate Mr. Brandt's help in closing this case quickly."

"Well, by all means, Rich. If you know the guy, this Baron whatever, then say so. Trust me, Pride's a stubborn son of a bitch. When he wants something, he's like a starving dog, and you're a bone—he'll gnaw on you and gnaw on you until he has what he wants."

Pride turned back to Brandt. "Well?"

"I don't know him well. He's a friend—an acquaintance, I guess, of an acquaintance. I met him at a party once is all. I thought I recognized him in the makeup, and I said, 'Hey, man, is that you?'"

"Just like that?" Pride asked.

"Well, I might have said 'Who dat!' first. But you know, it was Mardi Gras."

"Nothing wrong with a little 'Who dat!' between friends," Pride admitted. "Or acquaintances of acquaintances, if that's how it is."

"That's how it is. He just said hey, and then he went on his way. I got the feeling he had someplace to get to, a party or something."

"He didn't say specifically?"

"I wouldn't expect him to. I don't know him that well, like I said."

"Yeah, you said. What is this friend-of-a-friend's name? Do you know that much?"

"Go easy, Dwayne," Hamilton said. "Rich is cooperating, right?"

"Sorry," Pride said. He modulated his tone, holding

back his natural impatience with political types. "Do you know his name?"

"It's Landry. Bruno Landry. Like I said—"

"I know," Pride interrupted. "You're not bosom buddies. Anything else you want to share about Mr. Landry?"

"If I knew anything else, I'd tell you. He's a guy I've met, period. We said hey, and he went on his way."

"All right, thank you, Mr. Brandt," Pride said. "If you think of anything else that might be helpful, Douglas has my number."

"I keep trying to forget it," Hamilton said. "But you won't let me."

Pride knew that Hamilton called him far more often than he called Hamilton. But if the small lie let the man retain some dignity or standing with his colleagues, after rolling over so quickly, he would let it go.

"Thanks for your help, Mr. Brandt," he said. "Mr. Robitaille, good to see you again so soon."

"Don't forget my offer," Robitaille said. "Any time you'd like."

"Not a chance of it."

"Ordinarily, Dwayne, I would wish a visitor a blessed day," Hamilton said. "But in this case—"

"Save it for someone deserving," Pride said. He nodded toward the strangers at the table. "We're sorry to interrupt, folks."

Lasalle was quiet until they reached the elevator. Then he caught Pride's eye, and grinned. "A starving dog, huh? That's choice."

"I didn't think the analogy made that much sense, myself," Pride said.

"I don't know. I've seen you just about chew

somebody's leg off to get what you want."

"That's—" Pride began. Then he decided against it. Hamilton could be as silver-tongued as the next politician, when he needed to be, but obviously he wasn't always as articulate as he might like. And Pride had to admit there was some truth to the comparison. Tenacity had to be one of the tools in an investigator's toolbox, and Pride made use of it whenever he needed to. If the mayor wanted to see him as some kind of slavering bulldog, that was just fine with him.

17

When Pride and Lasalle got back to the squad room, they found Sonja and Patton waiting with the lowdown on Bruno Landry. A mug shot was up on the screen, showing an African American man glowering at the camera. He would have been handsome, but for the anger etched on his face. His hair was in cornrows, close to his scalp, and he had a mustache and a close-trimmed beard. His eyes were half-closed, and there was a little scar at the outside corner of the left one that made it look longer than the right. As Melancon had said, gold glinted in his snarling mouth. "Cat has a rap sheet as long as he's tall," Patton said. "And that's almost seven feet."

"Six-six, to be exact," Sonja added. "Three twenty-seven."

"I hope the Saints are signing him," Pride said.

"I don't think they'd want a guy with his rep," Sonja replied. "He did play some ball in high school. Before he dropped out. After that, though, it looks like he went down some dark roads."

"How dark are we talking?" Pride put his gun back in the cabinet and closed the drawer, then sat down at his desk.

"Drugs, at first."

"Using or selling?"

"First one, then the other. Also assault, battery, auto theft, and armed robbery. He's been in and out of Rayburn so many times, I think they've got a revolving door with his name on it."

"And he's out now?"

"He's never done any really long bits," Patton replied. "Couple years here, six months there, you know. Somehow, when he's facing serious charges, witnesses have a tendency to disappear."

"It's funny how that happens with some of these characters," Lasalle said.

"Ain't it, though?"

"Anyway," Sonja continued, "it looks like lately he's been serving as an enforcer for various criminal enterprises. He doesn't seem to have a lot of loyalty—whoever's willing to fork over some cash can buy his services. That's the word on the street, anyway."

Lasalle chuckled. "On the street," he echoed.

Sonja whirled on him. "Something wrong with that, Country Mouse?"

"It's just—it reminds me of my first day in New Orleans, is all."

"Your first day, Christopher? What happened?" Pride asked.

"Well, I was on Royal Street," Lasalle said. "Just walking around, getting my bearings, you know. Figuring out what was what."

"As one does, in a new place," Patton said.

"As one does," Lasalle agreed. "Anyway, this little kid comes up to me. He couldn't have been more than nine, maybe ten." He held his hand about three feet from the ground. "No bigger than that. But he walks up to me like he owns the city, and says, 'Yo, I'll bet you five bucks I can tell you where you got your shoes at.'"

Pride started to laugh. "Oh, no," he said. "You didn't."

"I did! Hell, I didn't know. *I* wasn't even sure where I bought my shoes. Someplace in Mobile, but I couldn't say beyond that. So I said, 'Sure, I'll take that bet.'

"Then the kid goes, 'Okay, you got your shoes right here, on Royal Street.' I laughed at him, and said, 'No, man, I got these in Alabama.' And he says, 'You mighta *bought* 'em in Alabama, but you *got* 'em on Royal Street now! I can see 'em right in front of me. Now pay up!'"

"Hah!" Sonja laughed. "What'd you do?"

"What could I do? I paid up. Then I badged him and told him to be careful who he pulled that on."

"Kid taught you a good lesson," Patton said.

"What lesson is that? Don't trust anyone in New Orleans?"

"That any kid raised on the streets in the Big Easy is smarter than any college graduate from Alabama," Patton replied.

Sonja burst out laughing again. "Roll Tide," she said when she could manage it.

"Smarter?" Lasalle echoed. "I don't think so. More underhanded and devious, maybe. Also, Percy, that's twice."

"Twice what?"

"Twice you've pulled 'Roll Tide' jokes in the last couple days. That's all you get. Any more and I'll start talking smack about Tulane. Won't be hard to do."

"This is all very entertaining," Pride said. "And I'm always glad to hear about the exploits of young Officer Lasalle. But how is it helping us find Landry?"

"That's gonna be harder than conning five bucks

out of Lasalle," Sonja said. "If Landry has an address, nobody knows what it is."

"Plenty of known associates," Patton added. "But they ain't the kind of folks who talk to cops. At least not without some serious persuading."

"I can be persuasive," Lasalle said.

"I made a list of places he's reportedly been seen," Sonja added, lifting a printout off the desk. "It reads like a travel guide to the parts of New Orleans tourists should avoid."

Pride took the sheet from her and scanned it. "Strip clubs, dive bars, back-room gambling joints… Plenty of folks still come here looking for sin. This list would steer them right to those spots. On the right websites, you could charge money for this information."

"I can always use some extra money, Pride, but not that bad."

"Give it to me," Patton said, rolling toward her. "I could use some new electronics."

Pride handed it back to Sonja, who folded it and put it in her pocket. "Not a chance, Triple P. Anyway, I'm pretty sure you already know all these places. I think you keep some of them in business."

"Probably so."

"We can check those later on, when Landry's more likely to be there," Pride said. "First, I'll see if I can confirm Brandt's ID. Back in a while."

Orleans Parish Prison was a series of interconnected, bland, concrete rectangles surrounded by tall fences and high walls, both topped with coils of razor wire. It dwarfed the buildings around it, and the purpose of the structure couldn't be mistaken. Pride checked in, showed his ID multiple times, checked his gun and his phone, and was eventually taken to an interview room where Gilbert Melancon was waiting, clad in jailhouse orange.

"It's you," Melancon said glumly when Pride entered. "I was hopin' it was my lawyer."

"Who'd you get?" Pride asked. He sat at a table opposite Melancon.

"Some public defender dude. Name's Allard, Ballard, some shit like that."

"Darren Ballard?"

"Yeah, that sounds right."

"Whatever he advises, do the opposite," Pride said. "He pushes his clients to take whatever deal the district attorney offers first. It's easiest for him, and he gets paid the same regardless of whether you spend two nights in jail or the rest of your life."

"Then why's he do that job?"

"Louisiana doesn't have the greatest record with public defenders," Pride explained. "We don't have near enough, and the ones we do have are overworked and way, way underpaid. Most lawyers who can do anything else *do* something else. But Ballard's the worst we've got—bottom of the barrel."

Melancon looked gloomier than ever. "Well, all I can say is thanks a hell of a lot for puttin' me in here, then."

"You put you in here, Gilbert. I'll do what I can to help you, but that's all I can promise."

"In exchange for what? I know you ain't come up in here just to be friendly."

"You're right." Pride had known he wouldn't be able to bring his phone in with him, so he'd had a mug shot of Bruno Landry printed out. He passed it over the table. "Is that the guy who asked you to keep track of Alpuente for him?"

Melancon regarded the picture for only a few seconds. "That's him."

"His name's Bruno Landry. Does that mean anything to you?"

"Not a thing. He's some dude, slipped me some bills and asked me for a favor."

"And killed your friend," Pride reminded him.

"Yeah, you say that. But you can walk out of here in a few minutes, and I got to stay and hope Ballard can do somethin' for me. That don't exactly give me a lot of faith in you, you know what I'm sayin'?"

"I understand, Gilbert. Like I said—"

"Don't bother."

Pride rose from his chair, then stopped. "Oh, I meant to ask—when you had to come up with a name, how did you happen to pick J.B. Goodtown? It took me a while to realize it was a play on Jean-Baptiste Le Moyne de Bienville."

"Just came to me, I guess. My moms, she's a teacher, and she's pretty much drummed New Orleans history into me since I was a little squirt."

"A history teacher?"

"She got her degree from Dillard University. She must've taught just about everything at one time or another. Spent decades in New Orleans schools. Then after Katrina, a lot of schools didn't reopen."

"I remember." The lack of schools had been one of the factors that slowed the return to the city. Once people had their kids enrolled in schools in Houston or Baton Rouge, they didn't want to move back into houses where there were no schools.

"Especially schools in black neighborhoods," Gilbert continued. "She picked up work here and there for a couple years, but now, all a sudden, she's too old. And since she got hurt, it's even harder. Impossible. So a woman who's taught hundreds of New Orleanians—a fine lady, firm but fair, you know, and smart as they come—can't even get a job substitute teachin' at the worst schools in the city. It sucks."

"It does," Pride said.

"And I'm stuck in here, where I can't help her, and I'm just another expense, another pain in her ass. That sucks, too."

"Definitely. Listen, Gilbert, I appreciate your cooperation. Like I said, I'll see if I can pull some strings."

"Like you some kind of puppet master?"

When Pride tapped on the glass for a guard to let him out, Melancon was still laughing.

Heading back to the squad room, Pride called in a BOLO for Bruno Landry. Gilbert Melancon had no reason to like Pride or NCIS, but he had identified Landry without hesitation, as certain as anyone Pride had ever questioned. Between that and Rich Brandt's certitude, Pride was convinced. Landry was their man.

Or one of them, anyway. He might have been the killer, but they were still no closer to a motive. What was Landry's interest in the Navy lieutenant? How would their paths even have crossed? How did the voodoo angle fit in?

And maybe most important, was anyone else involved?

They had to find Landry, for starters. But even that wouldn't answer all their questions. And Pride wouldn't be satisfied until he knew the whole story.

18

"Lieutenant Alpuente's tox screen came back positive for something I never would have expected," Loretta said. She and Sebastian had arrived at the squad room just minutes after Pride's return.

"What is it?" Pride started to ask.

But Sebastian stepped on his question. "L-3,4-dihydroxyphenylalanine!" he blurted.

Pride raised his hands in mock surrender. "In English, please."

"L-DOPA," Loretta translated. "It's a naturally occurring chemical in the human body, synthesized from an amino acid called L-tyrosine. But there's nothing naturally occurring about these quantities."

"Isn't it used as an athletic performance enhancer?" Lasalle asked.

"It can be," Loretta answered. "By bodybuilders, primarily. It's used to help build lean muscle mass, and also by some folks as a sexual performance enhancer. But while Lt. Alpuente was in reasonably good shape, he was no muscleman. And again, we're talking concentrations far in excess of what a bodybuilder would use."

"What else is it good for?"

"It's often used in the treatment of Parkinson's disease," Loretta said, "and other dopamine-responsive conditions. Dopamine can't cross the blood–brain barrier, but L-DOPA can, so it's used supplementally, in situations where the body isn't forming enough dopamine on its own."

"And leg cramps," Sebastian said. "It's being tested to help relieve leg cramps. Which I've considered picking some up for. I get these terrible cramps in my calves sometimes, when I'm trying to sleep, and—"

"Just stomp 'em out," Lasalle interrupted.

"What, stomp on my calves? I'm not even sure how I'd—"

"No, stomp on the floor with the leg that's cramping," Lasalle said. "As hard as you can. It eases the cramp."

"Oh, okay." Sebastian, standing on his left foot, had his hands on Sonja's desk for balance as he tried to put his right foot flat against his left calf. "That makes a lot more sense."

"Or you could just stand there looking like a deranged stork," Sonja said.

"Yeah, no." Sebastian put both feet on the ground and released her desk, as if its surface had suddenly heated to an intolerable degree. "Anyway, you were saying, Loretta?"

"I'm not even sure I remember," Loretta said. "Oh, right. The concentration of L-DOPA in Lt. Alpuente's system was way beyond what would be medically prescribed for any condition."

"How did he get it?" Pride asked.

"It's sold over-the-counter at vitamin supplement stores and health food stores," Loretta said. "But you didn't find any in the hotel room. Christopher and Sonja brought me a list of all the medications they found at Lt. Alpuente's house, and it wasn't one of them."

"Pretty sure we wouldn't have missed that," Lasalle said.

"No way," Sonja agreed.

"Okay, so that's a mystery," Pride said. "Next question: if he was using it on the sly somehow, why?"

"I'm not sure he knew he was using it."

"Why's that, Miss Loretta?"

"The main thing is, it's just not something you would ordinarily use if you didn't have a very good reason for it. The side effects can be severe, especially for someone taking as much as he seemed to be."

"What kind of side effects?" Sonja asked.

"Extreme anxiety. Intense fear. Horrific nightmares. That's for starters."

"And we already know he was suffering from those," Pride said. "Because of the voodoo curse."

"Because of the supposed voodoo curse, yes," Loretta said. "But it's possible that it wasn't a voodoo curse, or even simply his imagination. His state of panic could have been a result of the L-DOPA."

"It's that bad?" Lasalle asked.

"In high doses, it can be," Loretta replied. "But Lt. Alpuente had another contributing factor. He was prescribed Marplan for depression and anxiety. No doctor would have prescribed Marplan if they'd known he was taking L-DOPA, and vice versa. Marplan is a monoamine oxidase inhibitor, an MAOI. There's a specific prohibition against taking MAOIs and L-DOPA together, because the MAOI would accentuate the effects of the L-DOPA. The levels of Marplan in the tox screen are well within normal, and fit with the prescription bottle you found in his hotel room, Dwayne. That also leads me to believe he wasn't aware that he was ingesting L-DOPA. The combination could have easily contributed to the state of mind his fiancée described."

"Or it could still be a voodoo curse," Sebastian said.

"Come on, Sebastian," Lasalle said. "Don't tell me you believe in voodoo. You're a scientist."

"Yes, I—thank you, Christopher, for recognizing that. Yes, I am, in fact, a scientist. And I'm not necessarily a believer. But sometimes, that's entirely beside the point."

"Meaning what?" Pride asked him.

Sebastian perched on a corner of Sonja's desk. "Meaning that curses can work whether or not the victim believes in them."

"Really?" Sonja asked.

"Look, in some places—south Florida, I know for sure, and for all I know maybe right here in New Orleans—there are hospitals that hire staff members whose whole job is to work with people who have been cursed."

"But if they believe—"

"That's exactly my point," Sebastian interrupted. "These are patients who believe in modern medical science. They went to a hospital, not to a shaman or some kind of voodoo priestess. They've been to medical doctors, and the doctors weren't able to figure out what's wrong with them. Neither can the hospital staff. There's seemingly no medical reason for their condition, but they're undeniably sick. At that point, the hospital might pass them off to a 'social worker' who's conversant with the local magical communities. That staff member will ask them questions, and eventually it might work around to the patient saying, 'Oh, yeah,

I ran over this guy's foot with my shopping cart, and he said he was putting a curse on me, but I didn't think anything more about it.' The hospital staffer will go out and talk to that person, and eventually they'll lift the curse, and the patient will feel better. All without ever believing in magic of any kind."

"Still," Lasalle said. "If they're from a culture where belief in curses is prevalent, they might believe, somewhere in the recesses of their mind, without even knowing they do."

"Even if they never consciously acknowledge it to themselves, they're still susceptible to curses? I'll buy that," Sebastian said. "And in this case, that might be true. We know Alpuente was aware that he had been cursed, though we still don't know why, or by whom. We know he had a *gris-gris* bag and a voodoo doll on him, and that he comes from a household where voodoo seems to be a regular practice. He might have been a true believer. I'm just saying, true belief isn't always a necessary component of successful curses."

"It's like I said last night," Loretta put in, "some things can't be explained in a way any of us would consider satisfactory. And when you don't have an explanation—well, that's where magic comes in."

"I can't believe we're talking about magic," Lasalle said, "in relation to a murder case."

"That's because you're not from here," Pride said. "It's hard to be from New Orleans and not accept the presence of magic in the world."

"I'm not from here, either," Loretta said. "But a world without magic in it is... I don't know, I suppose that would be a world I wouldn't want to live in."

* * *

On the theory that the easiest way to dose Alpuente with L-DOPA without his knowledge would have been through his food, Pride and Sonja headed back to his house in Tremé, while Lasalle and Sebastian went to the Buccaneer Hotel to see if they could find where Alpuente had eaten in the days leading to his murder. Loretta would analyze his stomach contents, looking for clues to his last meals.

At the house, Sonja fetched Meghan Webster, the landlady. She came over clutching a ball of keys, some spiking out from between her fingers like weapons. She smelled like she'd been rolling in alcohol and tobacco. "When can I dump all his crap and clean the house?" she asked. "I'm losing money every day it sits empty."

"We'll let you know, Ms. Webster," Sonja replied. "In the meantime, just don't let anybody in but us."

"Nobody would want to go in," the woman said. "Not into a dead man's house."

"You might be surprised," Pride said. "Has anyone else come around?"

"Not that I've seen."

The landlady found the right key and let them in through the kitchen door. "I'll be at home," she said. "Let me know when you're done."

If you're sober enough to care, Pride thought. Admittedly, having a tenant murdered could be a little nerve-wracking, but he got the impression that this was a more usual state for her than a reaction to that event.

"We didn't think this place was a crime scene when we were here before," Sonja said, "or we would have secured it and stationed a uniform outside."

"No reason to think it was, considering where Alpuente was killed," Pride said. "But if he was essentially poisoned, then it might be. We'll get an officer here if we need to."

"When we were here before, she was having her house painted," Sonja said. "Looks like it's all done."

Pride looked out the window at it. "Looks good," he said. "No wonder she's concerned about losing rent money—that doesn't come cheap." He opened a pantry door. "You start here. Take anything that's not factory-sealed. I'll tackle the refrigerator and the other cupboards."

"Right," Sonja said. "This guy wasn't exactly a health nut, was he?"

"What do you mean?"

"We got Twinkies, Frosted Flakes, six—no, seven—kinds of candy bars, Cheetos, Funyuns, pork rinds, and five different kinds of canned meat. And that's just on one shelf."

"Don't judge," Pride said. He opened the freezer. Meat, meat, and more meat. He closed it again, quickly, glad he'd taken this task instead of giving it to Sonja, the vegan. "Really don't judge."

"Oh, my God!" she said. "Do you know how many kinds of Pop Tarts there are? And who needs more than one jar of pickled pigs' feet?"

"He was an... let's call it adventurous eater. Just bag, don't inventory. We've got to get this stuff to the lab so they can check for traces of L-DOPA."

"Eew," Sonja said. Pride was almost afraid to ask.

"What now?"

"On the floor, he's got some plastic bins of bulk foods. Looks like oats, flour, sugar, trail mix. Probably down here because he doesn't eat those things much. But some of the bins are sticky. Something got on them. Is L-DOPA sticky?"

"That's outside my range of knowledge," Pride said. "Bag those too, but separately from the rest. Sebastian likes to solve mysteries."

"I'm sorry I even touched them," she said. "I'm gonna have to scrub a few layers of skin off my hands."

"Hands are the fastest healing part of the body," Pride said. He was half-submerged in the refrigerator, putting plastic containers of leftovers into a garbage bag.

"Pretty sure that's tongues," Sonja countered.

"Same difference."

"Pride?" Sonja said. "I think I've figured out why you're not dating anyone."

19

Gilbert Melancon had said that Alpuente never left his room at the Buccaneer Hotel for very long, so Lasalle and Sebastian focused their search at restaurants within a few blocks of the hotel. The man had only stayed at the hotel for a few days, but he didn't live far away, and he might have picked the Buccaneer because he knew the neighborhood. Anyway, it sounded like he had wanted to stay close to where the Mardi Gras crowds would be.

This being New Orleans, there were plenty of places around where the man could have eaten, from fast food chains like McDonald's and Rally's to bar-and-grills and working-class restaurants like Leo's Caboose, the Superior Grill, and August Moon, all the way to upscale establishments like Commander's Palace. "I vote we start there," Lasalle said.

"That's because you're a foodie," Sebastian replied. "I doubt that Alpuente would have eaten there. His meal would have taken a long time, and if he had wanted to keep a low profile, choosing one of the city's best-known restaurants would have been the wrong choice. People go there to eat delicious meals, but also to see and be seen."

"You're right," Lasalle said. "He'd probably go in for something quicker and less famous. Trouble is, this is New Orleans, so even the less renowned places are gonna remind me I skipped lunch."

"I could talk to you about intestinal parasites, if that would help," Sebastian offered. "You'd be surprised at some of the things we find at the lab. Stomach contents really is a fascinating area of study—"

"That's not necessary, Sebastian. Really. Thanks, but I'll be fine."

"Your call. If you change your mind, let me know."

Just the thought of Sebastian's lecture on stomach contents put Lasalle's mind off food for a little while, but it didn't last. The more restaurants he entered, and smelled the insides of, the hungrier he got.

They spoke to the wait staff at each place—or the counter staff, in the case of the fast food joints—showing pictures of Alpuente and asking if anyone remembered serving him. So far, their search had been fruitless. In part, that was a function of time of day. They were canvassing in the late afternoon, which meant that someone who had served Alpuente breakfast or dinner might not be on duty.

Finally, they struck pay dirt at Flanders' Pie Hole, on Conery. When they showed Alpuente's photo to a waitress with coils of red hair piled up on her head and a welcoming grin, her smile widened even more. She had a nametag with "Deb!" written on it, almost hidden on an apron full of random pins: superheroes, team mascots, advertising mascots, sayings pithy and not-so-pithy. "Oh, I remember him," she said cheerfully. "He's had breakfast here for the last few days. Nervous type. Nice enough, and a decent tipper—not great, but not terrible. But he had a weird vibe to him. That's why I remember."

"What kind of vibe?" Lasalle asked.

She chewed on her lower lip as she considered. "Like he'd already dropped one shoe, you know?"

"And he was waiting on the next one to fall?"

"Right. He didn't look like a guy who would skip out on the check. Plus, he was in uniform, and people in uniform just don't do that, usually. But the way he was acting; if he was somebody else, I might have worried about that. Jumpy, like. The kind of guy who might hit the deck if a car backfired."

"You said he had breakfast for the last few days?" Sebastian broke in. "Did you ever see him before that?" Lasalle understood the question. Sebastian had explained that one day, or even a few, wouldn't have been enough to dose Alpuente with L-DOPA—it had most likely been happening for a while. If he was a regular someplace, though, that could explain the concentration in his system.

"No. It's possible that he's been here before, but I don't remember him until a couple of days ago."

"So he's not a long-time regular."

"Not on any of my shifts. I usually work breakfast and lunch, though, not dinner."

"Did he eat the same thing every day?" Lasalle asked. "Do you remember that?"

"It's been super busy with all the Mardi Gras crowds, but..." Deb bowed her head, staring at the floor. Lasalle figured she was running through her customers in her mind. The place was quiet, at this hour, with only one table occupied by four obvious locals, older folks who probably met here on a regular basis. They were talking over each other in the manner of people who had known one another for years.

"Strawberry-rhubarb pie," she said at last. "Every day. I thought it was a little strange—we sell plenty of pie, obviously. That's kind of our thing. But every day, with breakfast? That's a little nuts."

"Is there any in the kitchen now?" Lasalle knew it was a long shot—this was a popular spot for pie, so they probably baked it fresh every day. If someone had been dosing Alpuente through the pie, they probably knew he was already dead, so hadn't bothered to treat today's strawberry-rhubarb.

But sometimes long shots paid off, and good police work often required going the extra mile to find clues where nobody expected them. If he had to take a slice of pie into evidence, so be it. He had done stranger things.

"Sure," she said.

"Strawberry-rhubarb," Sebastian said. "My favorite. Well, not my absolute favorite. One of my top five, though. Or ten. Definitely top ten."

Lasalle glanced at him, and Sebastian shrugged. "What? I like pie."

"Is there any left from yesterday?" Lasalle asked.

"Well…" She blushed. "Now that you mention it, I actually like the strawberry-rhubarb myself. We had some leftover after lunch yesterday, so I saved a couple of slices for later. They're in the walk-in."

"Any chance we could take one?"

"If you're hungry, I can—"

"It's not for me. It might be evidence," he said.

"Evidence? Why? Did… did something happen to that man?"

"Yes, I'm afraid so."

Her smile vanished completely for the first time since she had greeted the two agents. "Oh. Well, I guess so, then." She glanced around, as if to make sure they weren't being observed, but there was only one other waitress in sight, and she was sitting in an empty booth sipping coffee from a lipstick-marked mug and looking at her phone. She paid Deb and Lasalle no attention at all. "Come on."

Deb led them through the swinging doors and into the kitchen. A heavily muscled cook was at a cutting board, carving steaks. Tattoos covered his bare arms and neck, and his apron was stained with blood and grease. He looked up at their approach, and his face hardened into a scowl.

"Benny," Lasalle said, recognizing the man. The New Orleans metro area contained more than a million souls, and the population had come back to about ninety percent of its pre-Katrina levels, but it often felt like a small town where everybody knew one another. "You being good?"

"You ain't my P.O.," Benny said. "You checkin' up on me?"

"Oh, do you know Benny?" Deb asked.

"We've met," Lasalle replied. In fact, he'd arrested Benny for armed robbery, years earlier. The man had beaten a tourist almost to death with an ax handle, in the course of stealing a wallet containing ninety-one dollars and a couple of credit cards. Once he had come out of his coma, the tourist had mentioned seeing a "Born Dead" tattoo on his attacker's forearm, which had made it easy to identify the culprit. "How's it going, Benny?" he asked.

"I'm workin'," Benny said, glowering at him. "I'm keepin' outta trouble."

"Glad to hear it."

Deb took a couple of steps backward. Lasalle didn't know if she was consciously making sure she wasn't between the two men, or just reacting to the tension in the air, but he was glad she had. Benny's life had been defined by rage. It had always simmered just under the surface, occasionally breaking out in some act of incredible violence. Nobody had been able to pin a killing on him, but Lasalle believed he had killed, and probably more than once. Lasalle thought he viewed members of the law enforcement community as a former Confederate soldier might have the Union troops stationed in the South during Reconstruction: as hated enemies given power over his life by the force of arms and the weight of history. He could understand the law but would never perceive their cause as just, and he itched to make whatever personal stand he could in protest of what he considered the unfairness of the forces arrayed against him.

At his sentencing hearing, he had exploded, overturning his chair and threatening revenge against Lasalle. That revenge had never materialized, but that didn't mean it had been forgotten.

And he had a big, bloody carving knife in his hands.

Lasalle's instinct was to move his hand closer to his gun. Such a move might be interpreted as threatening, though. Less than eight feet of rubber-matted floor separated the two men; Benny could cover it in a flash. If he lunged, Lasalle might not be able to draw and fire fast enough to stop him before that blade did some serious damage. Sebastian's presence probably helped—even if Benny could get him, he would figure that Sebastian would take him down.

Instead, Lasalle kept his hands in plain sight, well away from his weapon. "I'm just here for some pie," he said. "Nothing to do with you. I'm glad to see you've got a good job."

Benny shrugged, but his expression didn't change.

"Where's the walk-in, Deb?" Lasalle asked.

"Right over here," she said, sounding relieved. She moved to the big stainless steel door and pulled down on the handle. A wave of cold air washed over Lasalle. Now he faced a choice: keep his eyes on Benny while he walked to the cooler, or turn away and give Benny the opportunity to make good on his threat.

He hesitated only an instant, then turned. Let him try.

Benny stayed put, glaring fiercely but making no aggressive move. Lasalle and Sebastian followed Deb into the walk-in. "How much you need?" she asked him.

"One slice would be good," Sebastian said. "You're sure this is the same pie that Lt. Alpuente ate yesterday?"

"Absolutely," Deb said.

"And you can spare a slice?" Lasalle asked.

She gave him a frown, but nodded. "There's always more."

"That's the spirit," he said. It was still unlikely that Alpuente had been dosed by pie, unless he had eaten other meals at the restaurant until the past few days, then switched to breakfast. And it would require his killer or killers to have known not only his schedule, but when it would change, and what kind of pie he preferred.

Still, seeing Benny in the kitchen made the long shot a little shorter. Given his violent tendencies, it might not have taken much incentive to convince him to poison someone.

Or even to throw him off a balcony. Benny wasn't a lot taller than Alpuente, but where the lieutenant was trim, Benny was powerfully built, with a weightlifter's deep chest and broad shoulders, and his arms were massive.

On his way out, his pie in a Styrofoam to-go container inside a paper evidence bag, he stopped in the kitchen again. He found a clean place to set down the bag, then took out his phone and showed Benny a photograph of Alpuente. Doing so required him to get closer to the ex-con than he was comfortable with, but that was nothing new in his line of work. Benny drew back defensively as he approached, but Lasalle made sure he could see the phone in one hand and that the other hand was empty, and Benny put down the knife and let him come.

"Do you know this man, Benny?"

Benny studied the photo. "Should I?"

"You tell me."

"He doesn't look familiar."

"Do you interact much with the diners, or mostly stay in the kitchen?"

Benny laughed. "Look at me, man. You think the boss wants me in the front of the house?"

That edge of tension remained, but Lasalle didn't get the sense that Benny was lying to him. "Good point," he said. "I'm glad you've got a steady gig." He meant it. His brother Cade had worked in restaurant kitchens, and had been in trouble with the law. Lasalle knew from hard experience with Cade that second chances—and sometimes third and fourth chances—weren't easy to come by, but they could make a world of difference. If working at the restaurant kept Benny out of trouble, that was good for Benny and the community at large.

"You and me both," Benny said. "Do me a favor, and don't screw it up for me, okay?"

"I don't intend to," Lasalle replied. "That power's in your hands, Benny. As long as you don't screw it up, you'll be okay."

Even as he walked out the door, he knew that was overly simplistic. It took a long time for an ex-con's life to become truly his own again, if it ever could. Most of them spent every day looking over their shoulders, half-expecting society to decide once again that they were irredeemable and without value. The taint of prison never really left them, and it affected where they could work and live and whether they could vote. It affected not just them, but their families, and through them their neighborhoods, their cities, and their country.

Lasalle had put plenty of bad guys behind bars. He had no problem with that. Whatever disadvantages they'd been born with or society had piled on them, they had still made the choices that brought the law down on them.

He also knew that incarceration created a spiral of its own, doing damage far beyond whatever any individual lawbreaker had done. Breaking that spiral could only be a positive act.

Anyway, he had to hope. Without hope, he was just treading water. If all he did was lock up criminals, new ones would always arise to take their place. In most cases, it wasn't the locking up that mattered, it was what happened after they had served their time.

He left the restaurant hopeful for Benny and glad that he had played a part in ending the man's cycle of criminality.

And also, starving. And now carrying a slice of pie he didn't dare eat.

20

Patton Plame was tired. He was generally an energetic guy, especially considering how much time he spent sitting in his chair. He was typically upbeat, even if on some occasions he had to fake optimism until it took root and became genuine.

But he had spent so much time over the past two days studying video clips, frame by frame in many cases, looking for Baron Samedi and Edouard Alpuente, and it was wearying work. Most of the video was terrible; for every minute shot by professional videographers or stationary security cameras, there were hours shot by amateurs using smartphones and cameras of varying quality and posted on social media. First, he had to search all the social media sites to find it, which could be excruciating by itself, and after too many hours, could make him feel despair at the future of civilization.

Once he found any potentially helpful video, as often as not, it was shaky and choppy. Sometimes it was out of focus, and sometimes it was *too* focused; for instance, the five-minute long video he came across that consisted entirely of shots of women's behinds as they stood watching the parade. He figured it had either been shot by someone in a wheelchair, since it was similar to the view he often had in crowds, or by someone carrying a phone casually, his arm hanging at his side as he walked. Patton had to admire the initiative even as he bemoaned the use to which it had been put.

That narrow, determined concentration, peering for hour after hour at images jumping and twitching on the screen, made his eyes hurt, which in turn made his head hurt. Between that and his disappointment at some of his fellow humans for the things they chose to capture on video, or the things they did that *were* captured, he felt the need for a long, hot bath and a longer, dreamless sleep.

But baths and sleep were still a long ways off, he knew. The team had returned to the squad room, each worn out to some degree by the events of the long day, but aware that they still had to get through the night. And Patton had to show them something that might or might not make their night longer still.

"So here's what I got," he said, forcing himself to project upbeat optimism. "Check it."

His fingers flew across the keyboard like they were born to it. The elevated plasma screens flickered to life and the video he had found appeared there. The scene was the lobby of the Buccaneer Hotel. Patton had found a figure moving through the shadows, at the edge of the surveillance camera's range. He'd isolated the figure and haloed him to draw attention to it.

"What are we seeing here, Patton?" Pride asked.

"This is the hotel lobby. That there's Alpuente, checking in."

"We've seen this before. Melancon comes to the

counter and checks Lt. Alpuente in."

"Right, King. But keep watching." He let the video run until the moment the figure he'd haloed stepped into the shot, then froze it. "Okay, see, that's Landry. He's only on the screen for a couple of seconds, almost just a ghost image passing through. This is the only shot where his face is recognizable, and even then not really until I enhanced it."

"That's definitely him," Sonja said. "Good job, Triple P."

"Don't I always come through for you guys? Anyway, that's how Landry knew to bribe Melancon. He was tailing Alpuente, most likely. When Alpuente checked in, he moved close enough to overhear some of the conversation. I'm guessing that Melancon and Alpuente didn't know him from Adam—neither guy gives any indication that they recognize him, anyway, and he's close enough that Melancon could see him, for sure. He even glances up once, like Landry has caught his eye, but then he looks back at Alpuente. So at that point, unless Melancon's an incredibly good actor, he doesn't know Landry. Chances are Alpuente doesn't either, or Landry wouldn't have risked getting so close, especially with Alpuente being as nervous as he is, constantly checking over his shoulder."

"Makes sense," Pride said. "So whatever Landry's motivation was, it probably wasn't a personal beef between the two. We know Landry does enforcement work for some of the local criminal element. Maybe Alpuente got in over his head, gambling or something."

"There's no evidence that he's a gambler," Lasalle pointed out.

"That we've found," Pride reminded him. "That doesn't mean it doesn't exist. I'm just saying, if someone is killed by a mob enforcer, it doesn't hurt to look at the mobs."

"But we need to remember that Landry's a free agent," Sonja said. "He's not tied to a particular organization. He works for whoever comes up with the money. According to what I've heard, he knows where the bodies are buried all around town, but he keeps it quiet. That way different players can use his services, knowing it won't blow back on them."

"Which brings us back to square one," Pride said. "We can't ask Alpuente how he wound up on the wrong side of Landry. So we have to ask Landry."

Sonja eyed the window. "Now's our chance," she said. "He's like a vampire. He only comes out at night."

"Everybody ready to crawl through the proverbial seedy underbelly of New Orleans?" Pride asked.

"That's my favorite neighborhood," Patton said.

"We need you here," Pride told him, "staffing the command center."

By which, Patton knew, he meant that in a chase or a fight, he'd be no help. His value to the team was in his intellect and his technical skills. Pride and the others appreciated his contribution—he had no doubt of that—but there was still an unbridgeable gulf between them. They could work in the field, taking risks, running down the bad guys. They needed him where he was, as Pride had said. He was glad to be needed, but that didn't negate the desire he sometimes felt to be out in the streets with the others.

Still, he put on a smile. "You know it, King. I'll be here. Y'all couldn't function without me."

That, he was certain, was completely accurate.

* * *

"Seedy underbelly," Pride knew, was a cliché. And like most clichés, it was rooted in truth. Every major city had one, or several. If you scratched deep enough below the surface, he figured small towns probably did, too. If someone wanted to spend enough money on anything, there would be somebody else who'd be happy to take it and provide the desired good or service.

New Orleans had always had a casual attitude about some activities that were widely considered to be sins. *Laissez les bon temps rouler*—let the good times roll—was, after all, the city's unofficial slogan. For many, especially residents of the country's Bible Belt, the Big Easy offered a seemingly guilt-free, anonymous opportunity to cut loose. Booze, drugs, and sex could all be obtained by crossing the right palms with the appropriate amount of cash. He figured Las Vegas fulfilled the same function for westerners, and parts of Manhattan or Boston's Combat Zone for those in the northeast.

In some ways, it functioned as an escape valve, letting people blow off steam that might otherwise be turned toward more destructive acts. But it also attracted precisely the kinds of people one would expect—those who were happy to profit from the less socially acceptable urges of others. Those were often criminals, and as a consequence, New Orleans had more than its share of them.

It was a tradeoff Pride was willing to accept. The city's freewheeling, libertine ways made it a colorful and exciting place to live, and he wouldn't trade it for anywhere else.

But it meant nights like this one, where he had to face the true nature of the city's dark side. The team split up to better cover ground, and Pride moved quickly through a nightmare dreamscape of drug addiction and human trafficking, situations about which he could, at present, do nothing at all. He was looking for the killer of a naval officer, and all other considerations had to take a back seat.

He started at a couple of floating poker games he knew of, high-stakes operations where the participants might well be armed, and might well be accompanied by bodyguards in case someone else's trigger finger was even itchier than theirs. One was held in a room above a bar that had, in one of the building's previous incarnations, been a prostitute's crib, another in a high-end hotel room. His badge and his familiarity with the city's underworld gained him grudging access to both. He eyed the high rollers at the table and their hired gunnies, sticking to the shadows, sipping beer or smoking pot, but not enough—theoretically, at least—to hamper their reflexes should violence be called for.

He saw plenty of tough guys, but no Landry. Chances were good that the man would visit at least some of his usual haunts. He'd want to continue living his life as he always did; changing things up or lying low would raise suspicion. Those were amateur moves, and Landry was a pro.

From a door at the rear of the high-end hotel, Pride entered an alley running behind it. Most guests of the hotel never knew the alley was there, and even if they noticed it, they wouldn't venture in. So they would never see the open doorway from which music blared, or push through the heavy hanging fabric blocking the interior from view. Pride did.

Inside was a long, wooden bar. Men occupied most of the bar stools, glasses of beer or cocktails in front of them. On top of the bar, a woman wearing only a skimpy G-string moved lethargically, out of rhythm with the music. Her expression was flat, her eyes glazed. Drugged to the gills, Pride guessed, which might be the only way a woman could expose herself this way. Some of the men sitting before her watched in riveted fascination, as if they had never seen a female body before, but others ignored her, chatting among themselves or simply staring into space.

A couple of the patrons spotted Pride and, apparently smelling cop, promptly left their stools and exited the premises. Others paid him no attention. He walked through the joint. More women, most of them at least partially dressed, were sitting next to men, or writhing on top of them. Toward the back were dark, curtained-off areas, "champagne rooms," which could only be accessed by spending an exorbitant amount of money to buy a bottle of something labeled champagne for a dancer, who would then escort her catch into the "room."

There, Pride knew, anything might happen, with the exchange of whatever price the dancer was able to extract. Most of her take would go to the house, so the joint not only made money on the cheap champagne, but on the services provided by the women. Pride suspected that at least some of the women were victims of trafficking, brought to New Orleans from other states or foreign countries and held in a kind of bondage, made to work off supposed debts that could never be fully repaid, until they were deemed too old or damaged to work anymore and were cast off on their own.

This was the side of the city that troubled him the most. This crime wasn't victimless—the women were without power, and the men who took most of what they made and kept them as virtual slaves were the real abusers. If he could, he thought briefly, he would shut down this place, and any others like it, at that moment.

But that wasn't justice, it was dictatorship. It would mean imposing his own personal morality over others, and he knew how he would react if that were done to him. Nobody had appointed him judge. He was police, and he had police work to do.

He didn't see Landry, so he caught the bartender's eye. "Need somethin', boss?" the man asked. He was skinny and pale, with short brown hair. He wore a dirty white shirt with the top two buttons open and a narrow tie, knotted loosely. He didn't look like an owner, and he didn't look much happier than the dancer on the bar to be stuck working in such an environment.

"I'm looking for Bruno Landry. Have you seen him?"

The bartender gave him a practiced blank look. "Never heard of him."

"Right," Pride said. "When you don't see him again, let him know that NCIS wants to talk to him. The conversation will be a lot easier if he comes to us."

"If I knew who you were talkin' about, I'd pass on the message."

"See that you do."

Before he reached the door, he felt the dancer's gaze on him. He met it, and she shot him a look that made his heart lurch. *Help me*, it seemed to say. For an instant, he wanted to; he could draw his weapon, show his badge, and take all the women out of the bar, gunning down anyone who tried to stop him.

But what then? Many of them wouldn't even have copies of their own ID. They might be here illegally, or they might be bound by "contracts" that would take months in court to prove fraudulent. They might be addicts, unable to find other work, unwilling to get clean. They might have family members under threat back home. They might know no one in the city other than those who had brought them here and put them to work, might not even have bus fare to get home, and home might be an abusive household that even this kind of employment looked better than.

Then there were the jurisdictional issues, and the fact that some of these places kept NOPD officers, prosecutors, and judges on the payroll. Pride's Sir Galahad move might just make life harder for some of the women, and could prove fatal for others. The momentary satisfaction it would bring him would pale in comparison to the hardship that trying to "rescue" them, with inadequate resources and preparation, might bring.

Instead, he mouthed "Sorry," to her, and set a twenty on the bar at her feet. Inadequate at best, but all he could do at the moment. He would try to come back, try to press his counterparts at NOPD and the DA's office to do something for the women who worked here and at dozens of similar places in the city. But it had to be a coordinated effort, with social service agencies involved that could help the victims once they were free.

Pride was a cop, not a superhero. He couldn't save everybody. Some people didn't even want to be saved. The best he could do was the best he could do, and he always did that. It was grim reality, but reality it was.

He walked out, and a few minutes later, he entered the next place and did it all over again.

21

In New Orleans, especially around Mardi Gras, it was sometimes hard to tell the streetwalkers from the college girls, at least based on what they were—or weren't—wearing. College girls typically had more expensive clothes, better skin, and healthier hair, but they often showed more skin than the hookers did.

That said, Sonja recognized the three women hovering around a dark corner just off Bourbon Street for what they were. She approached them with her badge clearly on display. "Evening, ladies," she said.

"You a cop?" one asked, looking her up and down. "You could maybe do better on this side of the street."

"But not on our corner," another said with a chuckle. "We don't need that kind of competition."

"Not interested, thanks," Sonja said. "I get health insurance and retirement with my job."

"I got health insurance, too," the third streetwalker said, slipping a pack of condoms from a tiny purse.

"Make sure you keep using it," Sonja said. "Do you ladies know who Bruno Landry is?"

"I'll know who anybody is for the right price," one said. A scar ran down her right cheek, as if she'd been cut with a knife. Even in New Orleans, where prostitution was far more commonplace than in most cities outside Nevada, it was a dangerous business.

"Or forget who they is," said another with a laugh.

Sonja showed Landry's photo around. "Have any of you seen this guy?"

"That phone's the bomb," the one with the scar said.

"Yeah, I'll be needing that back," Sonja said.

"Remember 'keep-away?'" another one asked. "In school, how you'd take somethin' belonged to one of the other kids and you and your girls would throw it around, so the girl that owned it couldn't get it?"

"All I remember about school is Mr. House puttin' his hands where they didn't belong," the scarred one said.

"I'd love to stay and reminisce," Sonja said. "But I'm kind of busy. If you haven't seen Landry, just say so and I'll be on my way."

"You ain't gon' bust us?" the scarred one asked.

"You're not even on my radar. I'm pretty sure none of you are in the U.S. Navy."

"Well, I knows him, but I ain't seen him in a while."

"How long of a while?"

"Three weeks, maybe more."

"You know where he hangs out?"

"Here, there. When I see him, he finds me. I don't go lookin' for him."

"Anybody else?" Sonja asked.

She was met with blank faces.

"Okay, thanks. Stay safe, you hear? If you need anything, let me know."

"Anything like what?" one woman asked. "How about some foldin' green?"

"Anything like help," Sonja said. "If you want out of the life, or you don't feel safe, I'm around." She passed out business cards. The one with the scar immediately shredded it and dropped the pieces to the ground, but the other two hung onto them.

Baby steps, she thought.

Sebastian and Lasalle had drawn the short straw, or so it seemed. While Pride and Sonja were working the Quarter, they were about to walk into a shooting gallery in Central City. The yellow walls of the house were peeling away at the bottom, as if wood rot had dissolved whatever had held them to the frame. Plywood sheets had been nailed over the windows. In other spots, the walls had buckled like wet cardboard, leaving gaping holes. Iron bars fronted the only visible door. The house looked abandoned, but Lasalle said it was a drug den, usually occupied by a dozen or more hardcore addicts who made their purchases and shot up on the premises, too desperate to even wait until they got home. If they even had homes to go to.

Sebastian figured he knew what he was talking about. Anyway, it didn't look like a place someone would voluntarily live, so drug den made as much sense as anything else.

Where there were drugs, there was cash; and where there was cash, there were guns, and people ready to use them. Landry had been known to work here as a guard from time to time, and in the no-stone-unturned search, the place had to be checked.

"You take me to the nicest places," Sebastian said. "First to meet your pal Benny, and now this."

"You knew what the job was when you took it," Lasalle said. "Beats staying in the lab all day, doesn't it?"

"It does. Definitely. Not that I didn't love working with Loretta. But the smell in there—antiseptic and ammonia and dead people—that can get to you, you know? Especially if you have sensitive nasal passages."

Usually, Lasalle had explained, entering such an establishment was a major police operation, employing tactical vehicles and overwhelming force. That kind of operation required plenty of advance planning and coordination between NCIS and NOPD, sometimes with the DEA and JPSO involved. They didn't have time for anything like that, or even probable cause to get a warrant. They were alone, with only one another for backup, and would have to rely on whoever answered the door—if anyone—not to shoot them on sight. They were wearing Kevlar vests, but that was as close to tactical gear as they dared show.

Instead of knocking the door in with a dynamic entry ram, or simply driving through it, Lasalle reached through the iron bars and knocked. He kept his body to the side in case the knock was met by gunfire, and Sebastian waited on the other side. Nothing happened. Lasalle waited, then knocked again.

After another minute or so, Sebastian heard the floorboards on the other side of the door creak, and a male voice said, "Yeah."

"NCIS," Lasalle said. "This isn't a raid, and we're not here to jam anybody up. We're just looking for Bruno Landry. He here?"

"Why would I tell you?"

"Because like I said, we come in peace. This time. Turn him over and we can keep it that way. Mess with us and we'll be back with tanks, and we'll flatten this place and everyone inside it. Your choice."

"He ain't here."

"Convince us. Can we come in?"

A muffled laugh came back. "You kidding?"

"Do I sound like I'm kidding?"

"You sound like you're suicidal."

"Long way from it," Lasalle said. "I'm doing a job, same as you."

"Little different."

"Different objective, maybe. We're both trying to make a living."

"You sure you're cops?" the voice asked. "You don't sound like one."

"Open the door and we'll show you our badges."

"Man, you crazy."

"It's not the first time I've heard that."

"Not even the first today," Sebastian added. "Crazy Chris, they call him."

"Not surprised."

"So is he here?"

"I told you, no."

"I'm still not convinced."

"I open this door, I might just shoot your ass."

"People have tried that before," Sebastian said. "I'd tell you to ask them what happened, but you'd have to be able to speak to the dead."

"You're a couple of badasses, huh?"

"That's one way to look at it. Bad enough, anyway."

"Maybe I'll test you."

"Give it a try," Lasalle said. "Open up and we'll see what happens."

Before the man on the other side of the door could respond, Patton Plame's voice crackled in Lasalle's ear. "Guys, we just got a hit on our BOLO. NOPD says Landry's been spotted at the Ronday-Vous on Dauphine."

The Ronday-Vous was a notorious dive bar. It was

the kind of place where someone could get cheap booze at any hour of the day or night, where fights were as commonplace as spilled beer, and where it seemed that one could catch sexually transmitted diseases just by breathing the air.

Just Landry's kind of place, in other words.

"We're on our way," he said.

"I'm close by." That was Sonja's voice.

"Sonja, I'm not too far off," Pride said. "Don't take any chances."

"Patton," Sonja said, "is the officer who spotted him still on the scene?"

"Checking," Patton said. After a moment's silence, he said, "He's right outside, waiting for us."

Through the radio, Sebastian could hear Sonja's feet slapping against the pavement, hear the stutter in her voice as she talked and ran at the same time. "I'm almost there," she said. "I'll meet the officer there."

"Be careful," Lasalle said. He was already running for his truck, Sebastian close behind.

Behind him, he heard the door open, and the man inside say, "Okay, badasses, come on in and see how you do. Hey, where you goin'?"

22

Sonja had been inside the Ronday-Vous once before. She had been working undercover for the ATF, trying to bring down a dealer who made a specialty of selling large quantities of guns to criminal organizations. Her cover had been as a representative of a party in Central America—she had implied, without coming right out and saying it, that she was fronting for a drug cartel—that needed a large supply of military-grade automatic weapons and ammunition. The dealer she was trying to buy from had insisted on meeting there. She'd put it down to wanting to make her uncomfortable, put her on edge, to try to force a slip-up. She had swallowed her nerves, pretended the place was just fine with her.

She had made the deal, and the gun dealer had been arrested. He was still serving time in Angola. The bust was one of the proudest moments of her ATF career.

But after forty minutes in the Ronday-Vous, she had wanted to bathe in muriatic acid. For hours afterward, she had still felt the eyes of the patrons on her, and the touches of those men who'd grazed past her or grabbed her outright (at least one of whom would never walk the same). The place held a stink that seemed to stay with her for days, a miasma of booze and flop sweat and piss and desperate loneliness, of forgotten dreams and lost hopes. It was the smell of people who had given up and those who'd never had anything to give up.

Going back into that hole was not high on her bucket list.

But if that's where Landry was, then that's where she needed to be.

She rounded a corner at a full sprint, and there it was. It loitered on the edge of the Quarter like a panhandler waiting to accost anyone who strayed too near. The name was hand-painted on the wall and barely legible, and she had never known whether the misspelling was intentional. There had once been a window, but it had been boarded over and pasted over with beer posters that graffiti had largely obscured. The door was always closed but never locked, as far as Sonja knew. For bartenders, the owners tended to hire ex-cons, people who wouldn't be intimidated when the frequent fights broke out, when knives or guns were pulled, when customers were too drunk or high to make it to the bathrooms, or when people started having noisy sex on a table or in a booth.

She was glad to see a uniformed cop standing outside. He was a young guy, big, with shoulders like a refrigerator carton. His features were tiny, almost lost in the fleshy slabs of cheeks, forehead, and chin. He wore a nametag that said Cooke.

"Is he still in there?" Sonja asked as she approached, her badge out. She was a little out of breath from the run, but not a lot.

"Unless there's a back door."

"Of course there's a back door," she said,

exasperated already. "This kind of joint always has a back door. How long have you been on the job?"

"A year, I guess. A little less."

"They should teach you that at the Academy. Lot of people who go into a dive like this don't want to be seen leaving."

"Well, I didn't know. You still want to go in and look?"

"Hell yes," she said. "If he's in there, let me deal with him, okay? I mean, back me up if there's trouble, but I'll do the talking."

"Fine with me." Cooke looked down the street. "I got backup on the way."

"So do I," Sonja said. "But if he's already gone, it's a waste of time. I need to check. You go around to the alley and come in that way. I'll give you thirty to get there, then go in the front."

"Got it," he said. He didn't move.

"Hustle! I'm counting down."

As if only then realizing what he was supposed to do, he hustled. She could hear his feet against the pavement, his duty belt creaking and jingling, all the way around the building. When he was in position, she walked in.

If the place had changed at all, it was for the worse. Lighting was almost nonexistent, and much of what was provided was in the form of red or blue bulbs, offering "atmosphere" rather than illumination. The stench was worse than Sonja remembered. The hardwood floor felt like it had been greased instead of mopped, and her feet slipped under her.

By the time she spotted Landry, hunched over a table with a couple of beers on it, seemingly deep in conversation with an aging, bearded barfly, Cooke had come in from the back. Landry, facing Sonja, didn't see him, but his drinking companion did. He said, "Cop."

Landry rose instantly, ready to bolt.

Sonja showed her badge and drew her weapon. "NCIS, Landry!" she said. "Freeze!"

He didn't. Instead, he flipped the table toward her with one sweep of his muscular arm. Beer bottles flew, splashing her, and she had to fend off the table itself with her left forearm.

By the time she could see Landry again, he was halfway to the front door. Cooke was closing on him, but other patrons, on their feet now because of the commotion, stood between them.

"Landry!" Sonja called. "You're surrounded. On your knees!"

Instead, he kept going. He flung a chair at her, blocking any chance of a clean shot, even if she'd had cause to shoot. She batted that threat away, but he was already out the door.

"He's on the run!" she cried into her radio. She burst outside and spotted him racing down the street. "On Barracks, headed toward Bourbon!"

"I'm almost there," Pride said. "Don't lose him!"

"I'm getting close," Lasalle added.

"Okay, I have eyes on him," Patton said. "I'll try to keep tabs, too."

She heard Cooke behind her, but his breathing was already ragged, and she couldn't wait for him to catch up. She tore after Landry, who glanced once over his shoulder, then hung a right onto Bourbon Street.

Sonja reached the corner a few seconds later. The street was narrow here, mostly residential, and Landry was running into the one-way traffic. She was fast, but on the straight stretch his long legs gave him the advantage and he was pulling away from her.

Pride was on the far side of the Quarter, questioning the participants in a back-room craps game near Dorsiere and Canal, when he heard about Landry being at the Ronday-Vous. He was still wondering if Alpuente had been a gambler, so even though Landry wasn't present, he had been showing a photo of Alpuente to the players. Nobody admitted to knowing him.

As soon as Patton reported the police officer's spotting of Landry, Pride took off at a run. He had been on foot; his SUV was still parked at the squad room, blocks away, so he hoofed it across the Quarter. He took Iberville to Chartres and turned right, racing toward the Ronday-Vous, on the far side of some of the most historic and beautiful city blocks in the nation. The sidewalks were crowded; he ran with his badge in his hand, announcing himself, but even so he sometimes had to dart into the road to dodge around clumps of pedestrians.

He was almost to Jackson Square when Sonja reported that Landry was on Bourbon Street and outpacing her. He swung left on St. Peter, hoping to head off their quarry on Bourbon. St. Peter was busy, too, with cars and trucks heading up the same way he was running, and others lined up against the right-hand curb. Knots of merry-makers clogged the sidewalks, and there was less space on this narrow street to avoid them.

Crossing Royal, he was almost struck by a taxi barreling through the intersection. Swerving away from that, he ran headlong into a parked pedicab. The driver dropped a cigarette butt to the street, stomped on it, and asked, "Lookin' for a ride, mon?"

"No, thanks," Pride said as he disentangled himself. Backing away from the pedicab, he was honked at by the driver of an SUV almost too large to negotiate the Quarter's narrow lanes, trying to make a right from St. Peter onto Royal.

Pride took off up St. Peter again. "I ran into a slight stall," he said into his mic. "Anybody got eyes on Landry?"

"I had him on a security camera from Lafitte's," Patton said. "But he's in the wind now."

"What about you, Sonja?" Pride asked.

"I haven't been able to see him at all for a couple of minutes," she reported. "Sorry, Pride. That sucker's fast."

"Don't worry about it, Sonja," he said. "As far as we know, he's still on Bourbon, right?"

"I'm checkin' all the cameras around there," Patton said. "But yeah, I haven't picked him up anywhere else yet."

Pride could see Bourbon Street dead ahead. "I'm almost there," he said. "St. Peter and Bourbon. If he's still coming my way I should have a visual in a couple of minutes."

"I'm on Loyola Ave," Lasalle announced. "I'll be there soon."

Pride dashed into the road to get around a group of presumably drunken college kids, holding onto each other for support, then back onto the sidewalk. "Okay," he said. He heard music spilling out of Cornet, smelled the steaks grilling from The Embers. "I'm on Bourbon. Let me know if anybody spots him."

Bourbon Street was jammed, as he'd known it would be. The Mardi Gras crowds didn't leave the day after, and the partying didn't stop immediately.

Discarded beads from broken strings littered the ground like promises made in the flush of the evening and forgotten by morning; go-cups and wadded-up napkins and other detritus had blown up against the curbs. Cars had to slow for the pedestrians thronging the road. Making progress was even harder than it had been on Chartres, but Pride forged ahead, determined to stop Landry.

When he reached St. Ann, he glanced down the street. The squad room was just a block away, as was his SUV. No reason to get it now, though; he would make better time on foot than behind the wheel, on these streets, and the side trip might give Landry time to escape.

Instead, he stopped on the corner. Landry had to be somewhere close, heading his way. He peered down the street, eyeballing the patches of light washing out of shops and restaurants and the headlights of the cars. "Where is he?" he demanded. "Does anybody see him?"

"I don't," Sonja said. "I'm almost to Dumaine."

If she was there, then Landry had to be almost on top of Pride. Had he missed him, in the split second he had peered down St. Ann? He whirled around, checking his back trail, but there was no sign of the man.

"Wait, I got him again," Patton said. "This is from a couple of minutes ago, though. There's a space between the buildings, on Bourbon between Dumaine and St. Philip. Next to 920 Bourbon. He went down there, headed toward the river."

Pride knew Patton didn't mean he was literally headed for the river. That was still blocks away. But New Orleanians didn't use "north" and "south," they used "lake" and "river." Someone moving north was heading toward Lake Pontchartrain, and someone going the other way was headed for the Mississippi.

"Do you have eyes back there?" Pride asked.

"Not for a while, no," Patton said.

"What's his lead?"

"Almost two minutes, now."

"Damn."

"Pride, I can see you now," Sonja said.

He looked up the street. He'd been scanning for Landry, a big man, but now he spotted Sonja coming his way.

"I got you, Sonja," he said. "Christopher, where are you?"

"Rampart and, ahh, Bienville," Lasalle replied.

"Take Conti toward the river," Pride said. "Then take Decatur to Dumaine and leave your truck there. Work your way up toward us, and we'll be trying to flush him your way."

"Got it, King."

"If there's a change in plans, I'll let you know," Pride said.

"Roger that."

"Come on, Sonja," Pride said. He nodded toward the gap between the buildings that Landry had taken. "Let's catch us a killer."

23

Minutes ticked by as Lasalle fought the French Quarter traffic. He used his siren to clear intersections, but even so, the going was frustratingly slow. Any time of the year, the Quarter would be crowded, he knew, but this was the worst week to have to try to move quickly through its streets.

Finally, he reached Decatur, right where it narrowed from an expansive, divided street to a single lane in each direction. Pride's instructions had made sense; of all the cross streets down here, Decatur would be the one with the fastest-moving traffic and the fewest pedestrians. At least this far west—when he got closer to the center of the Quarter, that would change.

Again, he used his siren and swung a wide left. After the first block, though, between the cars parked along the curbs and the people on the street, the cars in front of him had nowhere else to go. At intersections, they could pull off, but in mid-block, he was stuck.

"Progress, Chris?" Pride asked in his ear.

"Getting there," Lasalle answered. "But not as fast as I'd like."

"What happened to NOPD?" Pride asked. "Patton?

Be nice if they could pick up some of the slack."

"I'm on the horn with them," Patton said. "They had a patrol car en route, but there was a fatality accident on Esplanade, so they got rerouted. There's another one on the way."

"And maybe they'll get here before Easter," Pride said. Lasalle could hear the aggravation in his voice, and he shared it.

"Any more sign of Landry?" he asked.

"Hang on," Patton said. "Yep, I got him. He's on—hold on just a minute, here."

"Patton?" Pride said. "Patton, where'd you go?"

For several seconds, Patton hadn't quite believed what he was seeing. Landry had appeared on a remarkably high-def video camera. Patton could see him clearly: a tall, broad-shouldered, heavily muscled African American man. He had cornrows and a beard that hugged his lean cheeks and narrow chin, and he was wearing a Jazz Fest T-shirt from 2013—the blue one where the text formed a box around some brass instruments. The camera was good enough to let Patton read the words.

It dawned on him that the only surveillance cameras in the neighborhood that crystal clear were their own, the ones mounted discreetly outside the squad room. Then he realized that the backdrop behind Landry was Royal Street, approaching St. Ann. Landry must have taken a circuitous route, no doubt hoping to shake his pursuers.

He pulled off his headset and rolled out the door and onto the sidewalk.

Immediately, he saw Landry. He was moving fast, but not sprinting, not doing anything to call attention to himself except being a head taller than almost anyone else on the block. He was working his way across Royal, as if intending to turn left at St. Ann. Still working toward the river.

Patton couldn't run after him, but that didn't mean he was helpless.

Ignoring oncoming traffic, he eased his chair off the curb right at the corner. Cars braked, tires screeched, the acrid smell of burning rubber reached his nostrils. He knew there had been a chance he'd be hit, or that he would cause an accident, but it was one he willingly took. He wheeled out into the middle of the street, angling toward the southeast corner, and timing it to get there just when Landry did.

The big man saw him coming—it would have been hard not to, since he had just nearly precipitated a multi-vehicle pile-up. Patton shot him a wide smile. Landry ignored it and tried to step around him, but Patton kept coming, ramming Landry with his chair. Landry stumbled and Patton lunged. His legs weren't much use to him, but his upper body strength was considerable. He threw his arms around Landry, and his weight and momentum bore them both to the ground.

Landry tried to wriggle free, but Patton held him fast.

"What the hell, dog?" Landry said, his voice an angry snarl.

"Give it up, Landry," Patton said.

A look of confusion crossed Landry's face, an expression so comical that Patton nearly burst into laughter. "Who the hell are you?"

"NCIS," Patton said. "You're under arrest, Bruno Landry."

"Fuck that," Landry said. He kicked free of Patton's grip, nailing him in the ribs a couple of times for good measure. When Patton snatched at him again, Landry punched him in the mouth. Patton felt his lips split under the blow, but he ran his tongue quickly across his teeth and determined that they were intact. That was something, anyway.

But Landry was back on his feet, and Patton was lying in the middle of the street. Landry kicked his chair, which skidded about five feet before tumbling over onto its side. "And fuck you!" Landry added.

That cogent comment delivered, he turned and started running down St. Ann. "I'm-a make sure you regret that!" Patton called after his retreating form. "Wait and see!"

Landry didn't slow or respond. "Yeah," Patton added. "Run, like the punk you are."

"That's Patton!" Pride shouted. He had heard brakes squealing up ahead, and wondered if Landry was somehow involved. But it wasn't until he and Sonja had worked their way through the sudden congestion on the sidewalks that they saw Patton's chair toppled in the street, and Patton dragging himself across the pavement toward it.

Other pedestrians were reaching to help, but Patton waved them away. Pride recognized Patton's tone as he said, "I got this!" Patton was proud, and he was as self-sufficient as anyone Pride had ever known. He'd probably made an attempt to stop Landry by himself, and had been unceremoniously dumped into the intersection for his trouble. Knowing strangers were watching him struggle would be humiliating for him; accepting their help would be unbearable.

He and Sonja reached him in time to right his chair.

"You okay, Triple P?" Sonja asked. "Or should I call you Batman?"

"If I had cuffed him, you could call me Batman," Patton replied. "I had him, but he broke loose."

"Looks like he did some damage," Pride said. He helped Patton up and into the chair. "He got blood all over your shirt."

"Yeah, well, I got a few licks in, too," Patton said. "But he got away. He's headin' down St. Ann."

"You might need a couple of stitches," Sonja said. "You want me to go in with you?"

"You stay on that bastard's tail," Patton said. "I'll be fine."

"You sure?"

"He's sure," Pride said. "Patton, get inside and get some ice on that. Call an ambulance if you need it."

"I'm fine, King," Patton insisted. He wiped his face with the back of his hand, looked at the blood there, and started toward the open door of the squad room.

"He'll be okay," Pride said. "Let's go." He started running down the street, with Sonja beside him. "Christopher, update?"

"Just parking," Lasalle answered. "At Decatur and St. Ann. Think I pissed off a couple of carriage drivers."

"They'll get over it. It's the horses you have to worry about."

"Did you hear that?" Sebastian asked.

"I've got the same comms unit on that you do," Lasalle answered. "Patton tried to intercept Landry, and became the man's punching bag. If I get my hands on Landry, I'll make sure to deliver some payback for that."

He parked the truck amid the horse-drawn carriages

in front of Jackson Square, and they started up St. Ann. Landry could veer off at Chartres, or he could go into a building someplace between here and there. But he had been heading steadily in the direction of the river, and Lasalle had no reason to think he would change course.

Despite the lateness of the hour, artists and other merchants were still out, with their wares up against the fence surrounding Jackson Square. At other times of the year, most or all of them might have given up for the night, but this was Mardi Gras week, and as long as there were tourists around, there would be folks trying to separate them from a few of their dollars. Lasalle and Sebastian hurried up the street, weaving in and out of the flock, trying to look casual and scan the way ahead for Landry.

Then Sebastian spotted the big man, bopping toward them at a rapid walk. "There!" he said.

Lasalle followed the other man's gaze and saw Landry. He shook his arms, loosening them for a fight. He touched his weapon, ensuring that he could draw it easily if it came to that. Landry was taller than he was, and looked like he'd been pumping iron since he was in diapers. But Lasalle thought about what he had done to Alpuente, and now to Patton, and he was ready to lay some hurt on the man.

He didn't know what tipped Landry off. Maybe it was the way the two agents' gazes bore into him, or maybe Lasalle just had a cop look that he couldn't get rid of—he didn't think that applied to Sebastian. Whatever it was, all at once, Landry changed course, crossing the flagstone-paved pedestrian area on Chartres, between the square and the Louisiana State Museum. Lasalle picked up his pace, hoping to cut him off before he reached the park, but Landry poured on the speed, covering the space in no time, and then he was up the steps across from St. Louis Cathedral, and inside the square.

Lasalle didn't bother chasing him to the steps. Instead, he headed straight for the fence. A silver-painted, silver-clad giant robot-man stepped in front of him, his motions jerky and erratic. Lasalle tried to sidestep him, but the man kept moving with him.

"Police," Lasalle said. "Out of my way or I'll make you show your license."

The robot-man stepped aside, bowing abruptly at the waist and crooking one arm, as if to say, "Right this way." Lasalle rushed past him and went to the fence. A not-very-good artist had hung oil paintings of New Orleans street scenes there, and he started to complain when Lasalle put his foot on the low wall and grabbed the upper spikes of the iron fence. Lasalle ignored him and tried to miss the paintings as he hauled himself up. He didn't try too hard, though, figuring that if he accidentally put his foot through one, the art world would applaud.

Then he was on the grass on the far side, landing hard but breaking into a sprint. Landry was already halfway across the park, racing past the statue of Andrew Jackson. Lasalle angled after him, darting across the first strip of grass, then vaulting the hedge. He almost fell on the far side—it had been higher than he'd expected—but he managed to keep his balance after a couple of unsteady steps. "He's in the park," he said into his mic as he ran. "Heading south."

Sebastian was far behind, still trying to work his gangly form over the fence. Lasalle couldn't help him, though; he had to catch up with Landry.

When he saw his prey again, the man was almost

on the Decatur side of the park. Lasalle thought that if they had just waited by his truck, Landry would have come straight toward them. Of course, if they hadn't spotted Lasalle, he might have gone straight down St. Ann, or either direction down Chartres, too, so that logic didn't hold water.

At any rate, Landry changed course again, heading instead for the south corner of the square. There was no exit there, but Landry went over the fence, even more easily than Lasalle had. Lasalle followed, almost a minute behind, and saw Landry angling toward the Jax Brewery.

"He's headed for Jax," Lasalle said.

"We see him," Pride said. "We're on an interception course."

"You are?" Lasalle asked. They had been behind him just minutes before.

Then he looked up and saw a yellow pedicab streaking across Decatur, right at Landry. Sonja was at the pedals, and Pride was in the back. Landry tried to veer away from it, but Pride jumped out and ran him down. Sonja abandoned the cab in the middle of the street and joined in the chase. Landry dodged and weaved like a running back working his way through a defensive line. He ran past the old brewery and across the train tracks separating the French Quarter businesses from the thin grassy strip of Woldenberg Park, and up the steps to the Moonwalk that ran alongside the Mississippi.

Pride got a handful of his T-shirt on the steps, slowing Landry down just enough. Lasalle and Sonja hurtled up the grassy embankment and tackled him together, Sonja going low and Lasalle high. Landry landed face-first on the walkway, right before the river. Lasalle grabbed his arms and twisted them behind his back while Sonja sat on him to hold him down. Sebastian raced up a moment later and pulled handcuffs from his belt.

When he was cuffed, Pride squatted in front of him and showed the man his badge. "Bruno Landry," he said, "you're a hard man to find. But now that we've found you, we need to have a little talk…"

24

"I want my lawyer."

Landry had said it the first time while he was still on the ground, with Sonja on his back. He said it again after he had been hauled to his feet, and a couple more times on the way to the squad room. Now, in the interrogation room, he was still handcuffed and still saying it.

"So you've said, several times. Your lawyer's been called," Pride said. "But you can still change your mind and talk to us. We can help you in ways your lawyer can't."

Landry didn't say a word, but his flat expression spoke volumes. Pride could already tell he would be hard to break. He had to give it a shot, though. He didn't know how long he would have Landry in his hands, and he wanted to make good use of the opportunity.

"You might not fully understand the kind of trouble you're in, Bruno. It's not just that you assaulted two of my officers in public places—on video, in one instance. We know you killed Lt. Alpuente. We have video of you going into his room before he took a header off his balcony, and coming out after."

"You got squat."

"I just told you—"

Landry cut him off. "You told me you have video of me going into some hotel room and coming out again. I don't believe you, because I was never there. But even if I was, you don't have any video showing me killing whoever it is you say I killed, because I didn't. And if you had video, or witnesses, you'd say that. But you can't, because you don't."

And that, Pride knew, was a concise summation of his problem. He had video of *someone* going into and out of Alpuente's hotel room at the time of the murder. He was convinced that it was Landry. But the flaws in the video would make it easy for a defense attorney to discredit in court, and the one clear shot, from the reflection in the framed painting—showing someone in full Baron Samedi gear—wasn't enough to convincingly prove that Landry was indeed Samedi. The other clips of Samedi, including the one of him talking to Rich Brandt, were persuasive enough to convince the NCIS team, but would still be easy for a lawyer to knock down. And Landry was correct about the most important point: despite the fact that the murder had taken place in broad daylight in front of thousands of witnesses, many of whom had their cameras trained at or near the event, not a single frame of video or any eyewitnesses existed that definitively connected Landry to the killing.

The case was circumstantial at best. No physical evidence—not a fingerprint, not a hair, not a trace of DNA—put Landry in Alpuente's room. No transfer DNA had been found on Alpuente's body linking it to Landry, although he had picked up DNA from various previous guests in his room, just by being there. In court, a lawyer would have a field day with that.

All the defense had to establish was reasonable doubt, while the district attorney had to prove guilt. In Landry's case, absent a confession, that was going to be hard to do. Pride not only didn't have enough to convict Landry, he didn't even have enough yet to charge him.

"We'll prove it," Pride bluffed. "Don't you worry about that."

"I don't see how, because I wasn't there and I didn't do it."

"You can keep saying that all day long, Bruno. We both know it's not true. What I don't know yet is the why—what you had against Alpuente, or whether you were working for somebody else. Murder one is bad enough by itself, but when you add conspiracy charges to it, things get a lot worse. If you want to make it easy on yourself, you'll just tell me you did it, acting alone."

"I want my lawyer."

"Your lawyer's on the way."

"Then you can leave me alone till she gets here. I got nothin' to say to you."

"I'm just trying to help you, Landry," Pride said. He had been sitting across the table from the man, but now he rose and walked around the room, ticking off each item on his fingers as he ran through them. "Maybe Alpuente wronged you in some way, or threatened you. Maybe you went to see him and an argument got out of hand. Maybe you were under the influence of alcohol or drugs. There are lots of mitigating factors."

"Ain't no mitigatin' this, because I didn't do nothin'."

"See, that's the sticking point. Because we know you did. We're going to prove it. Your trial will be a long, ugly thing, and since you killed Lt. Alpuente—a naval officer with a sterling record—in the most high-profile way possible, it's going to be on the news every single day. You'll be dragged through the mud. Every nasty, unpleasant thing you've ever said or done—and we know there are plenty of those—will become common knowledge. Even if—it won't happen, but even if—by some miraculous fluke, you got off, you'd be finished in New Orleans. You'd be recognized everyplace you went. Everyone would know you're a killer."

"Sounds to me like you're reachin' pretty hard because you got nothin' on me."

"Not reaching at all. As we speak, one of my agents—the one you attacked at the Ronday-Vous—"

"I didn't know she was a cop!" Landry blurted. "She don't look like one!"

"She's a professional, and I know she identified herself, so that won't fly. Anyway, my point is, she's executing a search warrant on your home, now that we know where it is."

"She won't find nothin'."

"She'll find whatever's there to be found. Meanwhile, another agent—the one you threw out of his wheelchair in the middle of the street—"

"Dude jumped me!"

"—is going through your phone records. He'll know everyone you've ever called, everyone who's called you. We're going to pick through your life like it was a Thanksgiving turkey and we're very, very hungry."

"What about *my* rights?"

Landry hadn't been Mirandized yet, because he hadn't actually been arrested. "I have a feeling you've heard your rights described plenty of times. I can run through them again, if you want."

Just then, the door opened, and a tall, elegant-looking woman walked into the room. Pride didn't know her well, but he recognized her in an instant, as would nearly every law officer, attorney, and judge in the city. Allyson Woodhouse, the newest partner at the white shoe law firm of Clement, Wilson, Becker, & Woodhouse, was the defense attorney typically called upon by mob bosses, business leaders, and politicians who found themselves on the wrong side of the law— who, in New Orleans, were often the same people. Despite the lateness of the hour, she looked like she had just stepped out of a TV studio's green room; her blond hair fell precisely to her shoulders, not a strand out of place, her makeup was perfect, and her tailored gray suit was clean and unwrinkled.

"I'm here to protect your rights, Bruno," she said. She stopped and glared at Pride. "Why is this man in handcuffs?"

"Because he tried to beat the crap out of two NCIS agents tonight, Ms. Woodhouse."

"So you're charging him with that?"

"For starters."

"May I have a few moments with my client?"

"I must say, I'm surprised to see you here, Ms. Woodhouse," Pride said. "Bruno is not your typical client."

"Based on what?" she asked. "His ethnicity? His socioeconomic status? I'm surprised at you, Agent Pride."

"Let's just say, I doubt that he's been inside a lot of corporate boardrooms."

"Everyone is entitled to the best possible defense, including Mr. Landry—a fact you seem to have forgotten."

"I haven't forgotten. It's just that I haven't forgotten

your usual rates, either. Is he paying you himself, or is someone else footing the bill?"

"You know that's out of bounds, Pride. I will ask you one more time, may I speak with my client in private?"

"Certainly," Pride said, starting for the door. "But the cuffs stay on as long as he's in my house."

He left the room, closing the door behind him.

"Thanks for bringing me along, Sonja," Sebastian said. "Working in the field—it's still pretty cool, you know?" He extended his index finger, making his hand into a gun shape. "All James Bond and bang-bang and everything." As he said "Bang-bang," he crooked his finger as if pulling a trigger. "I've always had a problem knowing what to do with a hand gun. Not a handgun, but, you know, a gun made out of a hand. The index finger is supposed to be the barrel, but then when you use it to pull the trigger, the barrel's kind of pointing back at you. So then are you shooting yourself? Or is the barrel still there, but suddenly invisible? It's a real quandary."

"Not if you only use a real gun as a gun," Sonja countered. "And you remember that it's a tool, not a toy."

"Well, yeah, there's that, too."

They had a limited time in which to search Bruno Landry's home, a fact Sonja had known as soon as she heard that Allyson Woodhouse was representing Landry. Woodhouse was as high-powered as defense attorneys got in Louisiana, and if anyone could quash the warrant, she could. Which meant they had to work fast, and they had to make sure whatever they found would stand up in court. Sebastian's lab experience would make him a valuable asset on a quick search.

Landry lived across the river in Terrytown. He had provided the address once they'd gotten him back to the squad room. Sebastian had run the address and discovered that the small brick house belonged to someone named Darlington Trower—Darling, to his friends. Darling was currently serving a twenty-five-year bit in Angola for aggravated manslaughter, so his sister Desire was taking care of the property for him. She had apparently rented it out to Landry without benefit of a contract or any other legally binding agreement, but she and her husband lived just a couple of blocks away, and when Sonja had knocked on the door, Desire had grudgingly, grumblingly complied with the order to open up the house.

It was set back from the road by a small rectangle of neatly trimmed lawn. A couple of trees stood in the yard, offering an additional level of privacy; from the street, only the driveway and a covered carport were visible. The house had two bedrooms, one bath, a living room dominated by a TV set that seemed slightly smaller than the average movie theater screen, and a kitchen with a breakfast nook. Sonja assumed the furniture had come with the place—Landry seemed like the type who traveled light and was ready to hit the road at a moment's notice.

"What are we looking for, exactly?" Sebastian asked her.

"Anything we can find. Ideally, something that connects him to Alpuente. Loretta said Alpuente didn't have any traces of Landry on him, but that doesn't mean there was no transfer the other way."

"So we could be looking for something as small as a fleck of saliva on Landry's clothing," Sebastian said.

"If Landry's Baron Samedi costume is here, that

would be a good start. Look, Sebastian, this is a long shot. Landry's been around the block a few times. He knows how to stay off the radar, and he didn't use a weapon to kill Alpuente, so we're not going to stumble across a gun or anything—or we might, but that wouldn't mean anything. Chances are, we won't find anything obviously incriminating. We just have to give the place a once-over and hope something turns up."

"The old once-over," Sebastian said. "Sounds like a plan."

One of the bedrooms looked like it was being used to store all of Darling's personal effects while he was away; a quick pass through it revealed paperwork in his name, school records, clothing far too small for Landry, and other items that were completely useless to Sonja. The only thing that hinted at criminality was an assortment of knives and ammunition in various calibers, but with no corresponding guns. They finished that room in a hurry and moved on to the other bedroom.

The clothing in that closet would definitely have fit Landry. It was mostly jeans and sports jerseys, with a couple of long-sleeved dress shirts, along with miscellaneous accessories like belts and shoeboxes. A dresser contained underwear, socks, and T-shirts. No Baron Samedi outfit, though.

They upended his mattress, checked the bottoms of the dresser drawers for anything taped there, looked under the bed and through shoeboxes in the closet. Sonja didn't like this part of the job. Suspects might well have committed crimes, but they were still human beings, and violating their privacy like this was an unpleasant task, even though it was legal and necessary. The things she found were often unpleasant, too. Criminals often kept pornography around, and drug paraphernalia, and some held onto souvenirs of their crimes, which was particularly disturbing in the cases of killers and rapists. Sometimes she came across items that humanized them—a high school yearbook with fond wishes scrawled on the pages by classmates, notes from their mothers, baby booties from their infancy. Most troubling were the cases where she found those things side by side with the porn and dope.

Landry, by comparison, was almost a phantom. He had moved in with some clothes and a few personal items. He was apparently well groomed, and took good care of his skin and hair, judging by the bottles, cans, and boxes crammed into the bathroom cabinets. But other than those things, he was barely a presence in the house he rented or borrowed from Desire Trower.

She was almost ready to give up. She and Sebastian were working in different rooms now, trying to maximize their time, and at one point, Sebastian had gone into the backyard. Sonja glanced out a window, but didn't see much of interest out there. Then he came back in and said, "I still can't really believe I get paid to look in people's trash cans. Of course, I can't tell Mom about that—she worries about me enough as it is."

"Knock yourself out," Sonja said. Sebastian went back out into the night, and Sonja could hear him rummaging through the cans.

She was working in the kitchen, amazed at the sheer number of takeout dishes of beans and rice Landry had started and put in the refrigerator, half-eaten, when Sebastian came back in. "Is this something?" he asked.

She closed the refrigerator door. "Dude has, like, six months' worth of old takeout in here," she said. "I'm pretty sure some of these dishes have new life forms growing in them. What'd you find?"

"This." Sebastian held up a clear plastic bag on a wire hanger. Printed on the plastic were the words DEVEARE'S COSTUME SHOP, TIMBERLANE, LA.

"Yeah, Stringbean. That could definitely be something. Good job, partner."

Sebastian beamed.

25

After fifteen minutes, Allyson Woodhouse emerged from the interrogation room. She stopped outside the door and fixed Pride with a fierce glare. "My client and I will be leaving now."

"I'm sorry?"

"I said, we're going."

"You can leave, Ms. Woodhouse, but Landry's not going anywhere. He assaulted two of my agents, and we suspect him of killing an officer in the United States Navy."

"Yes, Agent Pride, he told me all that. He also told me that he didn't kill the officer, and that he was nowhere near the area when it happened. He described your 'evidence,' such as it is. Furthermore, he said that when you picked him up, your agents didn't identify themselves. Some woman came into an establishment where he was having a drink with a friend and brandished a weapon. He reacted in self-defense, cleared himself a path, and instead of staying and fighting—which, given his admittedly spotty record, could have landed him in trouble—he vacated the premises. When his attacker pursued, he panicked and ran.

"Later, still in fear for his life, a stranger in a wheelchair apparently ran into him in the street. When he tried to apologize and get out of the way, the man grabbed him. My client extricated himself and once again tried to leave the scene before the situation could escalate. His actions throughout were perfectly reasonable, given the circumstances, and not remotely criminal."

"That's if you believe that the agents didn't identify themselves as such," Pride argued. "My agents are professionals, and that's a mistake they just don't make."

"You have witnesses, then?"

"In the first case, there was a uniformed police officer on the scene."

"Mr. Landry says he saw the officer only after the unknown woman drew a weapon on him. The officer came in a different door than she did, and didn't say a word throughout the incident. He didn't know if the officer was there in a professional capacity, or if he was in the employ of some enemy of Mr. Landry's. That's hardly beyond belief in New Orleans, is it?"

"No, I suppose it's not. But your client's timeline is a little on the imaginative side." In Patton's case, he knew the encounter would have been captured on video, but he also knew there wouldn't be any sound, so no way to determine for sure whether Patton had identified himself.

Woodhouse brushed back an imaginary stray lock of hair; a habitual act, Pride guessed, since it was still where it belonged. "Agent Pride, I have the greatest respect for Mr. Landry, as I do all my clients, but I would not describe him as a particularly imaginative fellow."

"I was trying to be polite, Ms. Woodhouse, but if you want me to call him a liar, I will."

"I don't want you to call him anything. Including a

taxi. I'll give him a ride home myself."

"He's not going any—"

"Yes he is," she interrupted. "Unless you'd like me to sue the federal government for false imprisonment, and name you as a party to the lawsuit. You don't have anything to hold him on. If you insist on holding him anyway, I'll have him out the moment we go before a judge, and the lawsuit will be filed within the hour."

"Look, Ms. Woodhouse—"

"You can call me Allyson, Dwayne. We've both been around this city long enough to know how this will play out, so let's quit wasting everybody's time. If and when you come up with something that will stick, you can charge Mr. Landry. Until then, if you need to reach him, you can call me at my firm. I'm sure you have the number."

Pride readied half a dozen arguments, but dismissed each one as soon as he'd thought of it. She was right. When Allyson Woodhouse came into a case, prosecutors turned timid. Eyewitnesses recanted their stories. Veteran cops trembled in their combat boots. She rarely lost, and she showed no mercy along the way.

Pride knew his case was weak. He'd have to have a lot more definitive evidence against Landry to charge him, and so far, he and his team had come up short.

"Okay, Allyson," he said. "You win. For now. I know Landry's guilty, and I'll prove it, I promise you. Not even you will be able to get him out of this one. But for the moment, he's all yours, and you're welcome to him. Just do me—and yourself—one favor."

"What's that?"

"Keep him on a tight leash."

* * *

"Was that…?" Patton asked after Woodhouse and Landry had gone.

"Allyson Woodhouse," Pride said, sinking into a desk chair.

"How does a dirtbag like Landry get a lawyer like Allyson Woodhouse?" Lasalle asked.

"That's what I've been wondering, too. She doesn't come cheap, and I don't think Landry is a particularly wealthy man."

"Somebody's paying her," Patton said. "She don't cross the street for free."

"And if we knew who that was, we'd have a better sense of what's going on here," Pride agreed. "But that's privileged information."

"I could find out."

"Not that way," Pride said, knowing what he meant. Hacking Woodhouse's private financial records would be a crime with grave consequences if it were ever discovered. Sometimes the unit had to finesse the law, but interfering with attorney–client privilege was another thing entirely. "Not yet, anyway. We'll nail him and we'll figure out who's behind him. And if we can't, maybe we'll revisit your idea."

"Whatever." Patton shrugged. Pride knew he could have done it in the time it took to tell him not to, but that was a line Pride wasn't ready to cross.

"I've been doing some research online, King," Lasalle said, "and I've got something that might be of interest."

"What is it, Christopher?"

"Seems Bruno Landry and your new friend Burl Robitaille go way back."

"Really? That *is* interesting. How far back?"

"High school, at least. They played football together, down in Chalmette. Robitaille was quarterback and team captain, and Landry was a wide receiver, and his go-to guy. They set a passing record for Jefferson Parish that held for eleven years."

"Now that you mention it, that does seem to ring a bell," Pride said.

"And guess who else was in school with them," Lasalle said.

"Who?"

"According to the school yearbook, he was called Ricky Brandt back then."

"Rich Brandt?" Pride asked.

"The one and only. Even in high school, he looked like a sleaze."

"A leopard can't change his spots," Patton said.

"Maybe in the morning you can take a deeper dive on Brandt, Chris, and I'll take Mr. Robitaille up on his kind invitation to visit."

"Uh, King?" Patton said. "I hate to break it to you, but it *is* morning. Has been for a couple of hours, now."

Pride had been vaguely aware of it, but now that Patton mentioned it, exhaustion felt like it would overtake him within minutes. "I guess it is, Patton. Maybe we should try to get some shuteye. Anyone heard from Sonja?"

"She's on her way back," Patton said. "She called a little while ago; I meant to tell you, but you were busy arguing with that shark in high heels. Said she found something that might help. Actually, she said Sebastian found it, but I assumed she was just hallucinating that part from lack of sleep."

His smile made clear that he was kidding. Sebastian was often the butt of jokes among the team, but no one doubted his skills as a scientist or as a field agent. He had already proved to be an enormous asset to the team.

"Okay," Pride said. "I guess we can stay up a little longer, to see what she's got. But then we all hit the sack for a while. And that's an order."

"Need more coffee," Sebastian grumbled. Everyone gathered around the wrought-iron table under the Café du Monde's green-and-white striped canopy was looking a little bleary-eyed, except Loretta. Pride glanced past her, through Washington Artillery Park's screen of massive oaks toward the Jax Brewery building, not far away from where the long chase of Bruno Landry had ended on the other side of the Moonwalk.

Pride took a sip from his mug, tasting the chicory that separated New Orleans' version of café au lait from that of everyplace else, and swallowed it down with a smile. "Some days there's not enough coffee in the world," he said. "But we got through yesterday, and we'll all get through today, too."

"I'm not so sure," Sebastian said.

Loretta gave him an encouraging shove on the shoulder. "You'll do fine!" she said. She looked as chipper as could be, as if she had just slept for twelve hours. Maybe she had. "You've been out later at comic conventions and late-night gaming sessions."

"Those are different," he said. "There's an energy there that keeps me going."

"You saying I don't give off the right kind of energy?" Sonja asked.

"I'm saying digging through some stranger's underwear drawer and garbage cans isn't my idea of a good time."

"But you made the crucial find," Sonja reminded him.

Sebastian smiled. "Well, that's true. I do have a knack for coming through in the clinch, don't I?"

"You sure do," Pride replied. "Sonja, you'll be visiting Deveare's this morning, right?"

"They open at nine," she said. "I'll be there."

"And you're visiting Rich Brandt, right, Christopher?"

"I'm gonna try to get to his place before he goes to work, so I can catch him off guard. And without Hamilton and the city attorney around."

"Good idea." Pride put down his mug and picked up a beignet, laden with powdered sugar, from his plate. He tapped off some of the powdered sugar and took a bite, then noticed Loretta watching him.

"Seeing you eat that reminds me," she said. "The pie Christopher picked up at Flanders' Pie Hole was clean. No L-DOPA at all. And delicious, I might add."

"You didn't save me any?" Lasalle whined.

"You were right there. I assumed that you would have had the foresight to buy some to go, if you were going to want some."

"Guess my mind was on other things," he said.

"You go back there," Patton said, "grab a pie for me. Don't even matter what kind."

"A whole pie?" Lasalle asked.

"Hey, you only live once."

"As I was saying," Loretta began, a sure sign that she was shifting the conversation back to the business at hand, "the same is not true of the food from Lt. Alpuente's home. Some of that was *loaded* with L-DOPA. I think it's safe to say that whoever was dosing him with the stuff was doing it there."

"We'll need a list of everyone who had access to the house," Pride said. "Did he have a cleaning service? Gardener? Friends over?"

"I'll call Michelle St. Cyr," Sonja said. "She would probably know, better than his mother. I don't think his mother and uncle leave their farm much."

"That's definitely the impression I got, too," Lasalle added. "They'd see him if he came to visit, but they didn't go visit him."

Pride finished his last beignet and drained his mug. "I think everybody knows what they're working on today. I'm heading back to Plaquemines Parish to try my hand at some skeet shooting."

"Be careful," Loretta urged him. "When there are guns around, you have a bad habit of becoming the target."

"I'll watch my step," he promised. "He invited me down, and casual conversation is often considerably more enlightening than interrogation. You don't have to worry about me." He pushed his chair back and stood up. "It's a glorious morning in the most beautiful city on Earth," he said. "Everybody go. Learn things."

26

Traffic was on Sonja's side, for a change, and she got out to Timberlane early. She found Deveare's Costume Shop in a small strip mall, sandwiched between a mailing and shipping store and a sandwich shop. A subtle scent of meat permeated the parking lot.

Sitting in her car, she called the number Patton had given her for Michelle St. Cyr. When the woman answered, Sonja identified herself as an associate of Pride's.

"He was so nice," Michelle said. "Has he—have you guys found out anything?"

"We believe we're close," Sonja said. That was true; they were certain that Landry was the killer. But they were just as certain that they couldn't yet convict him. Meanwhile, he was still on the streets, and telling Michelle that would only frighten her. Since they had no reason to believe she was in danger, Sonja held that part back. "Very close," she added. "And of course, as soon as we make an arrest, we'll let you know."

"Thank you," Michelle said. "You have no idea what this has been like. Or maybe you do, I don't know."

"I've… lost people," Sonja said. "But not a fiancé. So no, not like that. I'm very sorry for your loss."

"I think everybody at work knows about us, but they're pretending that they don't. I don't know if it's because they think they're respecting our privacy, because we tried to keep it under wraps, or if it's just easier for them to avoid talking about it around me. But it's like they're making it like he never existed, already. It's horrible."

"I'm sure it is." Sonja was afraid Michelle would start to weep. She wouldn't blame her if she did, but she hated dealing with crying women. It always made her feel awkward. She knew the words she was supposed to say, and she could do it, as she had with Alpuente's mother. But as soon as someone started really crying, the words fled from her mind and she had to fight to get them back. She had faced down murderous drug lords who didn't scare her as much as a single crying woman did.

"Anyway," Sonja said quickly, hoping to fend off the tears, "I was wondering if you could tell me who might have had a key to Lt. Alpuente's house, or who had regular access to it. Did someone clean it for him, or—"

"Oh, no," Michelle replied. "I didn't even have a key. That wasn't Ed's home, it was just a local base of operations for him. He worked and ate and slept there, but his life was up here. I was only in that house a couple of times, when we did something down in New Orleans at night. Generally, if we were together on weekends, it was because he came home to Nicholson."

"So you can't think of anyone he might have had over or let in?"

"I mean, I guess his landlady had a key. Other than that? No, nobody comes to mind. He did his own cleaning, such as it was."

Something at Deveare's caught Sonja's eye, and after a moment, she realized what it was—an illuminated OPEN sign in the window had flickered on. "Okay, that's good to know," she said. "Thank you. If you do think of anyone else, you have my number, or you can always call Special Agent Pride. I promise, we're going to get you the answers you need."

"Thank you, Agent Percy," Michelle said. "It's good to know Ed's not being forgotten."

"Not a chance," Sonja said. "That's not happening."

She finished the call, then got out of her car and walked into Deveare's. The front window was full of Mardi Gras-appropriate costumes, rich and colorful, with plenty of shiny fabrics and glittering accessories. The store was good-sized and evidently profitable, and the rents here were surely much lower than they would have been across the river. The owners had used every available inch of space, it seemed, even installing a dry cleaner's-style conveyor belt to hang costumes in two layers and make them accessible at the touch of a button. Sonja could smell the heavy oil used to lubricate the machinery.

In the front third of the store, mannequins stood around wearing selected costumes. Interspersed with those were racks of accessories, tables of packaged costumes, and scattered pedestals holding thick binders full of plastic-covered pages showing the hundreds or thousands of costumes available, presumably on the conveyor belts in back. Off to the right were three fitting rooms. Masks of every description were mounted high up on the walls. Behind all that was the sales counter, where a short, pudgy man with wispy gray hair eyed her expectantly.

"Let me guess," he said with a lecherous grin.

"You need an Easter Bunny costume. Or maybe a sexy bunny. I've got both, in just your size."

When she showed him her badge, his smile vanished and his brow furrowed.

"All I need is some information," she said.

"That's a shame. Not everybody can pull off the sexy bunny costume quite as well as they think, but you—"

"Save it," Sonja said. "I need to know about a Baron Samedi costume."

"Which one? I must have rented twenty-five in the last week. Samedi's huge at Mardi Gras, you know. Are you interested in the deluxe? The fancy dress costume? The masquerade ball version?"

"You tell me." She took out her phone and showed him a photograph of Landry in the costume, pulled from one of the better video clips Patton had found. "This one."

The man took the phone from her and studied the image. "That looks like the traditional men's," he said, "in the largest size we've got. He did a pretty good job with the makeup, too." He handed back the phone. "The gloves are a nice touch."

"They don't come with it?"

"None of our Samedis have gloves. He added those himself. It works, though. Maybe I'll add them for next year."

"Can you tell me who rented it?"

"First, are you sure it came from here?"

"Pretty sure, yes."

"You wouldn't happen to have the receipt?"

"No, all I saw was the bag." She pointed to the conveyor belt behind him, where all the costumes hung in similar clear plastic wrappings. "Like those."

"That's kind of our hallmark," he said. "So you

know every costume has been cleaned and is ready for you. Or, you know, for whoever."

"Well, it had your bag, so I'm assuming it came from here. Can you look through your records?"

"It'll take me a few minutes."

"I can wait."

"All right," he said. He pointed to a push-button bell on the counter, next to a multi-line telephone. "If anyone else comes in, please tell them to ring that. I might not hear the door from my office."

"I will," Sonja promised.

"Very well, then. I'll be back directly."

He moved through the rows of plastic-wrapped costumes with a practiced stride, barely rustling the bags as he went. Somewhere behind those, a door opened and closed; Sonja couldn't see it, but she could hear it in the quiet of the shop.

When he was gone, she flipped through one of the costume notebooks. The front section was all Mardi Gras and Krewe costumes, but behind that were cowboys and princesses, pirates and superheroes and movie monsters, animals and clowns. She saw the "sexy bunny" costume he'd wanted to put her in. He was right, she would look good in it. But if he tried to push it on her again, she might have to shoot him.

Turning away from the book, she noticed that one of the phone line lights had come on. She stepped behind the counter and tried to move as silently through the forest of plastic bags as he had, but she couldn't; they crackled like dry leaves when she did.

Then she heard the office door open. She hurried to the other side of the counter and back to the costume book. The light on the phone was off. When the man returned, he was at least two shades paler than he had been.

"I'm sorry," he said as he approached. He stepped to the counter and put his hands on it. They were trembling, so he took them away, finally sticking them in his pockets. "I was mistaken. That Samedi costume didn't come from us."

"You were pretty sure a couple of minutes ago."

"I was wrong. We only have one traditional men's Baron Samedi in that size, and we didn't rent it this year."

"Would you take another look, sir? This is very important."

"Look, I can't help you. I made a mistake, that's all. You showed me a tiny picture on a phone, and I misidentified it. As I said, ours don't even come with gloves. Those gloves were pretty clearly part of the set."

"They're just black leather gloves."

"All the same. I wish I could help you, but I can't."

"Would a subpoena change your mind?"

"Do whatever you have to do, but that costume did not come from my shop."

"Whoever you're afraid of, sir, we can protect you."

"Please," he said. "Just go. I can't do anything for you."

"Oookay," Sonja replied. She started for the door. "You might see me again, though."

"Save yourself the trip."

"Oh, trust me," she said, stopping with the door half-open. "It's no trouble."

Rich Brandt's house was three stories tall and set well back from the road, near Audubon Park in one direction and Clancy's, one of Lasalle's favorite restaurants, in another. It was deep and narrow, as houses were in many of the city's neighborhoods, with a two-car garage on the ground floor.

Lasalle climbed a steep flight of stairs leading to a porch that looked more like a garden, with tomatoes and strawberries growing in planters on the floor, and ferns and other greens drooping from hanging wire baskets. Somewhere behind the jungle, he located a doorbell and pressed it.

The woman who answered the door seemed harried, which might have been due to the blood-curdling screams Lasalle heard coming from an infant somewhere inside.

"If you're selling something, I don't need it. If you're pushing a cause, I'm not interested. And if you're looking for a handout, screw off. I am not in the mood today."

"None of the above, ma'am," Lasalle said. He identified himself and showed her his badge. "Is Mr. Brandt home?"

She stared at him so long he started to wonder if he still had powdered sugar on his face from the beignets. Finally, she said, "You don't look like a cop."

"I usually hear that I look exactly like a cop, so thank you for that. I am one, just the same."

"He's upstairs," she said. "I'll fetch him." She started to close the door, then opened it. "How are you with colicky babies?"

"Pretty good, actually," he replied. He loved kids, and he found himself missing Tucker, if not so much Tucker's mother Melody, who had lied to him about the boy's parentage. Tucker had turned out not to be his son, after all, but in the short time they had been together, they'd bonded.

"In here," she said. He followed her inside, and she pointed toward the kitchen. "I would've been happy with the two older ones," she said. She rolled her eyes toward the ceiling as she said the next part. "They're already at school. But no, he wanted another. So that's Pammie. Do what you can with her, and Rich will be right down."

Lasalle looked inside as she clomped up the stairs. Pammie sat in a high chair, wearing a plastic bib that curled up at the bottom to catch any dropped food. The high chair's tray was covered in Cheerios and spit.

"Hey, Pammie," he said as he entered. He used a soft, friendly voice. Kids at the hospital responded to it. So did Pammie, looking up at the stranger. "I'm Chris. How you doin' today?"

She blinked a couple of times, and he was afraid she was about to start screaming again. He scooped her up out of the high chair and bounced her in the air a couple of times. "Cheerios not doin' it for you this morning? How about some crawfish étouffée? Dirty beans and rice? You're a New Orleans baby, you got to have something better than cereal out of some old box, don't you?"

He jiggled her a couple more times, and got a smile in return. Overhead, he heard two sets of feet coming back downstairs. A moment later, Rich Brandt appeared in the doorway, still knotting what looked like an expensive silk tie. His shirt was sky blue, and the slate gray jacket over his arm matched his pleated pants. His aftershave entered the room before he did.

"Detective…" he began.

Lasalle corrected him. "Special Agent Lasalle."

"Yes, right. We met yesterday in the conference room."

"Correct," Lasalle said. Brandt's wife squeezed past him and took Pammie from his hands with a look of gratitude.

"Let's step into the living room, Special Agent," Brandt said.

"That's fine."

He followed Brandt out of the kitchen and into a tastefully furnished room. From the huge windows that encompassed most of the exterior wall, Lasalle got a glimpse of the park two blocks west.

"It's much calmer here," Brandt said. "Would you like to sit down?"

"That's not necessary, sir," Lasalle answered.

"What can I do for you, then? I told you folks everything I know about that man at the parade."

"Not everything."

"No? I thought sure I did."

"You didn't mention that you went to high school with Landry."

A look of shock flashed across Brandt's face, but he erased it so quickly, it could easily have been missed or taken for a shadow going across the sun. "Did I? I don't remember him."

"You did. He and Burl Robitaille were the heroes of the football team. You didn't talk about old times when you met with Robitaille yesterday?"

"Burl Robitaille has four restaurant locations in the city of New Orleans," Brandt said. "When we're in conference at City Hall, we're usually discussing those."

"So Landry didn't come up."

"Why would he? Like I said, I don't even remember going to school with him. I admit, I wasn't much for school sports. I think I went to a basketball game once, because a girl I was dating wanted to see one."

"I see," Lasalle said.

"I was on the student council," Brandt said. "That's where my interests were. Senior class president."

"I saw that in your yearbook. I also saw a picture of the three of you sitting together on some bleachers. You looked pretty chummy."

He had to admit, Brandt was good at disguising his reactions. He guessed that was the politician in him, always on his guard and focused on what kind of impression he made. "Like you said, Burl was the star quarterback and captain of the team. I was class president. We had to spend some time together, especially for things like yearbook photos. If you say this other guy, Landry, was in a picture with us, I believe you. I honestly don't remember him."

"Excuse me if I find that a little hard to believe, sir," Lasalle said.

"You'll believe what you want to believe, I'm sure. Now that you mention it, though, when I said I'd met Landry at a party, I think it might have been at Burl's home. He throws some pretty big bashes there, though not so many now that his wife is gone. It's entirely possible that I met Landry there without even remembering him from high school. I doubt that he remembered me, either. A lot of water under the bridge; none of us look like we did then."

"No, we don't," Lasalle admitted. "And yet, you recognized him in full Baron Samedi makeup and costume, on a busy street, in the middle of a parade, when he just happened to walk by."

Brandt squeezed his lower lip. If that was a tell of some kind, Lasalle didn't know him well enough to speculate as to what it meant. "Something about his eyes," he said. "I noticed it and it just struck me."

"He has a scar on one," Lasalle said.

"Yes!" Brandt snapped his fingers, then touched the outside corner of his left eye. "Right here. That's what it was. I saw that—the makeup didn't disguise that—and I just knew who it was. I'm good with names, so it came back to me."

"You're good with names, except of people you knew in high school."

"I'm telling you, Agent Lasalle, I didn't really know him in high school. I had my clique, my group of friends. I knew Burl because we were both big men on campus, as they say, but we didn't hang out. My clique wasn't the jocks. I was a student council, debate club nerd."

Lasalle didn't want to believe the man. It was too coincidental—those two running into each other on St. Charles Avenue, just minutes before Landry threw Alpuente off the hotel balcony.

At the same time, he found Brandt's story convincing. He wasn't coming across as evasive or dishonest. He made a good point about the nature of high school friendships. Lasalle had hung with the jocks in high school, and now that he thought about it, he couldn't come up with the name of his senior class president. He remembered her face, vaguely, but if he saw her today, he couldn't say for sure that he'd recognize her after the passage of the years. And Brandt was a few years older than he was.

"Yesterday, Pride said this was all connected to the death of that naval officer during the parade," Brandt said. "Is this Landry a person of interest in that case?"

"I can't comment on an ongoing investigation," Lasalle said. His usual answer in such circumstances.

"I'm not the press, I'm a member of the mayor's inner circle."

"I understand that."

Brandt looked like he was about to raise another protest, but then he waved it away. "Never mind. I respect your position, Agent Lasalle. I'm sure when there's definitive progress in the case, Mayor Hamilton will be informed, and I'll hear it from him."

"I'm sure he will be," Lasalle said.

"Have I answered all your questions? I'm going to be late for work as it is. And Hamilton's a stickler for promptness."

"I think so, yes," Lasalle replied. "Thanks for your cooperation."

"Any time," Brandt said. "Have a terrific day."

"I'll try. You do the same."

Lasalle was almost out the door when Brandt's wife hurried over to him, still holding the baby. "Thank you for whatever you did," she said. "Pammie's feeling much better now."

"She just wanted some dirty beans and rice," Lasalle told her. Off her shocked expression, he stepped back into the jungle and closed the door behind him.

27

Pride was passing through Belle Chasse on Louisiana Highway 23 when Sebastian called. He considered letting it go to voicemail, just because he would be at Robitaille's soon, and brief conversations with Sebastian were less common than Bigfoot sightings. But the forensic scientist wouldn't call if it weren't important, so he took the call.

"Hello, Sebastian."

"Hi, Pride. It's Seb—well, you already knew that. Modern technology, huh? We're living in the future. Except without the jet packs and flying cars and tricorders. Though I'm still hoping those are coming soon."

"Do you have something for me?" Pride asked, hoping to prod the man closer to his point.

"Something?" Sometimes, Pride wondered why he seemed to make Sebastian nervous. The truth was, almost everyone made Sebastian a little nervous. But he saw Pride as the boss, the authority figure, and that seemed to ramp up his anxiety even further. "Oh, right. I do, in fact, have something. I've identified that substance you found on some of those food containers at Lt. Alpuente's house in Tremé. The kind of tacky, sticky stuff?"

"What is it?"

"It's oil. More specifically, it's crude oil. The unrefined stuff."

"He got crude oil on food containers? How did he do that?"

"I wasn't there, so I can only speculate, but you said those containers were on the floor, right? My guess is he brought the oil in on his shoes, and then set the containers down in it."

"I guess that could happen," Pride said. "Is there anything else?"

"You haven't asked me where the oil came from."

"I kind of did, when I asked how he did that. But okay, Sebastian, where did the oil come from?"

Pride could hear Sebastian's grin when he answered. "From the BP oil spill."

"Sebastian, that was, what, 2010?"

"That's right. The Deepwater Horizon rig blew on April 20, 2010."

"He didn't rent that house until late last year."

"I'm not saying it's been in the house since 2010. The vast majority of the oil from the Deepwater Horizon blowout has long since been cleaned up. But there's still some lingering in remote coastline areas, especially in St. Bernard and Plaquemines Parishes. Lt. Alpuente was supposedly working on wetlands issues out there, so it's possible that he got some on his shoes or boots, then came home and tracked it on the floor, or got it on his hands, and transferred it to those containers."

"Okay, I'll grant you that's a possibility. Is there anything else?"

"Anything else else?" Sebastian echoed. "That was already an 'anything else.' I thought that was some pretty good detective work."

"Sorry," Pride said. "You're right, Sebastian, it was. Do me a favor?"

"Sure thing, Dwayne."

"Call the squad room and let the team know. I'll be at my destination in a few minutes, and I don't want to be on the phone when I get there."

"Roger, Dodger. I mean, umm, over and out."

"Bye, Sebastian."

"Right, yes, that. Goodbye."

BP oil, Pride thought. The longer this case dragged on, the more it seemed to center on Plaquemines Parish and not New Orleans at all.

Approaching Belle Chasse, with Robitaille's house on the far side, he hoped he wasn't heading straight into the lion's den.

Patton had started going through Alpuente's work files on the laptop Pride had brought him, but then things had happened so fast he'd had to shift over to other tasks. Lasalle had taken over, but then he had been retasked, too. Sebastian's call, coming shortly before Lasalle reached the squad room, sent him back to the laptop. The missing component all along had been motive—why would anyone kill a Navy lieutenant working on issues of coastal degradation? What was it in his life that had made him a target?

But when oil entered the equation, things changed. Most murders revolved around passion or money, and the oil business meant big money. BP had spent billions to clean up the Deepwater Horizon spill—and although it ate up profits for a while, the company could ultimately afford it, because oil companies were some of the wealthiest businesses on the planet.

The idea that a major oil company had targeted Alpuente for murder was the stuff of potboilers and TV thrillers, but that didn't mean there weren't individuals who might have taken a dim view of his activities. Historically, much of Louisiana's economy had depended on the oil and gas industries, which employed tens of thousands of people and pumped huge amounts of money into New Orleans and other cities. The recent slump in oil prices had hurt the area hard, and with the high-profile oil spill essentially mopped up, those billions were no longer flowing into the economy. There were plenty of oil industry workers on the unemployment rolls these days, or working in menial jobs for far less than they'd earned on the rigs and pipelines. If the lieutenant's research revolved around the spill's effect on wetlands, plenty of local folks might have considered him a threat to their livelihoods.

Lasalle scrolled through the lists of files on Alpuente's laptop. Draft reports, photographs saved as JPEG images, scanned questionnaires, and spreadsheets. Lots and lots of spreadsheets. Lasalle was pretty sure nothing more boring than spreadsheets had ever been invented. Reading them made watching paint dry look like high-octane entertainment.

Sadly, he had no choice. Once he had skimmed the report drafts and checked out the photos, he opened the first spreadsheet and tried to keep his eyes from glazing over.

"You awake, Lasalle?"

Lasalle turned in his chair to see that Patton had quietly entered the bullpen. "Barely. This stuff is making my eyes bleed."

Patton laughed. "That's because you've never spent

an eighteen-hour day writing lines of code. Once you do that, nothing you encounter on a computer screen will ever faze you again. I mean, except this video I saw once of ostriches mating. Some things are just plain *wrong*."

"This probably isn't as bad as that," Lasalle said. "It's just spreadsheets from Alpuente's computer." He filled the other man in on Sebastian's call, and the possible oil connection.

"Did you find anything in the spreadsheets?" Patton asked when he was finished.

"It's hard to say. In the reports, there are a lot of calculations that I can't always follow. The spreadsheets clarify some of it, and between those and the text, what I'm getting is that he's studying the wetlands loss in a particular area of the St. Bernard Parish coast. He's got references in there to a proposed high-end resort development project owned by something called Southern Louisiana Holdings, LLC, but it doesn't look like he's been able to figure out who all is involved in that, and, from what I can tell, there doesn't seem to be any specific connection between that partnership and the oil industry. It looks like there are shell companies on top of shell companies—like those Russian dolls, you know, that fit into each other?"

"Nesting dolls," Patton said. "I can dig it. Lots of folks with too much money to burn hide their corporate identities that way. I think if you look deep enough, it turns out that all the money in the world belongs to some old geezer hiding in a cave someplace, and the rest of us are just borrowing it. Send me what you've got and I'll do some checking."

"Thanks. It's coming your way in a minute."

He transferred the files to an internal shared drive,

and told Patton where to find them. Then he shifted to another question that had been dogging him—the precise location of the development in question. Finding those coordinates was comparatively easy, once he had figured out how to navigate the parish's online records system.

While he was doing that, Sonja breezed in. "It's like study hall in here," she said. "What have you pod people done with the caveman and Triple P?"

Thankful for another break from the mind-numbing online research, Lasalle stood up and stretched. "Where've you been, Percy? Costume shopping?"

"Let's just say that Timberlane is not the most exciting part of the Gulf Coast," she replied. "I went to that costume shop. At first, the dude was positive that Landry's Baron Samedi costume was one of his. Proud of it, in fact. But when I asked for rental records, he went into the back and made a phone call. When he came out again, he said no way, the costume couldn't possibly be from there."

"So he's hiding something," Lasalle said.

"Somebody told him to hide something," Patton added.

"That's definitely how it looked. He was really nervous when he came back out. Hands trembling, the whole bit."

"He's afraid of someone," Patton said.

"Well, Landry's still on the loose, so I don't blame him."

"You think he called Landry?" Lasalle asked.

"I don't know. Sebastian didn't find a receipt or any kind of paperwork for the costume at Landry's house, just that plastic bag. I don't know if he rented it himself, or if it was rented for him."

"He don't seem like the kind of guy who'd check Yelp for the best local costume shops," Patton said. "Though Mardi Gras does bring that out in some unexpected places."

"He also doesn't seem like the kind who'd go all the way down to Timberlane to get a Baron Samedi costume," Sonja said. "Not when every costume shop in eight parishes carries those."

"Probably every costume shop in the state," Lasalle said. "But if he didn't rent it for himself, who did?"

"That's the million-dollar question," Sonja answered. "Which I had hoped to get an answer for at Deveare's. Did Landry kill Alpuente on his own, or was he working for somebody else? And if so, who?"

"Maybe we can figure that out from what's on his computer," Patton said, "but it's gonna take some time. Trying to narrow down this corporation's ownership is like trying to untangle the world's biggest ball of string, only some fool's dumped glue all over it so it don't untangle anymore."

"What have you got, Lasalle?" she asked.

He tapped the computer screen. "I think I've found this development that Alpuente mentioned a lot in the reports he was writing. There's some link between this place and the loss of coastal wetlands. Sebastian says the gunk on Alpuente's food containers was crude oil from the Deepwater Horizon spill, and it looks like that oil might have contributed to the disappearing wetlands. But according to his research, it's not just oil putting the wetlands at risk, it's also climate, and development, and other factors."

Sonja stood behind him and looked at his monitor, which showed a satellite map of the St. Bernard Parish coastline. "That area looks familiar," she said. "Isn't that near where we were the other day?"

"Yeah, I think you're right. I was so focused on the development's boundaries, I wasn't looking at the big picture." He switched to a satellite photograph of the area, then zoomed in on it. The land that was under development had been pristine when the photo was taken, with no sign of what was to come. But when he clicked over to the right, moving slightly down the coast, he saw a piece of property with cultivated fields and dirt roads cut into it, and a few small structures scattered about. He zoomed in further, and the largest of those structures was revealed as a ramshackle farmhouse. "That doesn't look like the kind of neighbor a fancy resort would want to be next to."

"Chris," Sonja said. "Look closer. That's Alpuente's mother's farm!"

"You're right," Lasalle said. "Again, I wasn't seeing the forest for the trees. That's why it looks so familiar." He zoomed out a little and eyed the proximity of the two properties. As far as he could tell on-screen, they were directly adjoining. "So maybe Lt. Alpuente had a personal reason for investigating this, as well as a professional one. Remember how his mother and uncle told us the farming and fishing had been bad for the last several years? Maybe it still hasn't recovered from the spill."

"Yeah," Sonja said. "And he had that Dan Petro voodoo doll—the saint who's supposed to protect farmers. Maybe it wasn't just for his own protection. I think we need another look at that place. And at the new next-door neighbors, it sounds like."

"I'm driving," Lasalle said.

"You always drive."

"That's because I love my truck more than you've ever loved anything with wheels."

Sonja pondered that for a moment, then nodded. "Okay, you drive."

28

"Special Agent Pride!" Burl Robitaille threw his front door open and stood with his feet firmly planted, his hands widespread. He was wearing a textbook Southern country-squire outfit: white linen pants with suspenders and a striped, pastel shirt. The cuffs were rolled back to show off his deeply tanned, strong forearms. "I feel like we're becoming old friends."

"We've certainly seen a lot of each other these last couple of days," Pride said. "You kindly invited me to visit, so I thought I'd take you up on the offer."

Robitaille moved out of the doorway, giving Pride space to enter. "Well, come on in. No need for friends, old or new, to stand on ceremony. Can I get you some sweet tea? Coffee? Something stronger? Mint juleps and this house go together like ducks and water, I must say."

"I imagine they would," Pride answered. He wanted to get Robitaille talking, to try to catch him off guard. But it seemed a little early in the day for mint juleps, even in a house that would have looked at home on any Southern plantation of the pre-Civil War era. He stepped into the foyer, and Robitaille pushed the door closed behind him. The space was grand and marble-floored, with a ceiling somewhere in the heavens above and a magnificent curving staircase leading up toward it. "Sweet tea would be great, thank you."

"We'll have it on the veranda," Robitaille said. He walked through the house, out of the foyer and into an expansive living room. The outside of the house looked traditional, but inside the rooms were far larger than would have been found in the old plantation houses. The furnishings looked like they'd been chosen by a decorator, but with some touches that were pure Robitaille, including a series of football jerseys framed in massive shadowboxes hanging on the walls. They all had his name printed on them. "It's a perfect day, isn't it? Nothing beats spring in Louisiana."

"I'm with you there, sir," Pride said. "This is quite a place."

"I've been very lucky. I'll tell you, sometimes I wish there was a Mrs. Robitaille to share it all with."

Pride felt a sudden but momentary pang of regret for his marriage. He didn't miss Linda every day, like he had once feared he might. But he understood something of what Robitaille felt. "I know what you mean. All this space, and no one to share it with. Must get lonely."

Robitaille chuckled. "It does, but I don't want to exaggerate. As I told you before, it's far too much house for me. But I entertain a lot. I was married once, early on, but it didn't take. I could have married again, if I'd wanted, but all the potential Mrs. Robitailles I've met were somehow worse than none at all. Probably I'm just a selfish cuss. I have my businesses to keep me busy, though, and my staff helps keep me from being a miserable old bachelor. And of course, the animals help, too."

He kept walking, toward a tall French door that led onto a rear veranda, but Pride stopped in front of a maroon jersey with a white "21" on the back. "This one's from high school, isn't it?"

Robitaille stopped. "That's right. Chalmette High."

"I remember hearing about you, even then. One of the best quarterbacks this area's ever seen. Who was that wide receiver you used to hit all the time with those long bombs?"

Robitaille's eyes narrowed, as if he were reappraising. It was subtle, but Pride noticed just the same. "There were several," he said. "I played JV and varsity. Four years of high school ball, four of college, then the pros."

"I mean in high school. There was one—you and he set a record, didn't you?"

"That was Bruno Landry," Robitaille said sharply.

"That's right, Landry! Whatever happened to him?"

"I have no idea. He dropped off my radar after high school. I don't think he went to college. It's a shame, too—he could have had a career in the NFL, with his hands."

"That's too bad," Pride said. "But typical. We make friends in high school, people we think we'll be close to for the rest of our lives. Then we just drift apart. College, work, family… next thing you know, you're my age, wondering where the years went."

Robitaille gestured toward the line of framed jerseys. "I know where they went," he said with a tight grin. "Every morning when I get out of bed, a lifetime of aches and pains vividly refresh my memory. Now, how about that sweet tea?"

* * *

Once they were settled in comfortable, cushioned wicker chairs on the veranda, an African American servant—the "Walter" one of the guards had mentioned on his previous visit—who Pride hadn't even realized was in the silent house at the moment— brought sweet tea out to them on a silver tray. The glasses were liberally iced and sweating, and the man set them on glass-topped tables beside each chair. Pride thanked him, and he nodded somberly. He moved quietly, for such a big man, and Pride wondered if he had also played football. He was decades older than Robitaille, so even if he had, they wouldn't have been teammates.

The view was glorious, reaching across the rear of the property out to what resembled some lost, primeval forest in the distance. From here, the walls of the animal compound were too high to see inside, but the sounds and odors were prevalent, making Pride feel like he was at a real, professional zoo. "How long have you been collecting those animals?" he asked.

"Since I started to make some real money playing ball," Robitaille said. "A lot of guys spend it on big houses and fancy cars and clothes and rivers of bling. Obviously, I got the big house, eventually. First, though, I traveled. I went on a couple of safaris, in Africa— photo safaris; I've never been much for killing things. I came to respect wild animals, but I also learned about the threats they faced. I decided that what I'd do with my money was to try to save them, over there in Africa, but also here at home. I could protect them, breed them, do my part to prevent extinction."

Pride sipped his sweet tea. It was delicious. "A noble cause."

"I suppose. I didn't think of it that way, necessarily.

It was something I was able to do, something I thought might possibly make a difference. In the long run, I don't know, maybe I'm fooling myself. But I had to give it a shot."

"I know the feeling."

"I'm sure you do. Law enforcement, in this wicked, wicked world? That must be an incredibly frustrating pursuit."

"Sometimes it is," Pride admitted. Despite himself, he was almost starting to like Robitaille. The man's concern for animals, at least, seemed genuine, and a person who truly appreciated animals, Pride thought, had to have something going for him. "You win some, you lose some. Ideally you win more than you lose."

"I guess maybe it's like anything else," Robitaille went on. "In football, no matter how well we played one week, there was another game on the horizon. If we had a winning season, it's, what about next season? You can reach what you think is your peak performance, play as well as you believe it's possible to play, but there's always another test coming up, another challenge. I suppose criminals are that way, too. You put one away today, but tomorrow there will be two more out there, doing things that are twice as bad."

"You can never catch them all, that's for sure," Pride said. "We have to prioritize, just like anyone else."

He hoped the conversation would continue in this vein. If Robitaille talked enough about crime and criminals, he might slip up and reveal something about Landry. For all Pride knew, he had been telling the truth, and he had no idea that Landry was still running around New Orleans, working as hired muscle for gangsters and throwing people off of hotel balconies. But he suspected their relationship had continued, albeit changed, as their economic and social statuses had shifted ever further apart. Someone was paying for Allyson Woodhouse's legal services, after all, and she didn't come cheap.

Instead, Robitaille swallowed the rest of his tea and put his glass down hard on the table, standing abruptly at the same time. "Time for some shooting," he said. "The sun's high enough that it won't get in our eyes. That is why you came, isn't it?"

Pride had almost forgotten about that part of the invitation, and he'd hoped Robitaille had. But the man eyed him expectantly, and Pride had no choice but to finish his tea and follow along. "Walter will meet us out there with everything you'll need."

"Sounds good."

"Would you like to see some more of the animals? You only saw the primates last time."

"Absolutely," Pride said, meaning it. Once they started shooting, conversation would become more difficult. "That would be great."

"Come on, then." He led Pride down the back steps and over a flagstone walkway and into the walled "zoo." The smell was much stronger within the walls; the mixed odors of different animals, different species, blending into a musky, pungent cocktail. Almost as pointed was the mix of sounds: chittering, chuffing, screeching, and more.

"Loss of habitat and animal populations has all kinds of consequences," Robitaille said, stepping quickly past the monkey cages Pride had already seen. Just in case, Pride scanned the capuchins again, but they still appeared intact. "Many of those consequences were completely unforeseen. In parts of Africa, for instance, lion and leopard populations have been severely depleted, through habitat loss and hunting. Those predators can sometimes be dangerous to people living in small villages, so at first glance, that might seem like a positive development, right?"

"I suppose," Pride said, unsure of where the man was going with this. They walked past enclosures that were slightly smaller, but otherwise comparable to, those in major zoos Pride had visited. Red foxes paced in one; the next held a pair of porcupines, and in the one after that, a gray wolf lounged in a sunny spot. "Beautiful animal."

"Another top predator," Robitaille said. "I admire them all. Anyway, it turns out that removing those feline predators from the wild wasn't quite the bargain people had hoped for. In some of those areas, baboons have become rampant—baboons that had previously been kept in check by the lions and leopards. Those baboons are passing internal parasites along to humans. We've had terrible diseases result from such monkey-to-human transfer—Ebola, for one—and someday soon, we could see the next pandemic come to light the same way."

"You've obviously given this a lot of thought," Pride said.

"Playing football is fun, Dwayne—I hope it's all right to call you that?"

"Of course."

"And I'm Burl, please. Anyway, it's a blast. And maybe it has some societal value, bringing people together as a community of fans, instilling civic or regional pride, that kind of thing. But in the end, it's two teams of grunting men slamming into each other. Ultimately, it's not very important. Building businesses is something altogether different. In my Burl's Place restaurants, I'm building community at the ground level. Well, you own a bar, right, so you know what I'm saying."

"Definitely," Pride said, though he still was having a hard time following Robitaille's train of thought as it slipped from track to track.

"I give people jobs. They interact daily, becoming a kind of family. Then their regular customers become extended family. All of it's grounded, with a physical location contributing to the local tax base, as well as providing people with good, healthy food options. I don't own them all; I'm a figurehead, really. They license my image and my reputation is all. Every one except the originals here in Louisiana are franchises, so I'm creating business owners all over the country. Those owners train people who learn new skills, which they take to other businesses, and the effects cascade from there."

"That's admirable," Pride said. He looked at the other captive animals that Robitaille passed without comment: a pair of hyenas, a sloth, a red panda, three black bears.

One enclosure held a couple of adult deer and a single fawn, reminding Pride of the fawn that Alpuente had found in his yard. "What kind of deer are those?" Pride asked.

"Bactrians," Robitaille said, with a certain amount of self-satisfaction in his tone. "There were only about four hundred left in the world in the 1960s, but conservation efforts have increased their numbers to around two thousand. I've successfully bred them a couple of times."

Behind all the enclosures were the high walls that shielded them from view except to someone standing right in front of them. The flagstone pathway wound through it all, but the walls made it resemble a maze.

Robitaille stopped, turned toward Pride, and extended his hands toward the enclosures. "But these creatures—they're more important to me than any of that. They're the future. Extinction is imminent for some of these species, and I'm fighting that with everything I've got, along with other individuals and organizations around the world. We're outnumbered, and it's an uphill battle—the forces of progress are arrayed against us. Economic development, a growing global population, habitat loss, sport hunting and fishing, pollution, climate change—these things all work against wildlife. So we do what we can, hoping to forestall extinction for another day or week or month or year. I'm not Noah and I don't have an ark, but I do what I can."

"A good cause, for sure," Pride said. Robitaille was on a tear now; Pride wasn't sure he even heard the response, or needed one.

"Most of the animals I take in were injured," he went on. "Caught in traps, limbs broken. Sometimes they're young ones, orphaned by hunters or accidents. I'm saving individuals, and in the process trying to save species."

He dropped his hands and kept going. The next enclosures were cages containing birds: peregrine falcons, a golden eagle, a pair of bald eagles. After that came a pond with half a dozen flamingos standing ankle-deep in still water. Pride could see fish in the water, and a pair of ducks that might have been visitors floated nearby. Across the walkway, in a deeper pool, river otters chased one another, diving and breaking the surface and then vanishing beneath the water again.

"Walter's ready for us," Robitaille said suddenly. The abrupt subject change came as a surprise. Pride wasn't sure how he knew; since he'd arrived, he hadn't heard the two men speak a word to each other, but Walter had known to bring sweet tea to the veranda, and now, supposedly, he had made preparations so Robitaille and Pride could do some skeet shooting. Maybe this was Robitaille's standard method of "entertaining guests"—a glass of tea, a hurried stroll through part of the zoo, and then on to the guns.

Robitaille led him to an iron door set into the high walls. "Through here," he said. "Shortcut." He turned the knob and the door swung open with a raucous squeal. On the other side, the flagstone path continued uphill toward the grassy flat where Pride had encountered Robitaille on his first visit.

Up there, the shotguns were waiting.

29

"Were you able to talk to the guy from Hamilton's office?" Sonja asked as she and Lasalle motored toward St. Bernard Parish.

"Rich Brandt," Lasalle said. "Yeah, I talked to him. He said he doesn't know Bruno Landry from Adam."

"Really?"

"No, not quite. He doesn't remember him from high school, though."

"But he recognized him on the street, during the parade."

Sonja was making all the same arguments Lasalle had been turning over in his head since his visit to Brandt's home. "That's right. He says he was introduced to Landry at a party, probably at Robitaille's place. He didn't remember him from school, though. It's possible, I think."

"Wouldn't whoever introduced them have mentioned something about them going to school together?"

"Depends on who it was. If it was Robitaille, yeah, probably. But if it was someone else who happened to know Robitaille and Landry, then that person wouldn't necessarily have known that Brandt went to school with them."

"Sounds like a stretch," Sonja said.

"I know it does. But I like to think I'm a pretty fair judge of liars, and I didn't get the sense that he was lying. There was one other thing, too."

"What's that?"

"He remembered that scar at the corner of Landry's eye. Says that's why he recognized him. I can see that—it changes the shape of his eye just enough to make it a very distinctive feature. But I've checked their high school yearbooks, and he didn't have the scar then. So the thing that makes Landry recognizable to him now doesn't ring any bells from the old days."

"Okay, maybe," Sonja said. "Still seems like a pretty huge coincidence. Brandt and Robitaille in the same meeting at City Hall, all three of them going to school together."

"I admit that," Lasalle countered. "It's a huge coincidence. But sometimes a coincidence is just a coincidence, right? After all, we don't have anything connecting Brandt to Alpuente. I'm not saying he's not involved, just saying there's no proof yet that he is. I want to keep an open mind is all."

"There's nothing wrong with an open mind, Lasalle."

"Do you remember the face of every single person at your high school, Percy? I sure don't."

"I remember the ones I want to remember," Sonja replied. "There are a lot of them I've tried for years to forget, and I think I'm making some progress."

"Exactly. Brandt says he and Robitaille weren't buddies then, and I believe it. There are a couple of pictures of them together in the yearbooks, but they weren't involved in any of the same after-school activities.

I'd like to see their personal copies of those yearbooks, if they exist. If they autographed them to each other—you know, 'To my partner in murder,' or something like that, well, that would make a big difference."

Sonja laughed. "Conspiracies usually fail because the more people who are involved, the more likely it is that somebody will blab about it," she said. "You're right—we should keep an eye on Brandt, but maybe we shouldn't convict him until we find some evidence connecting him to the murder."

"That's all I'm saying."

"Well, I'm agreeing with you for a change, so shut up." She sat quietly for a few seconds, watching the road pass by the windshield, then added, "Are we there yet?"

When they turned up the dirt drive toward the house where Donna Alpuente and Elmer Comeau lived, the first thing they saw was a pickup truck with beams standing up in the bed, and plywood sheets screwed into place between the beams. It all combined to make the bed about eight feet deep, and the space inside was filled almost to overflowing. Furniture had been placed at the bottom, and smaller objects piled in on top of that. A mattress had been lashed to each of the plywood sides. A wooden ladder stood open beside the vehicle. "Looks like they're moving," Lasalle said.

"Twenty-first century Joads," Sonja said. Whenever she saw families who had loaded all their worldly goods into the back of a truck—more often than not, families with children; bikes and Big Wheels were commonplace—she thought of John Steinbeck's fictional Dust Bowl family, heading west in search of a better life, only to find that moving on didn't necessarily mean moving up.

"Pretty accurate," Lasalle said. "I read that book in high school. I thought it was ancient history, then, but I guess it's not."

"Not so much," Sonja agreed.

Lasalle brought his truck to a stop a few yards behind the other one. As he and Sonja were getting out, Elmer emerged from the farmhouse with his beloved TV in his arms, a blanket draped over it. He saw the agents walking toward him and put the set gently down on the dirt. "You got news?" he asked.

"About your nephew?" Sonja said. She didn't want to disappoint him, but misleading him would be even worse. "Not yet. Soon, we think."

"Where are y'all heading?" Lasalle asked him.

The old man rubbed a gnarled hand across his forehead, which was wet with sweat and lined with age, like a roadmap of his life's struggles. "We got another sister, over outside Pascagoula. She's got room for us. Can't stay here no more, that's for sure."

"Why not?" Sonja asked.

Elmer looked down at the dirt beneath his feet. "We had this place a long time. Our folks had it first, then when we grew up and they passed, Donna and her husband got it. They let me move in after my wife passed. We raised up Eddie here and all, and we always thought he would take it, in time. But that's not to be."

"I know," Sonja said. "I'm so sorry."

The screen door banged open and Donna came out, arms laden with clothing. She walked past them, climbed the ladder, and tossed the bundle into the back of the truck. "What Elmer's sayin' is we tried to hang onto the place," she said. "But we just can't anymore. You'd think they would keep raisin' their offers, but instead, they're lower every time. Finally we figured we'd best take it before it was down to nothin'."

"Plus there's that curse," Elmer added. "Y'all might think we're ignorant trash, but that's the real thing. Baron Samedi got Eddie. What if we're next? It ain't safe, stayin' here."

"We don't think any such thing," Lasalle said. "But I can tell you for sure, it wasn't Baron Samedi who killed your nephew. It was someone dressed as him, in a rented costume."

"So you say. I know different."

"Who told you that?" Sonja asked. "That wasn't in the news."

"Don't matter," the man said. "It's true, anyhow."

"Who's buying y'all out?" Lasalle asked.

Donna pointed toward the property next to the farm, with a motion as exaggerated as if she were throwing a rock at it. "Who else? They been after us for a year, now. Little more. Elmer's right, after what happened to Eddie and all, we just couldn't take the chance."

Sonja remembered the voodoo paraphernalia scattered around the house, the elaborate altar. Anyone who had been inside that house would know they were susceptible to threats of voodoo curses. "You shouldn't do anything rash," she said. "We're close to finding out who's behind all this."

"Rash?" Donna echoed. "We've been holdin' on by the skin of our teeth. What with as poor as the farmin' and fishin's been, the rash thing was tryin' to stay. We're done. We signed the papers and got the check and we're out."

"Who'd you sign the papers with?" Lasalle asked.

"Some company," Elmer said. "Southern Louisiana somethin'."

"Southern Louisiana Holdings, LLC?"

"That sounds right."

"Do you know who they are? Did you talk to them in person?"

"Somebody from them," Donna said. "Some real estate guy. Real slick, but young and dumb as a box o' rocks."

"Do you have his name?" Sonja asked.

Donna nodded toward the overloaded truck. "It's somewhere in there."

"Is there anything you can think of that would tell us who's behind the company?" Lasalle asked. "We've been trying to untangle it, but they've got the ownership hidden behind dozens of different corporate entities."

"I don't know nothin' 'bout that," Elmer said. "But if you go back out on the road you come in on, and turn right instead of left, they've cut a dirt road into their property. It's 'bout three-quarter of a mile from our gate. You'll see it; it's fresh cut. Next to it there's a big sign. I don't know if the fella on the sign is one of 'em, or just some actor or whatnot, but you can't miss his big, grinnin' mug."

"I hope you got a decent price for the place," Sonja said. "I'm sorry we couldn't have done something more to help you keep it."

"Ain't nothin' to be done," Donna said. "When it's time, it's time, and our time's come."

Lasalle handed her a business card, and Sonja did the same. "Let us know if there's anything we can do," he said. "And let us know how to reach y'all, so we can keep you informed on the investigation. We think we're close to knowing what happened."

Donna pocketed the cards without comment. Sonja hoped she would hang onto them, and would indeed stay in touch. Some family members of murder victims called constantly, even to the point of becoming pests. Others never wanted to hear from the police again, as if not knowing would somehow make the tragedy have never happened. She suspected Donna Alpuente would fall somewhere in between, not agitating for answers where there weren't any, but interested in knowing that some kind of justice had been done.

At the same time, she knew there was no such thing as justice that would make up for the loss of a loved one. Such a loss only time could heal, and that only imperfectly. Time was a bandage, which became a scab that could too easily be yanked off, and finally a scar, there as a forever reminder of what had been.

Ten minutes later, they had left the Alpuente property and turned right—farther from the main road—as Elmer Comeau had directed them. Stakes with pink ribbons on them marked off the boundaries of the resort-to-be. "There's the road," Lasalle said. It was wide and heavily traveled, the earth churned up by the huge tires of the construction vehicles visible over near the lakeshore.

"And there's the sign," Sonja added. A billboard stood next to the road, right where the old man had said it would be. They couldn't see its front from this angle, just its side and the posts that held it high.

But as they drew closer, it came into view. It was mostly yellow, with huge red letters. COMING SOON! it said. A SPECTACULAR BURL'S PLACE LAKESIDE RESORT HOTEL GOLF COURSE & MARINA! Inset next to that was the smiling face of Burl Robitaille, with the words "You have my word on it!" printed underneath.

"I was just about to call y'all," Patton said. Sonja and Lasalle were still sitting in Lasalle's truck, with Sonja's phone on speaker. "It took me long enough, but I finally got through the bureaucratic nightmare. Southern Louisiana Holdings is a corporate entity that Robitaille and some partners set up to finance his next move."

"Into the hotel business."

"Hotels, resorts, golf courses, you name it. Here's the beauty of it, as far as he's concerned—he hardly has any of his own money in it. He's licensing his name and his face, and the other partners are putting up most of the funding. That way, he gets his initial licensing fee no matter what. Even if any individual resort flops, he still makes a killing. If it does well, he collects royalties as long as it's in business. Say he can set up ten of these around the country—which looks like a conservative estimate—the deal's worth hundreds of millions to him if it goes forward as planned."

"Nice work if you can get it," Sonja said.

"There's one catch, though," Patton said. "This first one has to fly. Once it's a success, that triggers the licensing payments. After that, they start pitching Burl's Place resorts all over the country, and he gets his piece of the action as soon as the ground's broken."

"You didn't find all that out just by figuring out the corporate ownership," Lasalle said.

"Ask me no questions," Patton replied. "But listen

up. I kept going on Alpuente's files, and I found out what he was really onto."

"Was there something I didn't see?" Lasalle asked.

"You didn't see it because you weren't looking for what *wasn't* there."

"What does that mean?"

"It means his computer was hacked, and the hacker deleted the files."

"Wait, how do you know Lt. Alpuente didn't delete them himself?" Sonja wondered.

"Trust me. The hacker probably figured his work was invisible, but he wasn't counting on the mad skills of Triple P. Also, I was able to follow some threads he left back to an IP address inside the business premises of Southern Louisiana Holdings."

"You rock, Patton," Lasalle said. "So what's the big secret?"

"Dig this: Alpuente figured out that the resort was going to have to do some heavy-duty dredging to build the marina that's critical to the plans. Lake Borgne opens up to the Gulf, and the resort wants big yachts, maybe even some of your smaller cruise ships, to be able to dock there. That will require seriously heavy-duty dredging. And his calculations show that the dredging would have disastrous impacts on the surrounding wetlands. There's already been major wetlands loss over the past few decades, but it would get a lot worse a lot faster if that dredging goes forward. Or that's what the preliminary draft of Alpuente's report shows, anyway."

"And that's the draft that got deleted?" Lasalle asked.

"That and all the calculations behind it. The conclusion of his draft report was that he wanted the

Navy to completely block the resort. He wrote that, otherwise, the loss of wetlands would be 'irreversible, with drastic consequences for New Orleans and the entire Gulf Coast.' His words."

Sonja sat silent for a moment, stunned. Then she said, "Wow. An already very rich man can become super-rich, unless the Navy decides to pull the plug on the whole thing. That's worth killing over."

"Not just killing," Lasalle pointed out. "But by using the voodoo angle, convincing the nearest landowner—whose property would definitely not be visually appealing to the resort's guests—to sell out. Maybe acquiring that property was part of the plan all along. More space for the golf course."

"He probably figured that killing Alpuente and deleting all the data would be good enough to keep the Navy from getting involved," Patton speculated. "Even if they assigned someone else to carry on Alpuente's work, by the time that research was done and the calculations made again, it would be too late. The dredging would be finished and the resort would be built. Robitaille would get his first licensing payment, and from then on, he'd be on the gravy train for life."

"We've got to let Pride know," Lasalle said. "He's there now, at Robitaille's place."

"Hold on, there's one more piece," Patton said. "I pulled the banking records of Alpuente's landlady, just for fun. Guess who's been depositing four thousand bucks, twice a week for the last six weeks?"

"Small enough to not raise red flags," Sonja said. "But forty-eight grand is a nice payday for someone like her. No wonder she could afford to paint her house."

"And that's about how long Loretta thinks

Alpuente's been getting dosed with L-DOPA," Lasalle added. "By the only person with a key."

"We'll pick her up," Sonja said. "Drive, Lasalle. I'll call Pride."

"Text him," Lasalle suggested, already putting the truck in gear. "If he's standing there with Robitaille, he's not going to want to have this conversation over the phone. Tell him we're on the way."

30

As Robitaille had predicted, Walter had arranged everything for the skeet shoot. The electric thrower was humming softly, ready to go. Two shotguns leaned against the stone wall, which was about three feet high and presumably made of local stone. It looked like it had been here for centuries, and maybe it had been. Two pairs of electronic noise-canceling earmuffs were positioned on top of the wall, along with safety glasses and leather gloves. Two boxes of shotgun shells were open and waiting.

"Walter's very efficient," Pride observed.

"He's been with me a long time," Robitaille said. "I prize efficiency above all."

Efficiency and apex predators, Pride thought. Then he decided that characterization was unfair. Robitaille obviously did value predators, but his concern for other animals—even those that were more typically prey— appeared genuine. It was almost enough to make Pride wish he wasn't involved in Alpuente's murder.

He didn't really believe that, though. By now, he was nearly convinced that Robitaille was behind the young officer's death. He didn't know the whys and wherefores, yet, and he was still willing to be persuaded otherwise, if a better theory came along. He didn't expect that would happen. Robitaille might have been an animal lover, but from where Pride stood, he also looked like a man who had contracted at least one murder.

Appearances could deceive, of course. But the other side of the matter was that nobody fancied himself the villain in his own story. Whatever Robitaille had done, he presumably believed his motivation was a just one.

"Why are you really here, Dwayne?" Robitaille asked. Pride was astonished by the change in tone. The man had been a gracious host, up to this point, but it was almost as if he'd read Pride's thoughts, and there was a new, bitter edge to his tone. "We'll do some shooting and then you'll go on your way. But I can't help thinking that you didn't come just for some casual conversation and to shoot a few clay pigeons."

"You invited me," Pride reminded him. "I've been working hard lately, and I thought that a morning off might do me good. Clear my head."

"In Hamilton's conference room yesterday, you mentioned that you're still working the case of that officer who was murdered at the Mardi Gras parade."

"That's right."

"Given your reputation, I have a hard time believing that you'd let something like that rest while you go visiting people."

"NCIS isn't me, it's a team," Pride said. "I have good, capable agents working on it. Nobody's resting until we close that case."

"Yet here you are."

"Like I said, clearing my head. Sometimes it helps me to get a fresh perspective. To do that, I need a little distance from the work. Let my subconscious work while my analytical mind takes a break."

"Uh-huh." Robitaille didn't sound convinced, but he seemed willing to let it slide. Pride was left wondering what had prompted the exchange. Had he said something that had given away his true purpose? He hoped not. Robitaille was a suspect, but Pride still had plenty of unanswered questions, and he was hoping this visit would clear up some of those. For one thing, Robitaille was a successful businessman. What would he have against someone like Lt. Alpuente? Where would their paths even have crossed? And what would be so important to him that he might risk all his wealth and influence by getting involved in murder?

Robitaille put on his safety gear and started loading his shotgun, so Pride donned his muffs, gloves, and safety glasses, and picked up the gun left over for him. It was a Remington 870 twelve-gauge, a weapon he was familiar with. He clicked on the safety and pulled back the pump slide to open the chamber. He selected a shell from the same box Robitaille was using and inserted it, shoving it up into the loading flap. Once he heard the usual click, he withdrew another shell from the box and repeated the process until he had loaded five of them into the gun. With the safety still on, he swung the barrel well away from Robitaille and sighted into the air. The weapon seemed true, as far as he could tell without firing it.

As he turned it back toward the earth, he caught a glimpse of what appeared to be a dark figure darting across the grass, mostly hidden beneath the curve of the hill, but heading in their general direction. Walter? He couldn't imagine the old man moving so fast. Who, then? Or had it simply been a trick of the light?

What really disturbed him was that it had looked more like Landry than Walter.

Inside his pocket, he felt his phone buzz. He ignored it, but then it buzzed again. Robitaille was still busy loading, so Pride slipped off a glove and checked his phone.

Two texts had come in, from Sonja. The first said:

Robitaille's our guy. Be careful.

The second added,

On our way.

She hadn't specified on their way from where, though. Pride tucked the phone back in his pocket.

"Something important?" Robitaille asked.

"Fairly."

"I hope you don't have to leave. That would be a shame."

"Maybe a break in a case," Pride said. "But I don't have to go right now."

"A break, really? Tell me."

"I can't talk about an investigation in progress, Burl, you know that."

"It's just us here. You and me."

"Burl..."

He didn't like the way the other man was looking at him. All trace of friendliness had vanished from his face. His mouth was set in a grim line, his jaw thrust forward aggressively, his eyes narrow.

And he didn't like the fact that he had seen someone apparently sneaking up on them. Pride took a step toward the wall, reaching for the shells, as if to pocket one or two for later.

"You asked about Bruno Landry before," Robitaille said. He nestled the butt of his shotgun into his elbow. His right index finger rested on the outside of the trigger guard. "Would it surprise you to learn that Walter is his father? Bruno and I were a team in high school, but Walter worked for my family before that. Now that it's just me, he's still with me, as loyal as ever. It was a little strange in high school, when Bruno and I were a team, for me to come home and have my dinner prepared by his mother and served by his father. Bruno rode the bus to school and back with me in those days, but I didn't see him much outside school hours. Of course, our place wasn't as big as my house now. My father was well off, but I've done much better than he ever did. Still, Walter and his family lived in our servants' quarters."

"You know, Burl, there's not much that would surprise me about you anymore." Pride brought his own weapon up into a shooting position. "I think you'd better put down that Remington."

"Why?" Robitaille asked.

At the same moment, he swung the barrel around to point at Pride. Pride—certain now—squeezed his trigger. Nothing happened.

He leapt over the low wall and hit the ground on the other side, just before Robitaille's shotgun boomed and shot sprayed the area where Pride had been standing.

Pride rested the barrel of his shotgun on the wall and worked the trigger again, hearing only an ineffectual click.

His gun was inoperable. Probably the firing pin had been removed.

And Landry was out there somewhere.

Robitaille, just on the other side of that wall, fired again. Pride ducked just in time.

Head low, Pride scuttled about twelve feet down the wall, drawing his Colt revolver as he went. When he stopped, he risked another look over the wall. Robitaille was nowhere to be seen, but he couldn't be far away. In the distance, two more men headed his way from the direction of the house. They looked like the two guards, who had once again been staffing Robitaille's front gate when he had arrived. Both had what looked like military-style rifles strapped around their necks.

Just in time, Pride caught the glint of sunlight off Robitaille's gun barrel as the man rose up from below the hill. He ducked again, and Robitaille's shot peppered the other side of the wall, some of it flying overhead. Pride rose up, snapped off a shot in Robitaille's direction, then ducked down and kept moving, away from Robitaille and Landry. After another thirty feet or so, he stole another glance.

The two guards were closer now. It made sense that if Robitaille were trying to draw him into a trap, he wouldn't do it alone, or even with just him and Landry. Landry apparently hadn't had much problem killing Alpuente alone, but despite his naval record, the officer had never served in combat. Plenty of people had tried to kill Pride, but he was still standing. He couldn't be counted on to be an easy target.

As Pride had noted before, the guards both carried themselves like ex-military. Now they were security guards, but from the looks of things, they had additional duties as well. They were essentially mercenaries, or what people called "military contractors" these days, as if changing the name could change the nature of what they did—fighting for money instead of country or ideology.

The nearer they came, the more they spread out, making themselves harder to take out of play. If he shot one of them, he would pinpoint himself for the other.

He took stock of his situation. The wall seemed to mark off Robitaille's property line. If he kept following it the way he was going, eventually he would reach the road. Then he would have to backtrack to Robitaille's front door to get to his SUV.

But going the other way would lead right toward where he had last seen Landry. And, of course, hopping the wall would make him a target for Robitaille and the guards, coming from that direction.

He put his back to the wall and pulled out his phone.

How long?

he texted in response to Sonja's texts.
Her answer came in seconds later.

20 min?

Send backup. 4 armed men.

Then he pocketed the phone. He thought he could hold out for twenty minutes. But until then, he had no one to count on but himself.

31

"Pride!"

The voice was Robitaille's. He sounded a little farther away than he had been, but in the same general direction. Closer to the house, perhaps. Pride didn't bother to answer.

"You might as well come out! You're done!"

Not as long as I'm breathing, Pride thought. *And not as long as I'm holding Sweet Charmaine.*

Undeniably, though, he was in some trouble. Possibly a great deal of it.

There was one option to which he had given no consideration before, which was hurtling over the wall, gun blazing. He hadn't considered it, of course, because there was virtually no way that it wouldn't end in his death. And given that the men who would be shooting at him were apparently still some distance away, their shots might not be clean, so that death could be prolonged and painful. There was always the chance that he could hit each of them with a well-placed shot from his pistol before they could fire back, despite the fact that he would be jumping over a wall and running down a grassy slope and firing one-handed with little opportunity to brace his hand or to take careful aim. He had seen it done, in cowboy movies, when he was a kid.

All in all, it seemed like the least appealing of his options.

The wall offered at least a modicum of cover— good enough to stop Robitaille's shotgun pellets—and if anyone approached it, he could see them. His spine was starting to feel the strain of running at a squat, but it would hurt a lot more with a bullet in it. He kept going the way he had been, toward the distant, unseen road.

One more long stretch of crab-running. He could take it.

He went as fast as he was able, his head down and his back low. He wasn't silent, but he was quiet, and the men were making their own sounds, rustling through the grass as they approached. Had they simply rushed the wall, they probably could have finished him, but they were trying to do it without risking death themselves. He figured that strategy was Robitaille's doing—he likely wasn't used to killing, or to opening himself up to being killed, so he was probably urging stealth and caution.

Finally, the wall dropped into a dip, which was even deeper than it had looked at first. That was good for him, as long as he used it expediently. He couldn't see the other men, and for the moment, they couldn't see him. He slid a round into Charmaine's cylinder, to replace the one he had fired, then took a deep breath.

Hurdling the wall, he broke into a sprint, following the line of the dip. It veered away from the driveway and toward the house, but that was fine. It would put him closer to his vehicle. If he could escape, then return with Lasalle and Sonja and maybe a SWAT team, it might still be possible to end all this without bloodshed. That was always his preference.

So far, so good. As the land flattened out, Pride could see the house before him, on the far side of the walled zoo.

But the last forty yards he had to cover were on a level, grassy lawn, and his opponents held the high ground. He started across that bare stretch, wishing there was some kind of cover. Before he had covered fifteen yards, a burst from one of the rifles chewed up the earth near him. The guards were still far off, and firing downhill, but they were coming on fast.

He zigged, then dropped and swung around in the same motion, bringing his revolver up and firing a shot. The range wasn't in his favor, but luck was with him—either that, or years of hard-fought experience. A spray of blood jetted from the guard's right shoulder and he took a step back, almost dropping his gun. Pride could see the second guard, Landry, and Robitaille running toward the wounded guard, but none of them were in position yet to fire. He stayed where he was, crouched in the grass, for a few more moments. Willing his heart to slow, he took in a breath, pushed it out, and held it there. Bracing his gun hand with the other, he sighted on the wounded guard and fired again.

This one hit the man center mass, just above the sternum. The guard took three wobbly steps, then sat down heavily in the grass. After a few seconds, he flopped backward.

Pride hoped he hadn't killed the man. Law enforcement personnel were trained to aim for center mass, because stopping an attacker any other way was too risky. Arms and legs were hard to hit, and didn't necessarily eliminate the threat. So Pride was constantly torn—he knew what was safest for him and for others, so he took the shots that needed to be taken. But he didn't like having to do that, and he preferred to settle trouble without violence when he could.

Robitaille, Landry, and the other guard rushed to the man's side, distracted for the moment from their prey. Pride took advantage of that distraction to start running again. He knew now that he would never make it to the house, but he could, he hoped, at least reach the shelter of the zoo walls.

He was almost there when another, longer burst from the hillside came much closer to him. A round tore through his jeans leg—it felt like a child's quick tug—and he made a last, desperate dive. He landed facedown on the grass, but safely behind a corner of the high, whitewashed wall. More rounds chewed up the corner, just behind him.

He pinned himself against the wall and took a few moments to catch his breath. Only then did he realize that the round had grazed his calf. It wasn't bad, but it was bleeding, and it was starting to feel like someone had held a knife over an open flame and then pressed it against his flesh.

In a sense, by killing the guard—if, in fact, he had— he had raised the stakes of this whole encounter. But they had clearly intended to kill him, probably as soon as Robitaille figured out if he was indeed a suspect in Alpuente's murder. Sonja's text had moved up the timeline a little; he doubted that Robitaille had actually intended to fire the killing shot, but just to hold him there until Landry and the guards arrived. Once he had seen Pride bolt, he tried to take matters into his own hands.

Still, Pride understood human nature. Planning to kill an officer of the law in cold blood was calculated, almost like a business decision. Just an unpleasant task that had to be done. Actually doing it was a different story.

The fact that he hadn't gone quietly, but had rather been the first to draw blood, had elevated everyone's sense of urgency. There was nothing cold-blooded about it anymore. Instead, tensions were running high, anxiety was at fever pitch. Nobody was calm. Now it was kill or be killed, all the way around.

Pride got to his feet, bracing himself against the wall. His leg was still bleeding, but he couldn't tend to it now. They would be here in seconds, and if they came around that corner, he would be exposed again.

He didn't think he would have time to reach the house, but one of the zoo doors was just about fifteen feet ahead. He stepped forward, trying to put his weight on the wounded leg, and it almost gave way beneath him. He caught himself on the wall and limped the rest of the way. The door was unlocked. Careful to minimize the squeaking, he passed through, noting only as he closed the door again that he had left a clear trail of blood behind him.

There was no lock on the inside of the door. Why would there be, Pride figured, when the entire property was walled in and protected by armed guards? The animals were safely enclosed, and even if they got out, they wouldn't be likely to open the closed doors. Pride looked for something he could move in front of the door, to buy himself at least a couple of minutes when the others tried to follow his blood trail, but the only thing he saw was a boulder inside an enclosure containing a pair of bobcats.

Chances were they were used to humans feeding them and wouldn't attack if he entered the enclosure. But the scent of blood might change that calculation. And even if they left him alone, he wasn't sure he could rock the boulder free of the surrounding earth and carry it over.

Instead, he sat on the low wall of the enclosure and ripped off a strip of his torn jeans, then tied it tightly above the wound for a makeshift tourniquet. That done, he started hoofing it down the zoo's walkway.

He was surprised to see a tiger pacing in the next enclosure. Robitaille had told him he had a lynx, but no big cats. Pride realized he should have expected it—Robitaille was a murderer, so telling lies to hide the fact that he kept animals that were illegal for private citizens to own was a minor offense, by comparison. On reflection, Pride decided that his surprise was directed at himself, that he hadn't seen through the lies, that Robitaille had seemed friendly and open at first. All along, Robitaille must have known why he had come, but he hadn't shown any hint of guilt or even nervousness. That further confirmed Pride's hunch that Robitaille had never intended to do the killing himself.

Pride tried to remember the layout of the zoo. Robitaille had obviously taken him out a side door before they'd reached the tiger, because he hadn't wanted Pride to see it. The pathway wound back and forth in an almost maze-like fashion, so it was hard to gauge how far he was from the door nearest the house. If he could make it that far, he thought he could get to the house, take shelter there, and hold his hunters off long enough for reinforcements to arrive.

There was nothing to do but try. Limping, his leg beginning to throb, still leaving a visible but diminished blood trail, he kept going.

32

Pride had made it around three more corners when he heard the door he had entered through squeal open and then bang shut.

They were just over a minute behind. Two at the most. But they could move faster than he could, and they not only had a trail to follow, but once they were inside the walls, there was only the one path.

Unless, he thought, *you're willing to enter an enclosure.* That might be unexpected enough to throw them off. There could be cover in there, a place to hide. Maybe he could wait there while they went right past him.

It was a Hail Mary, but it was worth considering. He started watching for an enclosure with the right kind of cover and harmless enough residents.

He was almost past some monkey cages when he realized that they weren't the ones near the front of the zoo. These contained more monkeys than those had, of different types, some of them caged together.

Alone in the next cage, all by itself like some kind of social pariah, sat a capuchin wearing the most pathetic face Pride had ever seen.

Its right paw was missing, and the tissue of its

stump was still pink and raw.

"Sorry, fella," Pride said softly. "Don't worry, I'll let you come to court for his sentencing. Maybe you can even testify against him."

It was hard to precisely locate sounds within these walls, in part because of the constant racket the animals made and in part because the way twisted so much, and sounds bounced off the walls. But he was sure something had changed behind him. He had heard the door and then advancing footsteps, but now he didn't. He thought he heard the door open and close again. Were they splitting up? Someone coming up behind him, the others going for different doors, hoping to catch him in a crossfire?

He was turning away from the capuchin when he heard, or sensed, motion behind him. He spun, his gun ready to fire. But it wasn't Robitaille or one of his thugs.

It was the tiger.

Loose, and following the blood trail.

It stopped, its golden-eyed gaze fixed on him.

How fast could a tiger charge? He didn't know the answer to that. He tried to remember wildlife documentaries he had seen, but those were years, decades, in the past. The most recent had probably been when Laurel was five or six. He hoped he would get a chance to watch another movie with his daughter someday.

The other tiger-related question that occurred to him was: what would it take to stop one? Could his .357 Magnum do the job? Maybe if he emptied it, aimed well, and got very lucky.

But then he would have an empty gun, and enemies who knew exactly where to find him.

He couldn't risk checking to see how much time had elapsed since Sonja had promised to arrive in twenty minutes. He had been hoping backup would show up before that, but as yet, he hadn't heard any sirens or seen any signs of help.

"Nice kitty," he said quietly. He suspected that turning his back on the tiger would be suicide, so he backed up slowly, carefully, holding the cat's gaze with his. Robitaille had said his animals were rescues, which might have been another lie. Either way, there was a chance the tiger had spent at least some of its life in the wild, hunting to survive. Even if it hadn't, even if it had spent its entire life feasting on giant-sized helpings of Meow Mix, it had instincts. Those instincts would tell it that here was wounded prey. Easy pickings.

The tiger had frozen when Pride had turned to face it. Now, seemingly recognizing its advantage, it started forward again. It moved slowly, deliberately, placing one giant paw on the path, then the next. Its muscles rippled under its sleek, striped fur. It was an impressive creature, a beautiful beast, and Pride couldn't help admiring it.

In a way, being its lunch would be preferable to falling before the guns of Robitaille and his cronies.

Still, he hoped to avoid either fate.

He was going to have to come up with a plan of action quickly, though. The tiger was starting to move faster. Any second now, it would close the gap, leap, and Pride would be done for. Or Pride would have to shoot and hope for the best.

If he moved, the cat would get him. If he didn't, it would still get him.

He moved.

The door to the capuchin's cage was on the side nearest Pride and farthest from the tiger. He hadn't studied it, wasn't sure how it opened or whether it was locked, but the time for such considerations was gone. He snatched at the handle, realized it was just a simple latch on a chain-link gate. He yanked open the door, swung inside, and tugged it closed.

The tiger slammed into it a split second later, snapping some of the links and caving it in several inches. Pride backed away from the door, then whirled around in case the capuchin attacked him from behind.

But the capuchin was behind yet another door. This one had a padlock on it, presumably because monkeys could figure out simple catches. The two-door system, Pride realized, made sense—a single door would give the monkey an escape opportunity every time a keeper entered. So he had nothing to fear from the monkey, which was currently clinging to the far wall of the cage anyway, screaming, panicked by the tiger's proximity.

The tiger, though, was another story. He didn't know if the beast understood how easily it could open the unlocked door, or tear it from its hinges, or just batter through it.

It had backed up a few feet, and it paced there, eyeing Pride. He wondered when it had last been fed. Maybe it wasn't hungry, but riled by the scent of fresh blood. Maybe having been released from its enclosure, hunting down the first available prey was what came naturally.

Regardless of what the tiger did, Pride was trapped. If he left the cage, the cat would get him. Staying in it, he was a sitting duck. And now, thanks to the capuchin's howling and the tiger's presence, they would know precisely where he was. "After I promised you a court appearance, too," he said. "Some thanks."

The minutes ticked by, and nobody showed up. Pride watched the tiger tire of pacing and lie down, close enough to be at the cage door within seconds if Pride tried to escape. It gradually dawned on him that the tiger had to have been set free intentionally, so maybe Robitaille and the others were just watching the doors. If Pride didn't show up at one of those, eventually they would expect to come in and find the tiger happily dining on him.

Maybe that knowledge could buy him a couple of minutes—if he could come up with a way to bypass the big cat.

Even the capuchin started to settle down. It was trembling, still clinging to the side of the cage with its left paw and feet, eyes wide, but it stopped its caterwauling, and Pride appreciated that. Thinking was a little easier in the relative silence.

He wondered if he could slip out the door and climb to the cage's roof before the tiger reached him. It seemed unlikely, especially with his wounded leg. A more realistic scenario was that he would be most of the way up and the tiger would leap, sink those enormous claws into his flesh, and pull him back down.

The capuchin's cage contained some chains and a water bottle and a couple of plastic children's toys. What had Robitaille called them? Enrichment items. The water bottle could be accessed from this section of the cage, for easy refilling. But it was just light plastic—even if he threw it at the tiger, it wouldn't do any damage. And it would require opening the main door enough to get his arm out, which might be enough for the tiger to take his arm off.

If he could unlock the capuchin's cage, he could sacrifice the monkey, tossing him over the tiger as a distraction. But unless he wanted to shoot the lock off, he wasn't going to be able to do that. And shooting a lock didn't always work like it did in the movies—as likely as not, given the quality of the padlock and the way his luck had been running this last twenty minutes or so, his round might just ricochet back into him.

Life in New Orleans imbued its people with a certain kind of optimism. The Crescent City had suffered tyrants and scoundrels, devastating poverty, unspeakable violence, and heartbreaking storms. But the people always bounced back, forgiving if not forgetting. *Laissez les bon temps rouler* was more than a motto, it was a way of life, a reminder that no matter how hard today was, tomorrow there would be music and laughter, good food and drink, friendship and family and fun.

Just now, however, Pride's optimism was on the wane. Alone, trapped in a monkey cage with a hungry tiger outside, outgunned and outnumbered by his enemies, he was in as much peril as he had ever been.

It took a moment for his mind to sift through the sounds of the zoo animals and recognize that something had changed, and another moment to recognize what that change signified.

Sirens.

Still distant, but growing nearer by the second.

At last, the cavalry was on the way. All he had to do was survive until it showed up.

Pride smiled, gave the capuchin a thumbs up. The monkey looked at him quizzically, but didn't return the gesture. Then again, it only had one thumb, and that was wrapped around the chain-link.

In his moment of respite, Pride pulled his phone out and wrote another text for Sonja.

At least 3 armed men & 1 tiger. Careful.

As he put the phone back, a shadow fell across the cage. Pride looked up and saw the bearded security guard standing atop the wall, a short distance away, aiming his rifle.

"Guess you're still alive after all," the guard said. "Looks like I'm gonna have to change that."

33

"Tiger?" Lasalle repeated when Sonja read him the text. "Does he mean, like, a *tiger* tiger?"

"I don't think he means Tiger Woods is gunning for him with a seven iron," Sonja said. "Do you know any other kind of tiger?"

"We know Robitaille has himself some kind of private zoo," Lasalle replied. "So if Pride says there's a tiger, I'm guessing he means there's a tiger."

"Drive faster!"

Lasalle was already topping ninety on the narrow country road, dodging cars and the occasional farm truck or tractor. "I'm doing what I can," he said. "We won't do Pride any good if we wind up dead before we get there."

"Okay, drive faster but safer."

"You want to take the wheel?" he offered. Secretly, he was relieved that Pride had texted at all. It meant that for the moment, he was alive and not under fire.

On the other hand, the fact that it had been so long between texts likely indicated that he had been in danger. And the nature of the most recent text meant that he still was.

He pressed down on the accelerator, then eased up for a blind turn. Coming out of the curve, he was starting to speed up again when he saw a pair of riders, teens from the looks of them, on horseback at the grassy edge of the road. A truck laden with hay barreled toward him from the other direction, so he couldn't swerve into that lane. Instead, he braked, eased past the riders, then stomped on the gas.

The mounted teens reminded him of why he and his fellow agents did what they did. As he hurtled toward a situation in which people could potentially die—and those people were just as likely to be him and his partners as the bad guys—they were a sign that life went on, that the good guys outnumbered the bad, that most people just wanted to live their lives unscathed by evil. Lasalle and his team were part of the thin line that tried to separate the evil from the innocent, to ensure that for the vast majority of Americans, crime was something they read about in the news or saw on TV, but not part of daily existence.

Dwayne Pride was the best lawman Lasalle had ever known. He had devoted his life to the cause they all served.

But there was more to Lasalle's sense of urgency than that. It wasn't something Lasalle thought about often, but it was never absent from his awareness just the same. His relationship with his own father had always been strained. By necessity, his parents had to devote more of their attention to Lasalle's troubled brother, Cade, than to him or his sister. They weren't strangers to their parents, but they weren't as close as they might have been—especially to their father, who was never around much to begin with.

But the strained relationship came closer to breaking

altogether when Lasalle made clear to his father that he wasn't following him into the oil business. The old man had never understood why his son would want to be a cop. Pride, on the other hand, not only understood it, but embraced it.

Lasalle admired Pride. He appreciated the things that Pride had taught him, the encouragement Pride had given him, and the unconditional acceptance the older man offered. If he wasn't an actual father, he was as much a father figure as Lasalle had ever known, and he had no intention of letting the man down. When the road finally straightened, he poured on the speed.

The security guard was still talking when Pride raised his Colt and squeezed the trigger three times. The first round was deflected slightly by glancing off the chain-link—just a fraction of a centimeter, but by the time it covered the distance between gun barrel and guard, that was enough to make it miss by inches.

The other two were on target. The guard flinched when the first one hit, and his finger tightened on the trigger of his automatic rifle, sending a spray of bullets into the path below him. When the second round hit him, his hands went slack. The rifle fell, but dangled on the strap around his neck. His mouth dropped open, forming an O shape, and he pitched forward. When he landed, it was facedown on the path, on top of his gun.

The tiger watched with interest as he fell, and was at his side in two long bounds. Sniffing at the man's unmoving form, it hardly looked up when Pride opened his cage door.

Pride climbed to the roof of the cage. Once again, the panicked capuchin screamed, and the monkeys in the big cage next door joined in. The general uproar spread throughout the zoo until the racket was almost deafening. Pride couldn't hear the sirens anymore; he had no idea how many there were, or how near.

From the cage roof, he was able to haul himself up to the top of the wall. It was about six inches wide—comfortable enough for him to negotiate under normal circumstances, a little harder with a wounded leg that sent bolts of pain through him every time he put weight on it.

But it gave him elevation, and he took advantage of that to get his bearings. Most of the zoo still lay between him and the house, off to his left. He saw Robitaille, shotgun in hand, bolting for the veranda as if the devil was on his tail. He considered shooting, but decided against wasting a bullet. Running away, Robitaille was no imminent threat. On the other hand, he didn't know where Landry was, and firing a shot would give away his own location.

He could try moving along the wall, but it was precarious footing, and outlined against the sky, he would be an easy target. He scanned for Landry, but to no avail. Maybe he had already taken off, and that was why Robitaille was dashing for cover.

Pride holstered his revolver, crouched down, then lowered himself gingerly from the wall. He would still have to drop a couple of feet, but that wouldn't hurt nearly as much as jumping from the top. He braced himself for the shock, then released his grip.

When his left leg hit the ground, it buckled under him and he went down. He shook off the lancing pain, got his hands and knees under him.

And then Landry bolted from the corner and delivered a roundhouse kick to the side of his head.

Pride crumpled in the dirt, stunned by the blow. Landry was on him in an instant, dropping down onto his back and looping a powerful arm around his throat. Pride sensed his gun being yanked from its holster, and readied himself for the inevitable shot. Instead, as Landry tugged his head up, he saw Charmaine soar up and over the wall. It landed with a thump on the other side, discharging once from the impact.

"I don't much like guns," Landry said. "I mean, I use 'em when I got to, but I'd rather do things the old-fashioned way."

"Like throwing people off hotel balconies?"

"That was a lucky shot, I gotta say. I meant for him to land on the street and break his neck. Hittin' that trident? Hell, I wished I had that on video."

As he spoke, he demonstrated what he meant by "the old-fashioned way." He had a knee pressed against Pride's spine, and the arm encircling Pride's neck was gradually pulling his head back. Under more than three hundred pounds of weight and pressure, Pride couldn't breathe, and the agony was almost unbearable. In another few moments he would pass out, but whether that happened before or after his neck or spine snapped was anybody's guess.

In what would surely be his last instants of consciousness, he reached back and grabbed fistfuls of Landry's hair. He jerked Landry's head forward and threw his own back at the same moment. The shock of the collision made lights flash in Pride's eyes, but Landry's grip loosened, and Pride knew he wouldn't get a better chance. With his hands still tangled in the bigger man's hair, he bucked Landry off and wrenched him to the side.

With Landry's weight off him, Pride lurched to his

feet, back against the wall for support. He sucked in a few deep breaths and fought a wave of nausea. Landry gained his feet, too, and when he rose to his full height, he loomed over Pride.

"That hurt," Landry said. Blood ran from his nose, but he ignored it.

"Then we're even," Pride said. "Make this easy on yourself and surrender."

Landry gave a menacing chuckle. "Don't think so."

Pride had only a moment to prepare himself for Landry's next move. The big man lowered a shoulder and charged. The force of his attack expelled the air from Pride's lungs and smashed him into the wall. He struck back, but Landry followed up with a jab that caught Pride under the chin and drove the back of his skull—still tender from the jolt against Landry's forehead—into the wall.

Dazed, Pride managed to raise his arms in time to partially defend himself against a flurry of punches. He was under assault from a man who was bigger, stronger, younger, and, at the moment, not nearly as damaged as Pride, a man who was using him as a speed bag.

If he was going to survive the next few minutes, he was going to have to do something drastic, and he was going to have to do it soon.

So he collapsed.

He dropped to a crouch as Landry's right fist was flying in for a savage uppercut. Instead of finding Pride's face, it smashed into the wall, splitting knuckles and drawing blood. Slightly off-balance because Pride was no longer between him and the wall, when Pride pushed off and slammed his shoulder into Landry's midsection, the big man lost his footing. He tumbled over backward, catching Pride on the way down.

They both wound up on the ground again, but this time, Pride was on top.

And he was hurting.

He swung again and again, pummeling Landry with punch after punch to the jaw, the cheekbone, the still-bleeding nose. Landry flailed in response, but with his back against the ground, his swings were without momentum, wild and ineffectual.

"Give up!" Pride said. "I don't want to hurt you."

Landry snarled something and spat at Pride, writhing and bucking beneath him.

Pride held on, raining blows down, wishing the man would surrender.

Then Landry found the wounded spot on Pride's leg. The wound was shallow, just a scrape and burn, but Landry dug his thumb into the spot and electric agony shot through Pride. Landry took advantage of the moment and threw Pride off, then regained his own feet.

Pride was slower to rise. Landry delivered a snap-kick to Pride's chest, knocking him to the ground again.

Pride got to his hands and knees. His breathing was ragged and painful. Every part of him hurt. Cells that he had sloughed off in grade school hurt.

Landry kicked him in the jaw, and he went down.

But he got up.

Landry waited until he was almost on his feet, then fired a left hook, catching Pride just below his right eye. He went down.

And he got back up. Slowly, unsteady on his feet, almost blind from the pain.

"I'm tired of this," Landry said. "Time to wrap it up." He stepped forward, took Pride's throat in his huge hands, and lifted him off the ground, squeezing all the while.

Pride couldn't breathe. The world turned dark at the edges, and the darkness was closing in. His legs dangled uselessly.

It would be easy, he thought, to give in, accept his fate. Landry was a giant, and he was used to taking physical punishment. He seemed to thrive on it, in fact.

There was only one problem with that idea: Cassius Pride hadn't raised any quitters, and Dwayne Cassius Pride shared more than his father's name.

Through the encroaching darkness, Pride glimpsed Landry's own throat. The man had a bull neck, corded with muscle, but it was still vulnerable. Pride bunched his fist and swung under Landry's extended arm with everything he had. He slammed it into Landry's Adam's apple, feeling cartilage give under the blow.

The effect was immediate. Landry's grip relaxed, and Pride dropped several inches but kept his balance. The bigger man bent over, trying to breathe. Pride didn't think he had broken the cartilage; Landry would live, but he would be hurting for a good long while. Landry went to his knees, fighting for breath, his eyes starting to bug out. Pride locked his fists together and swung like a home-run hitter, smashing them into Landry's temple, and the man sank to the ground, unconscious.

Pride knelt over him. Now that he wasn't struggling to breathe, his chest rose and fell. Breathing would be difficult, painful, but his larynx wasn't crushed.

Pride swept a hand across his face, wiping stinging sweat and blood away from his eyes. He was taking out his phone to check in with Sonja and Lasalle when he saw Walter coming toward him, carrying yet another shotgun.

34

"You all right, sir?" Walter asked. He held out a hand. Pride clasped it and let the man help him to his feet.

"Been better," Pride said. "Guess I could say the same about your boy, but he'll survive."

"He never has been any good," Walter said. "I don't know what his mother and I could've done different, but whatever we did, it didn't work too well. I'm just glad she died when he was little so she didn't have to see what he became."

"Fathers and sons," Pride said. "I have a daughter. She's the light of my life."

"I expect she is." Walter indicated his fallen son with the shotgun barrel. "This one could have played ball, gone pro. But he found himself at a crossroads somewhere along the way, and he chose the wrong path. Brought shame on me and his mother, rest her soul." He eyed Pride. "You'll need a doctor, sir."

"I expect we both will."

As if just remembering that he was holding the weapon, Walter said, "Mr. Robitaille, he insisted that I give you that particular shotgun. It's not one of his best, so I didn't know why. When I heard all the shooting, I reasoned that maybe there was something wrong with that one, and that was why he wanted you to have it. It was never my intention to put you in any danger."

"You know what kind of man Robitaille is, though."

"I knew what kind his father was, and I knew his mother, too. Both fine people, as good as you could want. I don't know what happened to their son, any more than I do Bruno here. Sometimes the apple falls farther from the tree than we want it to, I guess. Still, I never thought either of them would murder anyone."

"They both have," Pride said. "Your son directly, and Robitaille through conspiracy. He hired your son to kill a Navy officer, and he tried to kill me."

Walter nodded. His eyes might have been the saddest ones Pride had ever seen. They were big and brown and liquid, with heavy bags beneath them. Pride got the impression that he had been mourning the loss of his son for years, decades, even though he was still alive.

"I'm sorry to hear that. And sorry for that officer, and his family. What can I do to help?"

"Where's Robitaille now?"

"He came tearing into the house like a bat out of hell," the old man said with a chuckle. "Went straight to the gun safe and loaded his pockets with shells, then tore out the front. I don't rightly know where he got to after that."

Pride cocked his head. Over the ringing in his ears and the din from the zoo, he could hear sirens closing in. "Stay here and keep an eye on your son while I look for him. The police will be here any minute."

"Glad to," the man said. "I'd even put the handcuffs on him if they'd let me. Boy's got to learn someday what's right and what's not."

"Thanks," Pride said. Then he remembered that his Colt was still in the zoo, as was a loose tiger. "Borrow that?"

Walter handed him the shotgun, and Pride headed for the house.

When Sonja and Lasalle reached Robitaille's property, Lasalle had to slam on the brakes to keep from driving headlong into the iron gate. The truck shuddered and fishtailed in the drive, but stopped just short of it. Lasalle eyeballed the gate and said, "Hell with it. I'm goin' through."

"Hold on, Country Mouse," Sonja said. "There's probably a switch in that shack. Don't wreck your grille for no reason."

Lasalle started to argue, but wisely shut his mouth. She opened her door and hopped out, ran to the guard shack, and found the switch. In another few moments, she was back in the truck, and they were heading up a long driveway.

Just past a thick stand of trees, a sports car raced toward them.

"That's Robitaille!" Sonja cried.

"You sure?"

"I've seen that face on enough restaurant ads," she said. "And on that billboard. It's him."

"Okay." Lasalle braked and cranked the wheel hard right at the same instant. The truck swerved, its tail swinging up until it sat crossways, blocking the entire drive. The sports car had to come to a sudden stop to avoid ramming it.

Sonja and Lasalle lunged from the truck. Lasalle ran around to the other side and they both stood behind the front end, weapons drawn and aimed at the sports car. "NCIS, Robitaille!" Sonja shouted. "You've got nowhere to go!"

"Federal agents!" Lasalle added. "Step out of the car with your hands empty and extended."

Instead, Robitaille lifted a shotgun from the seat next to him and pointed it through his windshield.

"Oh no you don't!" Lasalle cried. "Don't you shoot my truck! You do, and I'll—"

"You'll what?" Sonja asked.

"He doesn't want to know. It'd give him nightmares for the rest of his life."

"Toss the shotgun out the window, Robitaille!" Sonja called. "This is the end of the line!"

Robitaille's hands were quaking, the barrel of the gun clacking against the windshield. Finally, he reached over, opened his door, and threw the weapon into the grass beside the driveway.

"Now get out, with your hands in the air," Lasalle instructed. "Spread your fingers."

Robitaille did as he was told, spreading his fingers and shoving them out of the car, then climbing out of his seat. He was shaking so much that Sonja said, "Look, jazz hands."

Lasalle chuckled and started around the rear of the truck. Sonja went around the hood, so they approached from different directions.

"On your knees," Sonja said. "Lock your hands behind your head."

Again, Robitaille followed their instructions. With his hands quivering uncontrollably, he could barely interlace his fingers. Sonja stepped behind him and clicked handcuffs closed over his wrists.

"Where's Pride?" Lasalle demanded.

Robitaille's mouth opened, but he couldn't manage anything more than a grunt.

"Where's Pride?" Lasalle asked again. "You were gonna shoot my truck! Don't give me another reason to make you regret being born."

"I don't know!" Robitaille said. "Last I saw, he was in my collection."

"What collection?"

"The animals! The zoo!"

"The tiger," Sonja said, suddenly afraid. She reached for her phone, and it started to buzz as soon as she pulled it from her pocket.

"Pride? You okay?"

"I will be," Pride said. "Look up."

"Up where?" she asked, glancing into the trees overhead.

"At the house."

She did. There was Pride, coming out of a huge front door and down a few steps. He tucked a shotgun under the arm that held a phone to his ear, and waved. From this distance, she wasn't sure, but it looked like he was wincing as he did.

"You sure you're okay?" she asked.

"I'm fine," Pride said. "Well, not fine. I'll be a lot better if you tell me that guy on his knees in front of you is Burl Robitaille."

"It is," she replied.

"Good work."

Vehicles Sonja couldn't see pulled into the driveway. Through the trees, she could only make out the lights, and the too-loud sirens wailing. "Did you get Landry?"

"Got him," Pride said.

"What about the tiger?"

"Somebody might need to call Animal Control.

I'm not in any shape to arrest a tiger. And he might be armed with a .357 Magnum."

"The tiger?"

"I'll explain later," Pride said. "Make sure Robitaille knows how lucky he is that he surrendered to you instead of making me catch him."

35

Once the prisoners were all accounted for—
Robitaille, Landry, and the first guard Pride had shot,
who would live after all; the tiger had finished off
the other guard—Pride paid a visit to his doctor. The
doctor taped him and patched him and prescribed
painkillers that Pride wouldn't take, not because he
savored the pain, but because he didn't like the way
they made him feel—loopy and out of control. Pride
would get by on over-the-counter remedies and the
occasional beer and the support of his friends.

Then, bandaged and bruised and still aching, he
drove to the Lower Ninth. Mama T hadn't told him
precisely where her community center was located, but
the first local person he asked knew what he meant,
and directed him. He recognized the place when he
arrived; there had been a store there, which had been
abandoned after Katrina and had gradually fallen
victim to the elements. Now it had been razed, the lot
cleared, and a new structure had been built in its place.
The walls were concrete block, painted a cheerful mix
of gold and purple, and the roof was pitched and
covered with shingles. In the large, fenced backyard

stood a colorful play structure for kids, several picnic tables, and a big propane grill. In front, a hand-painted sign read NINTH WARD COMMUNITY CENTER. ALL ARE WELCOME, ALL ARE LOVED.

Pride grinned. Sounded like Mama T, all right. New Orleans could use a few more like her. So could the rest of the world, for that matter.

A tall black man wearing overalls and no shirt came out of the door, carrying a steel toolbox, as Pride walked up. Pride recognized him. "Clayton," he said. "What are you doing here?"

"Just a little plumbing problem," Clayton replied. "One of the kids flushed a diaper, toilet backed up. Nothing to it."

"Hardly worthy of your skills," Pride said, shaking the man's rough-skinned hand. "How's Mae?"

"She's doing right well, sir. Thank you for asking."

"Give her my love," Pride said.

"I'll do that. You look a touch banged up." Clayton put a finger under his right eye, where on Pride a butterfly bandage held the skin together.

"Occupational hazard."

"I hear that," Clayton said with a chuckle. "Keep the faith, Dwayne."

"You too, brother," Pride said. Clayton held the door for him, and Pride went inside.

The center still smelled new; the lingering scents of sawdust and fresh paint and recently turned earth were, to Pride, optimistic odors. They smelled like growth, hope, and a tomorrow that was better than yesterday. A little boy he didn't know looked up at him. Pride gave him a smile and asked, "Where's Mama T?"

The boy wouldn't meet his gaze—Pride couldn't blame him, given the way he looked—but he pointed toward an open door on the left.

"Thanks, son," Pride said. He went to the doorway and peeked in. Mama T sat behind what he guessed was a surplus government-issue steel desk, poring over paperwork.

"Hey, Mama T," Pride said.

She marked her spot with a finger and looked up. "Agent Pride!" she said, beaming at him. Then her expression changed to one of concern. "You look like you been dragged behind a horse for about twenty miles."

"That's why I came over," he said. "I'm still happy to talk to your people, but I think it should wait a few weeks, until I don't look quite so awful. I'd hate to give people the impression that law enforcement is a dangerous profession."

She laughed. "I'm pretty sure it is."

"Okay, well, you could be right about that."

"You look awful. Does it hurt?"

"Only when I laugh." He touched his jaw, gingerly. "Or talk. Or, you know, breathe."

"You get who you were looking for, though?"

"Oh, we got him. Them, really."

"That's what it's all about, then."

"Yes, it is."

"Don't worry about us. I've got some other speakers lined up, so we can get to you in a couple of weeks. Will that work?"

"I should look mostly human by then, so sure."

She glanced down at the paperwork covering her desk. "I still could use some help here, especially on the educational side. I'm no school administrator, I'll tell you that. I don't suppose you've thought of anyone could help me out?"

As soon as she said it, a thought that had been nagging

at Pride for a couple of days—but had been pushed to the rear by more urgent considerations—suddenly shot to the forefront. "As a matter of fact, I might," he said.

"Really?"

"I don't know for sure that she'd be interested, but I expect she might. She's a former teacher—just about every grade, from the sound of it, and every subject at one time or another. She's out of work, though, and at her age, the schools won't hire her anymore."

"How do you know her?"

"Her son's in jail, awaiting trial. I'm going to do what I can to get him sprung, though. He's not a bad kid, just got mixed up in something beyond his control. His name's Gilbert Melancon. I don't know hers, but I'll get it from Gilbert for you."

Mama T rose from her seat and came around the desk. "That would be fantastic, Dwayne!" She enveloped Pride in a hug that elicited an involuntary yelp.

"Sorry," she said. "Sometimes I get carried away."

"It's okay."

"You sure?"

"Sure I'm sure. I've got to get going, Mama T. I'll call or swing back by when I have Mrs. Melancon's information for you."

"You keep helpin' me out, we might have to name a wing of this center after you. Or a room, I guess, since it don't got any wings."

"That's entirely unnecessary," Pride said. "The whole place should be named after you, from the looks of it."

"Ain't about me," she said. "It's about the Lower Ninth. It's about the people. The community."

"In that case," Pride said, "it already has the perfect name."

She laughed. "I guess it does, at that."

* * *

With Landry and Garrett Michaels, the security guard, being treated at the hospital, under the watchful eyes of the NOPD, Pride paced the floor of the interrogation room. Allyson Woodhouse huddled with Burl Robitaille at one end of the table. She looked as glamorous as ever, but Pride noticed that she kept a few inches of space between her designer outfit and the bloody clothes Robitaille wore—blood that had come from the guard, since Robitaille was somehow the only person involved in the fracas at his property who had walked away physically unscathed.

"My client has nothing to say at this time," Woodhouse said.

Pride gave a heavy sigh. "Maybe he doesn't, but I do." He fixed his gaze on Robitaille, ignoring the presence of his high-priced attorney for the moment. "Burl, let me make a few things clear to you. We have you dead to rights on multiple charges relating to your attempt to kill me. First, I was there, I'm an officer of the law, and I know you gave me a non-working gun, then shot at me. That's attempted murder. I also know you involved three other people in the attempt. That's conspiracy. One of those people died, unfortunately, and you're also responsible for that death. There is nothing Allyson can do to get you out of that fix. You brought it on yourself, and you'll do hard time for it. If she hasn't told you that, she's committing legal malpractice and you should fire her."

"Dwayne, that's—" she began, but he waved her off.

"It's my turn now, Allyson," he said. "I'm just telling Burl the hard truth. He made some bad choices and he'll face consequences for that.

"But what I'm really more interested in is closing the case of Lt. Edouard Alpuente. I have a feeling that Bruno Landry will be plenty talkative once his jaw doesn't hurt quite so much, and I expect that he'll pretty much blame you for everything. That security guard will probably say the same. They're both looking at long prison stretches, too, so anything they can do to shift the responsibility to you will be in their best interest. Even with Allyson representing them, they'll understand that."

"Burl, ignore him," Allyson said. "He doesn't know what he's—"

"I've been doing this a lot longer than you've been lawyering, Allyson. I know the law, and I know human nature. Those men were both hired help, and they'll roll over on their employer in a heartbeat. What that means for you, Burl, is that you're faced with a choice here. You can keep quiet, like Allyson recommends, and if you do, I'll make sure you get sent to the worst hellhole you can imagine. The federal prison system has some real doozies, I can guarantee you that. Even at the worst prisons, there are varying conditions, and I can make sure you get the worst of those, too.

"Or I can pull some strings to ensure that you serve out your sentence somewhere easier. Maybe someplace with a comfortable climate, even right here at Lafitte. And I imagine you'd rather spend your time with the white-collar crowd than the hard-ass gangbangers and psychopathic serial killers, right?"

"Don't let him scare you," Allyson said. "He doesn't have the power to arrange that."

"Yes, I definitely do, Burl. The fact that I don't often choose to exercise it doesn't mean I don't have it. You're still a young man; with good behavior you could be out of prison while you're still in your fifties. Until then, the way you spend your years is in my hands. Which means it's in your hands, ultimately."

"What do you want from me, Pride?" Robitaille asked.

"Burl, don't—" Allyson began.

Pride talked over her. "I just need some answers to a few simple questions. That's all. You know you're going away, so make it as easy on yourself as you can. You help me, I help you. There's really not much Allyson can do for you at this point—not that it'll stop her from billing hundreds of hours at whatever exorbitant rate she's charging you. But there's a lot I can do for you, if you let me."

"What do you want to know?"

"Burl, if you talk to him, I'll..." She let the sentence trail off.

"You'll what, Allyson?" Pride asked. "Remove yourself from the case? From all three cases? You know how much you'll earn for representing these three men, even though they're all going to prison. If Burl here confesses, he'll save himself a nice piece of change, and you'll still have the other two cases to bill against. Or all three could confess, but even at that, you've made a nice piece of change, and there'll be more to come. Either way, you come out of this just fine."

"You want a confession, Pride?" Robitaille asked.

"I want answers."

"To what?"

Pride knew he had him, at this point. Woodhouse sat stiffly in her chair with her legs crossed and her arms folded over her chest, staring into the distance. Robitaille was looking at Pride like a drowning man being thrown a lifeline.

"We know why you had Alpuente killed," Pride said. "You needed to prevent the Navy from blocking the lakeside resort you were developing. But why was that so important that you would turn to murder? You're already a rich man. Yes, you stood to make a lot more, but you told me in your house that it was already more than you needed, that you owned it because you felt pressured by people's expectations of the wealthy. So why was amassing more wealth worth people's lives?"

Robitaille stared at the table while Pride asked his questions, and when he looked up, his eyes were moist. He knew he had made careless decisions, and Pride figured that if he didn't weep today, he would soon, once the full weight of his actions sunk in.

"I... I wanted more," he said. "When you play sports, it's all about winning. If you're not winning, you're losing. My restaurants are doing fine and I'm making plenty of money, but those are... those are a victory that's done. I needed the next victory. If the restaurants are the regular season, the resort business is the Super Bowl."

"I don't think most athletes would kill to win the Super Bowl," Pride said.

Robitaille gave a bitter laugh. "Maybe you don't know a lot of athletes. Anyway, the winning was important, but it was also the money."

"You have plenty of money."

"I do, but it's not enough. It's never enough. I told you what I'm trying to do for the animals, Pride. We're looking at massive species loss over the next century or so. A worldwide extinction event, maybe on par with what happened to the dinosaurs. The only thing that's going to help is money. Lots and lots of it. Money to buy land, to prevent development, and to maintain stable, healthy ecosystems. Money to raise public awareness. Money to hire armies to stop poaching. The world has turned capitalist, and don't get me wrong, I've got nothing against capitalism. But as the global population expands, the space left for the animals disappears. Forests are being cut down, land is being cultivated for crops or taken over by cities or used for manufacturing. A recent study warned that two-thirds of the planet's vertebrate animals—not counting humans—could be gone by 2020. To stop that from happening, those of us with money have to be able to match or beat the economic activity generated by those other uses."

"So in order to make money to preserve ecosystems in other parts of the world, you thought it was necessary to build a resort and dredge out Lake Borgne for a marina, ensuring greater devastation to Louisiana's wetlands?"

"Look, I understand what's happening here. I talked to Alpuente about it a couple of times, and he showed me his research. But you're not looking at the comparative scale. Louisiana could sustain some minor damage if it meant saving tens of millions of acres in Africa."

"I'm not sure that's your choice to make, Burl," Pride said. "But I am interested to know that you talked to Alpuente. What made you decide on the voodoo curse angle?"

Robitaille didn't even hesitate; once he had started defending himself, his words rushed out in a flood. Woodhouse shot him steely glances once in a while, but otherwise looked like she wished she were anywhere else.

"We bought up parcels all along the lakefront,"

Robitaille said. "But his mother and uncle wouldn't sell. I think Alpuente was telling them not to, because he hoped that if we couldn't get that one, we couldn't build. He was wrong—we'd have built anyway. But their place is an eyesore, and we'd have had to put a pretty high wall at that end of the resort to hide it.

"Anyway, one of my real estate guys, Jack Finnegan, was over there all the time, talking to them, trying to persuade them to sell to us. He came back once and told me about all the voodoo crap in their house. I figured that I could use that to scare them away. Then, when I realized that Alpuente would have to die, I thought that if it looked like he died as a result of the curse, it would make the curse seem all the more real to them. That part worked. When Finnegan told them that Baron Samedi had killed Alpuente, they couldn't wait to sign the paperwork."

"So this Finnegan knew that you'd had Lt. Alpuente killed? Because the Baron Samedi thing was never released to the press."

"I told him I found out from Mayor Hamilton," Robitaille said. "He had nothing to do with what happened to Alpuente."

"So that was just you and Landry? Nobody else?"

"That's right."

"Not Rich Brandt?"

Robitaille's mouth dropped open. "Rich? No way."

"Then who hacked into Lt. Alpuente's computer and deleted his files?"

"That was a kid who works in my IT department. Jackson Lokey. He didn't know about the killing, either. I just told him which files needed to disappear, and he did it."

"I'm afraid I'm going to have to have a talk with

Mr. Lokey, then. Destruction of government property is also a crime."

"Pride, he was just following—" Robitaille stopped in mid-sentence.

"Just following orders?" Pride finished. "You know how that sounds, right?"

Robitaille nodded. "Yeah. Look, I'm sorry all this happened. I'm sorry I let my ego and ambition get in the way of my common sense. It was like I started rolling a snowball downhill and it turned into an avalanche. I never wanted anyone to get hurt. I just wanted to help."

"And I'll make sure the judge takes that under advisement," Pride said. "I told you if you talked to me, I'd do what I can to make this easy on you, and I will. As long as you understand that you're going to be going away for a long time. Your resort deal's not going to happen. You'll still be a wealthy man, but maybe not as wealthy as you'd hoped."

"That's all right," Robitaille said. "If I had known what this would end up costing, I never would have started it anyway."

Finally, Woodhouse could contain herself no longer. "Burl, now that you've said all this, you have to understand that I won't be able to do much for you. I told you to keep quiet, but you wanted to talk, and now—"

Robitaille interrupted her. "It's okay, Allyson," he said. "When I chose to disregard your advice, I knew what I was doing. For the first time in quite a while, I think, I made a decision I'm okay with. Now I'm making another one. If Landry and Michaels still want you to represent them, I'll pay for it. As for myself, I don't think I'll be needing your services anymore. You know where to send the bill."

"Burl, don't—"

"You're done here, Allyson. Goodbye."

She shot to her feet, outrage etched on her face. "Dwayne, tell him that he still needs representation. He can't just fire—"

"Actually, Allyson, he can, and I believe he just did. You know the way out, right?"

She shot him a fierce look, then spun on her two-thousand-dollar heel and stormed from the room. After the door slammed, Pride met Robitaille's gaze, and for the first time in quite a while, saw a smile on the man's face. "I feel better already," he said.

"Enjoy it while it lasts," Pride replied. "You're likely to feel worse again before we're done."

36

"Unintended consequences," Pride said. He was back in the bullpen, and the whole group was there: Patton in his chair, Lasalle at his desk, with Sonja leaning against it. Pride was standing, as was Loretta. Sebastian's lanky form was sprawled in a spare desk chair, which he was swiveling back and forth.

"Sorry?" Sonja asked.

"That's what Robitaille was talking about, a little while before he started shooting at me. Something about the loss of leopard and lion populations leading to a baboon explosion, which could in turn lead to a new pandemic."

"A baboon explosion," Sebastian repeated. "I'd like to see that. I mean, not a real explosion, like boom, but like, a bunch of baboons stuffed inside one of those big phony cakes, and then they all burst out at once."

"They still put girls in those cakes?" Patton asked. "Because I'd rather see that, to be honest."

"*Anyway*," Pride said, endeavoring mightily to bring the conversation back to the general vicinity of reality. "I was thinking on the way back about how much this whole case revolved around that."

"Baboons?" Sebastian asked.

"Capuchins," Lasalle corrected.

"Unintended consequences. Our local economy has been fueled by—no pun intended—fuel. The petroleum industry. Drilling, refining, shipping. It's pumped a lot of money into southern Louisiana over the years. What we didn't know at the time was that it was gradually working against us, too."

"In so many ways," Loretta added. "Burning fossil fuels aggravates the greenhouse effect, warming the climate. Climate change makes storms and severe weather events ever more damaging. Add in wetlands loss due to the infrastructure required by industry, and that from spills in the Gulf, and we've been committing a kind of slow-motion regional suicide for quite some time."

"Maybe not quite suicide," Pride said, "because there's no coming back from that. But damage, definitely. Still, if you shut down the oil and gas industries overnight, you'd also shut down a major part of the area's economy. So what's the answer?"

"I guess," Sonja suggested, "part of the answer is gradually weaning ourselves off fossil fuels. While at the same time retraining the people who are still working in that field."

"A lot of oil workers don't want to do anything else," Lasalle said. "If you don't believe me, I can give you my father's phone number and you can check with him."

"So by researching wetlands loss in the neighborhood he came from, including at his momma's farm," Sebastian said, "Alpuente brought himself to Burl Robitaille's attention."

"That's right," Pride said. "And when Robitaille discovered that Alpuente was gonna advocate blocking the resort and the dredging, he figured he had to shut Alpuente up. Getting murdered was the unintended consequence of Alpuente's research."

"Yeah, and bringing NCIS into the picture was the unintended consequence of that murder," Sonja said.

"Including prison time for Robitaille, and hospital time followed by prison time for Landry and that one guard," Lasalle added.

Pride closed his eyes for a moment, thinking about the guard who hadn't survived, and the tiger that Animal Control had to put down, because it had been found feasting on the guard's corpse. At least the capuchin was getting professional veterinary care, and it looked like it would make it.

He thought, too, about Lieutenant Alpuente, targeted for death because he had served his country with the honor and dignity expected of a sailor. Lasalle had tracked down his aunt in Pascagoula and left a message for Donna Alpuente, letting her know that her son's killer had been arrested, and when she could claim her son's remains.

"You know," Patton said, "I think I understand everything that went down, except for one thing I just can't wrap my head around."

"What's that?" Pride asked.

"In that video from the hotel hallway, what happened to the footage with Landry in it? Why did that get fritzed out when the rest of it was fine? I've been over it and over it, and I can't come up with any conceivable explanation. It just don't make sense."

"I know the answer to that one," Sebastian said.

"You do?"

All eyes turned toward Sebastian, who sat up straighter in his chair, and stopped swiveling for the moment. "There's only one answer that fits the facts, given the circumstances. I mean, Landry was dressed as Baron Samedi, right? It was Mardi Gras. He had just killed someone who had a *gris-gris* bag and a voodoo doll in his room, and who fervently believed he was under a voodoo curse."

"Right…" Patton said. "So? What happened?"

"The only thing that can explain it," Sebastian said, "is voodoo."

The others burst into laughter. Sebastian's face turned bright red, and Pride knew he had meant it seriously, not as a joke. But Pride wasn't laughing.

After all, this was New Orleans. Things were different here, and he was glad they were. The usual rules didn't apply. New Orleans was a world unto itself, separate and distinct. Life in the Big Easy was colorful, loud, fragrant, filled with music, tinged with sadness but rich with celebration. To be a New Orleanian meant being a special kind of person, open and accepting of others' differences, not rigidly bound to the outside world's predetermined notions of right and wrong.

If voodoo was going to work anywhere, in other words, it would be here.

And here, Pride knew, surrounded by his friends and with his favorite city on Earth right outside those doors, was exactly where he wanted to be, for as long as he lived.

And then some.

ACKNOWLEDGMENTS

Every novel is its own challenge, and few challenges are met entirely alone. I need to thank my family for giving me the time and space to meet this one. Thanks also to Natalie and the whole Titan Books crew; to Maryann and the team at CBS-TV; to Howard and Kim-Mei; and to Gary Glasberg, Scott Bakula, and the cast and crew of *NCIS: New Orleans*. Thanks also to the Crescent City itself. Every time I'm away from it, I can't wait to get back!

ABOUT THE AUTHOR

Jeff Mariotte is the award-winning author of more than sixty novels, including thrillers *Empty Rooms* and *The Devil's Bait*, supernatural thrillers *Season of the Wolf*, *Missing White Girl*, *River Runs Red*, and *Cold Black Hearts*, horror epic *The Slab*, and the *Dark Vengeance* teen horror quartet. Among his many novels set in existing fictional universes are *NCIS: Los Angeles: Bolthole* and *Deadlands: Thunder Moon Rising*. With his wife, the author Marsheila Rockwell, he wrote the science fiction/horror/thriller *7 SYKOS*, and numerous shorter works. He also writes comic books, including the long-running horror/Western comic book series *Desperadoes* and graphic novels *Zombie Cop* and *Fade to Black*. He has worked in virtually every aspect of the book business, and is currently the division chief of Visionary Books.

NCIS:™
LOS ANGELES
Extremis

JEROME PREISLER

A brand-new original thriller tying in to the hit TV
show, *NCIS: Los Angeles*. When an 85-year-old retired
rear admiral and two-term California senator is found
murdered in his home—the place ransacked, and
his computer's hard drive stolen—the NCIS: OSP
team is called in to investigate. They soon uncover a
connection to several other mysterious homicides and
break-ins, and a top-secret U.S. Navy project dating
back to World War Two.

For more fantastic fiction, author events,
competitions, limited editions and more

VISIT OUR WEBSITE
titanbooks.com

LIKE US ON FACEBOOK
facebook.com/titanbooks

FOLLOW US ON TWITTER
@TitanBooks

EMAIL US
readerfeedback@titanemail.com